DARK WHISPERS FROM AFAR

THE CHILDREN OF THE GODS
BOOK SIXTY-THREE

I. T. LUCAS

Copyright © 2022 by I. T. Lucas

Published by Evening Star Press

EveningStarPress.com

ISBN-13: 978-1-957139-30-2

WILLIAM

"*B*ecause I'm falling for you, my handsome, immortal prince."

Those were the last words Kaia had said to William before closing her eyes and letting out a sigh.

Reeling from the impact of her proclamation, he took a brief moment to bask in those words and to come up with some of his own, but by the time he was ready to tell her that he'd fallen in love with her the first moment he'd seen her, she was fast asleep.

With her glasses perched crookedly on her nose, her long blond hair tangled, and her lush lips parted, Kaia looked so adorable that William just wanted to keep watching her so he could memorize everything about her. But even though she was sleeping peacefully, she couldn't be comfortable.

As he took her glasses off and put them on the nightstand, it occurred to him that he hadn't told her that she would no longer need them after transitioning.

There were still so many things he needed to tell Kaia, and now that he knew how receptive she was to his version of history, he was looking forward to it instead of dreading it.

There had been no disbelief, no shock, not even awe. Kaia had listened to his fantastic story as if she hadn't been surprised to hear that the mythological gods had been real, and she hadn't batted an eyelash when he'd told her that they'd taken human lovers and produced immortal offspring.

But he'd only given her a brief overview of the history of gods and immortals, and he hadn't gone into detail.

In preparation for the grand reveal, William had collected several articles discussing the Biblical narrative and how it echoed more ancient tales describing real events. He'd even stored them on an app on his phone to show Kaia, but she hadn't needed convincing.

He'd just been confirming what she'd suspected all along.

When his phone buzzed with an incoming message, William was tempted to ignore it, but he had a feeling it was from Kian, and the boss probably wanted an update.

Reluctantly pulling his arm off Kaia, William turned around and picked up the device. As he'd suspected, the text was from Kian, and it was one word long. *Update.*

When the boss was down to single-word commands, it was better not to keep him waiting.

Gently pulling his other arm from under Kaia, William managed to get out of bed without waking her. Last night, the girl hadn't slept more than two hours, and she'd still worked all morning as if she were already a supercharged immortal.

That was the power of youth. Even humans felt invincible at her age.

After pulling his pants on, William padded out of the bedroom and closed the door behind him as soundlessly as he could.

When he placed the call, Kian answered right away. "How did it go?"

William knew what the boss was worried about, so he opened with that. "I didn't mention knowing anyone on the island. Kaia assumed we had an informant, and I just confirmed without saying who the informant was. We didn't go into any details about the Doomers either. I just told her that the original immortals had split into two opposing camps, good and evil, and that I'm on the good team."

"Did you tell her about Annani?"

"I told her that our clan is led by a goddess."

William had made the mistake of telling Kaia that there had been more than one survivor, but since he didn't fear that any of the information would leak from her, he wasn't worried about it.

"How did she take it?" Kian asked.

William chuckled. "As if I was confirming what she already knew. Kaia thinks that there is a very high probability that sightings of unidentified flying objects are real, and that aliens could be hiding in the depths of our oceans or on the dark side of the moon. Compared to that, my story of gods and immortals was tame. She didn't even ask me to show her proof and just accepted everything I told her at face value."

"Lucky you." Kian let out a breath. "Most Dormants have a real hard time suspending their disbelief. Did she ask you if we can get her friend out?"

"She did. I told her that we couldn't. Then she asked if we could relay a message to Anthony. I said that I'm not sure because I'm not the one dealing with the informant, and that I doubt my boss would authorize it."

"The boss wouldn't," Kian said. "If Anthony gets a message from Kaia, he will wonder how she knew where he was, and how she managed to relay the message. He's under Navuh's compulsion, so even if he swears to keep it a secret, he won't be able to hold on to it."

"You're absolutely right." William was embarrassed about his failure to think it all the way through, but he wasn't going to admit to Kian that his acuity suffered when he was near

Kaia. "I preferred the nameless, faceless boss to take the blame for refusing to send the message to her friend."

Evidently he wasn't immune to the effect a testosterone spike had on males.

Kian snorted. "If Kaia is a Dormant, I won't remain nameless and faceless for long. She'll come to live with you in the village."

William winced. "She hasn't given me an answer yet, and since she's so young, there is no rush."

"No one says no to immortality unless they are afraid of dying during the transition, and at nineteen, Kaia has nothing to fear."

"It's more complicated in her case." William sat on the couch and propped his feet on the coffee table. "She's very attached to her family. They are so important to her that she might give up immortality to avoid separation from them."

"How old is her mother?"

"Karen is young enough to transition, provided that she has no health issues, but she's in a loving, committed relationship, and she has five kids, two of them being one-year-old twins. She might not want to risk it either."

"Obviously. But let's worry about that when the time comes. Step one is to confirm that Kaia is a Dormant, and that means inducing her. When she transitions, we will move to step two and see what can be done about her mother and her siblings."

KAIA

*A*s Kaia's brain started waking up, she turned on her side and reached for William, but he wasn't there. Had she fallen asleep in his arms, or had it been a dream?

And what about all the things he'd told her?

Was all that part of the dream as well?

She remembered William telling her that he was an immortal and that she was a carrier of godly genes, but Kaia had had strange dreams before, so that wasn't out of the ordinary for her.

Chuckling, she turned on her back and looked at the ceiling. She had lucid dreams of her prior life as a man, so nothing William could have told her in a dream or otherwise would surprise her.

She remembered him carrying her to bed and helping her undress, but she didn't remember them making love, and since she had her T-shirt and underwear on, it was proof that they hadn't done anything more than cuddle. She could've fallen asleep in his arms and then dreamt up that conversation.

It was one hell of a vivid dream, though.

Kaia sighed and turned her head to look out the window.

It was still day outside, but it was getting dark, and given how empty her stomach felt, that seemed about right. She'd missed dinner, and William must have gone without her.

Hopefully, he would bring her a plate. If he didn't, she would demand to be taken out on a proper date and fed a proper meal, and by that she meant a juicy hamburger with a double order of fries.

As Kaia's mouth watered, her stomach made an angry, demanding sound that got her out of bed in an instant.

Grabbing her neatly folded jeans off the dresser, she smiled. They'd been tossed on the floor when she and William had gotten in bed, and he must have picked them up and folded them for her. It was a very sweet gesture from a guy who needed help remembering where he'd put his glasses.

When Kaia was done freshening up and walked into the living room, William was there, and as he turned to her with a big grin spreading over his face, a mirroring grin spread over hers. She hadn't expected to find him there, and she'd expected even less to realize how happy it would make her to see him there waiting for her.

"Good morning, Princess." He walked up to her and pulled her into his arms. "I hope you're hungry."

As Kaia glanced at the small dining table William had set up for two, noting all the little details he'd added to make it fancy and romantic, her heart swelled with love for him. The table was covered in a white cloth, and a slim vase with two red flowers peeked from between the pile of covered plates he'd brought from the kitchen.

"This is lovely. Where did you get the flowers?"

William chuckled. "The flowers were easy. Emmett has them growing in his little private garden next to the cottage that he no longer uses." He pulled out a chair for her. "The tough part was finding a round tablecloth. Darlene cut it out from a large bedsheet."

Instead of sitting down, she lifted her arms and wound them around his neck. "If you keep doing such sweet things for me, I'm going to fall in love with you."

"I'm counting on it." He put his hands on her waist and pulled her against his body. "Are you okay? I mean, given all you learned before your nap?"

Kaia tilted her head up and pressed a soft kiss to his lips. "When I woke up, I wasn't sure I hadn't dreamt it. You are a three-hundred-year-old immortal, right?"

"A little older than that. I'm three hundred and thirty-two years old, but who's counting?"

She laughed. "So that's where the thirty-two came from."

"It's coincidental. I've been using thirty-two since I originally turned that age." He steered her toward the chair. "Let's sit down and eat dinner before it gets cold."

"Thank you." She sat down. "What time is it? I left my phone in my bungalow."

"It's ten minutes to eight." He sat across from her.

"Wow. I slept for over six hours. You shouldn't have waited for me. You must be starving."

"I have enough reserves." He patted his stomach. "I can afford to lose some weight."

Kaia grimaced. She hated when William referred to himself as overweight. So what if he had a little padding? The small layer of fat cushioning the hard muscles underneath felt wonderful when his body was pressed against hers.

"You're perfect the way you are." Removing the lid off her plate, she lifted her fork but paused before spearing a piece of potato. "I find you very handsome." She stabbed the fork into the chunk and lifted it to her mouth.

William shook his head. "I used to be much heavier than this, and if I don't watch it, the weight will pile back on in no time. I like to eat, and I hate any form of physical activity. If left to my own devices, I would sit in front of the computer screen for sixteen hours a day while shoving sandwiches and snacks into my mouth."

Kaia reached for the can of Coke William had put in front of her plate. He must have gone to her place to get it, and wasn't that sweet?

The guy was a keeper for too many reasons to list.

"Don't worry. I'll keep you active and won't let that happen." She popped the lid.

William arched a brow. "Oh, yeah? How?"

"I have a physical activity in mind that you'll enjoy taking part in very much." She took a sip. "And I'll make sure that you engage in it at least once a day."

JADE

"*C*ome." Jade tugged on Kagra's sleeve. "I need to burn off some steam. Let's hunt."

Jade hadn't had a private moment with her second-in-command since discovering Safe Haven and its leader's true identity, and she burned with the need to share the news with the only person she could talk to.

Kagra's brow furrowed. "Just the two of us?"

"Yeah. We won't go far. I'm not very hungry. I'm just restless and need an outlet for my energy." Jade shrugged her jacket on and walked out the door.

Kagra followed. "We should take some of the young ones with us."

"Not today." Jade looked down her nose at the guard blocking her way. "Move. We are going hunting."

The guy didn't budge. "Your leave is not on the schedule, and therefore not authorized. I can't let you go without a badge from security, and you know that."

Jade bared her fangs at him. "I'm the prime, and Kagra is my second. We can go hunting whenever we please. If you need badges from us, go to the office and get them."

Her claim wasn't entirely true. As Igor's prime, Jade had more leeway than the others, but Kagra didn't. Nevertheless, the guard responded to her natural dominance as she'd expected, dipping his head and doing as she'd commanded.

Getting authorization to leave the compound wasn't a big deal, and all she needed to do was stop by the security office on the way and get badges from the officer in charge. There was nowhere to run, and even if there was, the compulsion and the collars around their necks made it impossible.

Igor just wanted to keep tabs on everyone in his compound and know where they were at all times.

In that, he and she were alike, and if he wasn't murderous, immoral, and irreverent scum, she would have agreed with his security measures.

When Jade had been in charge of her tribe, when she still had a tribe, she had similar procedures in place, but the difference was that she'd never murdered or enslaved her people, and the procedures had been put in place to keep everyone safe.

Nevertheless, she'd failed spectacularly to ensure her tribe's safety despite how careful she'd been, and she was still paying the price for that failure with her own flesh.

Staying on as Igor's prime and making sure that no other female took her place wasn't about pride, and it wasn't only about gaining information and helping the other females he'd abducted and enslaved either. It was also a self-inflicted punishment.

Not that she'd managed to learn much from him throughout her twenty-two years serving him. She still couldn't figure out how Igor had found her tribe or the others. She'd tried to get him to tell her, but regrettably, he wasn't one of those villains who liked to brag.

The guard returned with their badges. "Next time, go to the security office first."

As she took the badge and affixed it to her jacket, Jade cast him a glare. "Open the gate."

He opened his mouth but then quickly closed it and opened the gate without saying a thing.

Jade stifled a satisfied smile. She could still get most of the males to respond to her demands as long as they weren't in direct opposition to Igor's.

Over the years, she'd tried to use that small advantage, but Igor was too smart, and his commands to his men ensured that none of them would aid in her escape or respond to her attempts at stirring up resentment and making them rebel.

When they were on the other side, Kagra chuckled. "You haven't lost it yet. You are still the alpha."

"It's not something that can be lost. You're either born with it, or you are not." Jade let out a breath. "What you call my alpha power only works on the rank and file, and you have it too. But since Igor is immune, and so are his lieutenants, it does us no good."

"Still, Igor chose you as his prime even though you make it no secret that you despise him and want him dead."

"The only reason he tolerates me is that he wants strong offspring."

"You also offer him a good fight." Kagra grimaced. "He gets off on subduing an alpha female."

"That he does." Jade swallowed the bile rising in her throat and shook her head. "Let's run."

There was a very thin line between the Kra-ell sexual dominance dance and rape, and Igor and his cronies had crossed it by a wide margin. But the only way she could deal with her situation was to not dwell on it.

The day she allowed it to consume her, she would lose her mind.

Running and hunting helped, but today she had a lot to talk about with Kagra, and hunting had just been an excuse.

Slowing down, Jade sniffed for water and charged toward the river. The Karelian's woods were so dense that even though she'd hunted in them for years, she still needed the scent of water to orient herself.

At the riverbank, she found a fallen log to sit on and motioned for Kagra to join her. "Do you remember Veskar?"

"Of course. You hated him and made his life so miserable that he broke his vow of loyalty to you and escaped."

Jade kicked a rock into the river. "You were still so young back then, so it might have looked that way to you. Veskar was immune to my power, and I was hard on him to get him to fall in line, but he was untamable. He was a disruptive influence on the other hybrids, and I was glad to see him go."

Kagra nodded. "I'm glad that he left. I hope he and Vrog survived. If they were in the compound, they would have been slaughtered along with the other males of our tribe."

Jade swallowed the lump that had formed in her throat. "Veskar is alive, and he's done well for himself."

Kagra narrowed her eyes at Jade. "How do you know that? Have you always known where he was and didn't tell me?"

"I had no idea where he was or even that he was still alive. I just found out where he was this Monday. I was searching the internet for inspirational stories for the children, and I stumbled upon a commune called Safe Haven. They run spiritual retreats that teach humans how to become the best versions of themselves. The commune leader calls himself Emmett Haderech, and he's none other than our Veskar."

"Are you sure?"

Jade shrugged. "I'm fairly certain that it's him. He's grown an enormous beard and long hair, probably to hide the fact that he looks too young for the age he's supposed to be, but even though he's a hybrid, I recognize Kra-ell eyes even when they are half-human. The question I've been debating is whether I should contact him."

"What for? He can't do anything to help us, and you'll just put him in danger."

"You're right. He can't help us on his own. But he might be affiliated with other Kra-ell. We thought that we were the only pod that had survived, but we know now that many more made it. There might be more Kra-ell out there."

Kagra's eyes widened. "What if the royal twins survived? Either one of them could take on Igor."

Jade put her arm around Kagra's shoulders. "I wish they were still alive, but I know that they perished. Who do you think sabotaged the mother ship and why?"

"Igor," Kagra whispered.

Jade nodded. "That's what I suspect. He either planned a coup even before we left the motherland, killed the royals en route and sabotaged the ship to cover up the murders, or he just took advantage of the disaster to rise to power."

WILLIAM

*E*ver since Kaia's comment about the physical activity she intended to engage him in, William had been sporting an uncomfortable hard-on, but he refused to let it dictate his plans for the evening.

They still had a lot to talk about.

Pushing her plate away, Kaia leaned back. "I can't take another bite." She rubbed her stomach. "It's amazing how even goop tastes good when I'm hungry."

"Goop?" William got to his feet and started collecting the dishes. "Maggie is a gourmet chef. Don't let her hear you call her cooking goop."

Kaia shrugged. "So it's healthy and gourmet, but it's still mostly goop. When I woke up, I planned to make you take me on a proper date and feed me a proper meal." She followed him up. "But then I saw the table you set up for us and forgot all about it."

Damn. Kaia was right. He should take her to a nice restaurant and show her a good time. She deserved proper courting from him, and to be wooed and charmed.

"I should take you out. Where would you like to go?"

"It's nothing fancy. I'm dreaming of juicy hamburgers and fries." She glanced at the sink that was okay to rinse a coffee cup in, but no more than that. "Do we need to carry everything back to the kitchen?"

"We can do it after we have coffee." He put the plates into the paper bags he'd brought them in. "I'm sure you have many questions for me." He loaded the coffeemaker.

"I haven't given it much thought yet." She walked over to the couch and sat down. "I fell asleep before I had time to process what you told me, and I was too hungry to think about it while I ate."

His Kaia was a fast thinker, and she didn't need long to process what he'd told her, which hadn't been all that much to start with.

William eyed her with a frown. "That's not like you. What's going on?"

"I'm not the genius everyone thinks I am. It's just that some things come more easily to me than others. Everything that has to do with math and computations is intuitive to me. The rest is just as hard or as easy as it is for the average person."

"I doubt it." William leaned against the counter and folded his arms over his chest. "There is nothing average about you. What I have you working on requires much more than computational skills. It requires intuition and multi-faceted thinking, and what you've managed to do so far is nothing short of miraculous. I had the advantage of understanding at least some of the gods' language, and I still couldn't figure out the instructions. You had no prior knowledge, and you've done better than I have."

"You are not a bioinformatician." She closed her eyes briefly. "I knew what to look for. You didn't. Besides, I have a knack for solving puzzles." She pulled one leg under her and shifted sideways to look at him. "Now that I know that those journals contain instructions on how to build a cyborg, I'll probably decipher the rest in no time, but I need to know more about the Odus. You told me that those writings could contain information that would be greatly beneficial to humanity or just as greatly detrimental. I want to know what you meant by that."

He should have expected Kaia to focus on the science. Just like him, this was her comfort zone and what she was confident about.

"What do you want to know about the Odus?" He brought the two coffee mugs to the table.

"To start with, just some general information. How strong are they? How much do they weigh? What can they do? How do you control them?"

"They are incredibly strong, and they are nearly indestructible. I have no idea what they are made from. I assume that their outer layer is biological but that their inner organs are mechanical in nature, or maybe some of them are biological and some are mechanical." He rubbed the back of his neck. "I think that their creator based them on himself and used his genetics to create the outer biological layer. They can regenerate from injuries even faster than immortals, and if that's included in the instructions, we might be able to use that knowledge to give the same regenerating ability to regular human bodies, basically turning them immortal."

Kaia narrowed her eyes at him. "Do you have any doctors or scientists in your clan? Don't they know why your bodies can repair themselves so fast and why they don't deteriorate like all other living things?"

"Our chief physician has been trying to find the secret to our longevity for decades, but she's an MD, and what she knows about genetics is apparently not enough. We don't have any geneticists or bioinformaticians in our clan."

"Interesting." Kaia lifted her coffee mug and took a sip. "People thought that once the human genome was deciphered, we would have all the answers, but biological systems don't work like computer circuits. They adapt, systems take over for each other when needed because an area is damaged, and external factors determine gene expression. It's much more fluid than anyone had suspected. I'm not really surprised that your doctor couldn't figure it out. But a manual for building cyborgs might have the answers we are seeking."

"My thoughts exactly. But discovering how to make humans immortal without altering their fertility could be disastrous. Talk about overpopulation."

Kaia tilted her head. "What about your kind? Is your fertility altered?"

"It is. Otherwise, immortals would have overrun the Earth. That's why our enemy doesn't let the Dormants transition. As long as they are in their dormant state, they can produce children at a normal human rate. Once they become immortal, their ability to conceive drops to nearly nothing. Centuries can pass before an immortal female has a child."

KAIA

"Centuries?" Kaia's gut clenched. "So, if I turn immortal, I might not have children for centuries to come?"

It made sense that the procreation rate of immortals would be much lower to compensate for their incredibly long lifespans, but it hadn't occurred to her until William had brought it up.

"That's the downside." He gave her a tight smile. "The upside is that it's never too late. You can have children when you've lived for thousands of years. Annani, our Clan Mother, had her first daughter when she was over three thousand years old, and she continued to have four more children, but that's uncommon for an immortal female, let alone a goddess."

"That's terrible." Kaia's hand shook as she put down her coffee mug. "I always thought that I would have a big family. When it was just Cheryl and me, the house felt empty, and then Idina was born, and we came alive as a family, and two years later the twins arrived, and it became chaotic, but I love it." She wrapped her arms around herself. "There is so much love to spread around. I can't imagine living for thousands of years and having no children."

For a long moment, William seemed lost for words. "The clan is a family," he said after a while. "I know that it's not a substitute for having your own children, but once you become one of us, you'll never feel alone. I never felt the need to have kids of my own, and although I yearned for a mate, I wasn't lonely, not since my lab became a large enterprise teeming with people. When it was just me, I couldn't wait for someone to stop by for a chat."

His words had registered somewhere in the back of her head, and Kaia promised herself to talk to him about it some other time, but she was still stuck on the issue of waiting to have children for centuries or a millennium.

"If turning immortal means that I might not have children for hundreds or thousands of years, then I don't want to transition before I have at least two, and preferably four." She frowned. "My mother is a Dormant too, right?"

"Correct. And so are your sisters and brothers."

"What about Gilbert?"

"Probably not."

"Then how is my mother going to transition? She's not going to leave Gilbert. Can she transition and still keep him?"

William winced. "That would be problematic on several levels. First of all, transitioning at her age is risky, but it's probably still okay if she hurries up. Secondly, she will need an immortal male to induce her, which is a problem since she's with Gilbert. And thirdly, long-lasting relationships between immortals and humans are not possible for obvious reasons. Kian might make an exception and allow Gilbert into the village with his mate and his children, but his mortality would be heart-wrenching for your mother."

It would be terrible, and Kaia didn't want to think of how it would affect them. Hopefully, the journals would supply the answer for turning regular humans immortal, so she could keep her stepdad with them forever.

If only she could go back in time to save her father, turning him immortal before his heart gave out. But not even William or his Clan Mother, the goddess, could perform a miracle like that.

Reminded that the lives of her loved ones could be snuffed at any moment, Kaia resolved to ensure that everyone else in her family turned immortal as soon as possible.

"What about my sisters and brothers? How are they going to be induced? Cheryl could have sex in a few years, but what about the little ones?"

"Idina is probably still young enough to transition just from being around the goddess, and the boys will be induced when they reach puberty. For males, it's less problematic. All they have to do is fight an immortal male and spur him into biting them and injecting them with his venom."

She lifted her hand. "Hold on. How is Idina going to transition just from being around the goddess? And how is she going to spend time with her?"

"I don't know how it works, but it does. The little girls go with their mothers to the sanctuary, and they turn immortal in no time. I assume it's easier for the girls because they don't only possess the immortal genes but also transfer it to the next generation."

Kaia shook her head. "That doesn't make any sense. Adult women need both venom and semen, pubescent boys need just venom, and little girls can be induced just by the goddess's presence? You're a scientist, William. Does that make sense to you?"

William shrugged. "Not everything can be explained by science. We don't know how thralling and compulsion work, and immortals and Dormants have other paranormal talents that can't be scientifically explained either."

As the puzzle pieces rearranged themselves in Kaia's mind, her eyes widened. "Is that why you have paranormals here? Do you think that they might be Dormants? Is that how you go about finding them?"

William snorted. "That would be at least semi-scientific, but that's not how it usually works. We hope to find Dormants among people with paranormal abilities, but so far, that's not how most of them were found."

"How does it usually happen?"

"The Fates bring Dormants and immortals together like they did for us."

"The Fates." She grimaced. "Are you serious? The Fates?"

"I am, and trust me, it wasn't easy for me to accept, but we had so many pairings that were the result of seemingly random encounters that I could no longer deny the facts."

The truth was that she should know better than most people that paranormal phenomena were real. She not only remembered a past life, but she'd also found proof of it. So why should she find the idea of fate so outrageous?

Kaia lifted a hand. "I'm willing to suspend disbelief for a moment and accept that fate is a thing. But you are talking about The Fates. Do you mean the three Fates from Greek mythology?"

"Yeah." He rubbed a hand over his jaw. "I know how crazy that sounds. The Fates weren't invented by the Greeks. Like most everything else in their mythology, including their pantheon, they inherited them from prior civilizations, and the originals were the gods themselves and their belief system. I too thought that the Fates were just a fantasy, but I have been proven wrong."

Kaia groaned. "So, what am I going to tell my family? That the Fates want my mother to leave the father of three of her five children so she can turn immortal?"

"You shouldn't tell them anything yet."

WILLIAM

*K*aia glared at him. "What do you mean? They are coming here this Saturday. What am I supposed to tell them?"

William took her hand. "It's not certain yet that you are a Dormant, and we won't know if you are until you transition. Why worry them needlessly? And what's more, why dangle immortality in front of your mother and sister and then take that hope away?"

Letting out a breath, she pulled her hand out of his and slumped against the couch pillows. "So much for no rush and having children before transitioning. I might have time, but my mother doesn't."

William hadn't asked her who she planned to have those children with, and he didn't want to. His fertility wasn't any better than that of an immortal female, so him giving her a child in time before she needed to attempt transition was unlikely. Could he tolerate her having one with a human male?

If Kaia was a Dormant, her children would turn immortal no matter who the father was, so denying her that option because he was jealous would be criminally selfish.

He couldn't think of her with another male, but artificial insemination was an option he would be willing to consider.

Could he, though?

He wanted Kaia to have his children, not some random human sperm donor's.

She put a hand on his thigh. "What's going on in your head? You look as if you are chewing on a mouthful of lemons."

"I'm just trying to figure out how it can all work out, and I don't like any of the solutions."

"Care to share your musings with me?"

Not really, but now that Kaia was privy to his biggest secret, William had lost his excuse to keep things from her.

"You said that you wanted to wait until you had children, but you didn't specify who you wanted to have them with."

Kaia smiled suggestively. "Are you volunteering?"

As anxiety over baring his soul to Kaia dried out his throat, William swallowed. "I know that we've just met and that talking about mating and having a family is premature, but nothing would make me happier than having children with you."

"You are right. It is premature." She patted his thigh. "I don't want to rush into getting pregnant right away, but since I've already completed my studies and my financial future is secure, I don't intend to wait too long." She took a sip from her coffee that was probably already cold, grimaced, and put the mug down. "I might be old-fashioned in that regard, but unlike my mother and Gilbert, who have three children together and yet are happy with their nonbinding arrangement, I want a wedding ring first."

Fates, the girl was decisive, and she went for what she wanted, like a bulldozer.

"Are you proposing?" He must have gotten infected by her bravado to chance such a loaded question, and now that it was out of his mouth, he waited anxiously for her answer.

Kaia tilted her head and eyed him from under lowered lashes. "Are you saying yes?"

Sneaky girl. "It's unfair to turn the question around, but if you are proposing, then I'm saying yes."

She laughed. "Talk about being irresponsible. We've known each other for less than a week."

He clasped the hand she'd put on his thigh. "What does your heart tell you?"

The smirk slid off her face. "My heart tells me that you are the one and that I will never find anyone as perfect for me as you are. But if I'm not a Dormant, and I can't turn immortal, we don't have a future together. I might be terribly old-fashioned, even compared to my own mother, but I want to be married to the father of my children." She swallowed. "Even if he's not my perfect prince."

"Then your choice is clear. You need to allow me to induce you before having children, and if you turn immortal, you'll just have to wait patiently to have them."

Kaia closed her eyes. "You can't expect me to give you an answer now." She opened them and leveled her gaze at him. "I need to give it a lot more thought. It's not a decision that can be taken lightly."

"That's perfectly understandable." He lifted her hand to his lips and kissed her knuckles. "I just need to give you one more piece of information to consider." It was one of the hardest things he'd ever had to confess, but there was no way around it. Kaia had to have all the facts before making her decision.

"Don't tell me that there are even more caveats."

"Unfortunately, there are. Immortal male fertility is just as low as the fertility of immortal females. I most likely can't get you pregnant even in your dormant state. It kills me to tell you that, but if you want to have children before becoming immortal, you need to consider having them with a human male. If you are indeed a Dormant, your children could become immortal no matter who their father is. I wanted to suggest artificial insemination, but you made it clear that you want to be married to the father of your children, so I guess that's not an option, and neither am I."

As tears pooled in the corners of Kaia's eyes, William expected her to tell him that it was over between them. Instead, she cupped his cheeks and kissed him lightly on the lips before pulling back. "I can't fathom a future without you in it, and I will not be the one to walk away. My choices, whatever they are, will always include you. Regrettably, that's not true on your side. If I can't turn immortal, it will be over between us."

"It won't. I will not let it happen. If you can't turn, I'll take whatever time you have to give me."

Kaia shook her head. "I will not do that to you. Watching the people you love die while you live on is a hell I don't wish on anyone."

7

KALUGAL

"You're home early." Jacki looked up at Kalugal with anxious eyes. "Did something happen at work?"

She was sprawled on the chaise in their bedroom with a pillow propping her enormous belly.

"Nothing happened." He knelt in front of her and pressed a soft kiss to her lips. "I couldn't concentrate at work and decided my time would be better spent with my beautiful wife. How are you doing?"

Jacki was a week late, and he was going out of his mind with worry. Bridget had said that it was uncommon for immortal females to go more than a day or two over their due date, and she'd given Jacki a device to wear twenty-four-seven to monitor the baby's heartbeat. On top of that, their son was a big boy, which amplified Kalugal's anxiety. Bridget had prepared them for the possibility that Jacki would need a C-section, another rarity for immortal females.

The monitor was the only thing keeping him from losing his freaking mind.

"As well as can be expected." Jacki cupped his cheek. "I'm so glad that Amanda talked us out of going to Egypt. I didn't know the last two weeks would be so miserable. I spent the morning floating in the tub."

He frowned. "Is the heartbeat monitor waterproof?"

"It has a water-resistant probe that I used."

He let out a breath. "Our son loves his mommy so much that he doesn't want to leave her womb." Kalugal feathered a kiss on Jacki's stomach. "But Mommy is uncomfortable, and Daddy is anxious to meet you, so you need to hurry up and be born."

"He'll come when he's ready." Jacki put a hand on her belly. "I love you."

"I love you more than words can express." He took her hand and started kissing one finger at a time.

When she winced, he thought that he'd accidentally nicked her with his fang, although it was highly unlikely that it could happen when they were not elongated.

"I'm sorry," he murmured against her fingers, searching for the one he'd nicked to lick the hurt away.

"About what? Making me pregnant?" She winced again. "Or telling Junior that it was time for him to be born?"

Understanding dawning, he felt his heart sink down to his gut. "Are you feeling contractions?"

He'd been waiting for this moment for months, but now that it was here, he was terrified.

"I'm not sure." Jacki frowned. "Real ones wouldn't be coming so soon one after the other, so it's probably nothing. But I've had false contractions before, and Bridget said to call her anytime I felt them."

"I'm calling her right now."

Kalugal pulled out his phone and called the doctor.

She answered on the second ring. "Is it time?"

"We are not sure. Jacki had two small contractions, one after the other, so she thinks it's the false ones again."

"At this stage of her pregnancy, I prefer for her to come to the clinic. And just in case it's the real thing, bring an overnight bag with you."

"Yes, doctor. We have it ready, and we are on our way." He looked at Jacki's face, searching for signs of distress. When she seemed fine, he relaxed a little. "I'll carry you to the golf cart."

She shook her head. "I should walk. If this is the start of labor, walking will speed things up."

Kalugal wasn't sure that he wanted things to go faster than they should, but it was Jacki's decision. He was just glad that he'd bought a golf cart for his household's exclusive use, so he wouldn't have to send someone to search for one of the clan's that was available.

Pushing to his feet, he offered her both hands and gently heaved her up. When she tried to find her flip-flops and couldn't see where they were because her belly was in the way, he knelt on the floor again and put them on her feet.

Jacki threaded her fingers through his hair. "Thank you. That's very sweet of you."

He pushed up and leaned over the belly to kiss her cheek. "I don't kneel for anyone except for you, my queen."

She rolled her eyes. "I'm a girl who grew up in the foster system. If I'm the queen of anyone, it would be the queen of underdogs."

Folding his arm behind her back, Kalugal smiled. "Even if that were true, I would still be your perfect loyal subject. I'm the guy who had to run for his life from his father, so I might be viewed as an underdog." He led Jacki into the elevator and pressed the button for the ground floor.

"Your father wouldn't have harmed you. In his own twisted way, he loves you."

Kalugal had often wondered about that. It had been arrogant of him to think that his father hadn't known that he was alive and that he couldn't find him. With enough resources and dedication, Navuh could have discovered his whereabouts when Kalugal had lived in New York and then in the Bay Area. That he hadn't could mean one of two things. One, that his father didn't care enough, and as long as Kalugal didn't try to overthrow Navuh, he was content to leave him be. The second was that his father loved him and wanted what was best for him.

The latter was unlikely, but Kalugal could fantasize that it might be true and that his father wasn't a monster.

There was also a third possibility.

Life in the Brotherhood and the constant rivalry between the so-called brothers was dangerous, so perhaps Navuh wanted one of his two true heirs to be away and in hiding in case something happened to Lokan.

That his father hadn't found the clan yet was also puzzling.

Navuh probably could have done away with Annani and her people a long time ago, but then he wouldn't have a nemesis to dangle in front of his people and unite them in hatred of it. The Brotherhood needed a mighty enemy to keep from falling apart, and since no human army or regime fit the bill, that left only Annani and her clan of immortals.

8

JACKI

*S*ix hours later, Jacki held their son in her arms. "He looks like you." She smiled up at Kalugal.

Even though she'd done all the work, the poor guy seemed more worn out than her.

Men.

Hiding her smile, she kissed the top of their son's head. It was covered in the softest dark fuzz, and he had quite a lot of it for a newborn. That extra week in the womb hadn't been for nothing.

Thank God that she hadn't needed a C-section as Bridget had feared, but she couldn't have done it without the epidural. Junior's birth weight was nine and a half pounds, and birthing a child this size naturally would have been a nightmare.

"I think he looks like you." Kalugal put his hand on the baby's bottom.

Jacki caressed their son's downy head. "He has your coloring."

"This hair can still fall out, and he could turn blond."

Unlike most men, her husband seemed disappointed that his son looked like him.

"Let's ask Gertrude what she thinks," she suggested.

The nurse had been a wonderful midwife. Her calm demeanor and cheerful attitude had made the process almost fun. She'd kept making jokes at Kalugal's expense, which he'd taken without complaint, and the many words of encouragement and compliments she'd paid Jacki had compensated for not having a mother to hold her hand during the birth of her first child.

As usual, thoughts of her mother and what had prompted her to give up her child saddened Jacki, and this was not the time to get melancholy.

"I already have." Kalugal grimaced. "She said that Junior looks like me."

"You sound so disappointed."

His eyes widened. "The love I feel for him and for you could fill up the universe. It's just that I kept imagining a boy with soft blond curls and blue eyes. A little angel like his mother."

Jacki chuckled, her hand caressing the baby's incredibly soft back. "First of all, I'm not an angel, and secondly, I kept imagining a little dark-haired daredevil with a charming smile and smart eyes like his father."

"You think that my smile is charming?"

She laughed. "Despite your enormous ego, you're such a glutton for compliments."

"Only from you. I need to know that I please you, my love." He put a hand over his heart. "It's ingrained in my immortal male makeup."

"You are the best husband any woman could wish for and the wisest," she said, only semi-mockingly. "And that's why you need to name our son." She batted her eyelashes at him.

Jacki had come up with more than a dozen names that Kalugal hadn't liked, but he hadn't offered any suggestions of his own.

"We will name him together."

She sighed. "You didn't like any of the names I came up with."

"I don't want to call our son Jonah after David's brother. It's bad luck to call a baby after someone who died prematurely."

Jacki groaned. "We can call him Guntar after your professor persona." At this point, she was willing to work with that. Their baby boy needed a name other than Junior.

Kalugal shook his head. "It has to be an original name and none that I've used in my disguises."

"Then how about something simple like a good old-fashioned biblical name. Benjamin, or Abraham, or Jacob?"

"Knock, knock." Syssi stood at the open door with Kian behind her. "Can we come in and see the little prince?"

"Of course." Kalugal rose to his feet. "I wondered what was keeping you."

"Allegra woke up and got fussy." Syssi walked up to the bed and leaned down to kiss Jacki's forehead. "How is Mommy doing?"

"Awesome. I had an epidural, and Bridget and Gertrude were wonderful." She cast a smile at her mate. "Not so much to Kalugal, but it was all in good humor."

He shook his head. "They ganged up on me, but I didn't let them bully me. I wouldn't leave the room through all the checkups they did."

"Good for you." Kian clapped him on the back and then pulled a cigar out of his pocket. "Do you want to step outside and smoke a celebratory Cuban?"

"Thank you, but I'm not leaving my wife and son's side. I'll take a raincheck."

"As you wish." Kian put the cigar back in his pocket. "So, does Junior have a name yet?"

Jacki grimaced. "He doesn't. We are open to suggestions."

"How about Darius?" Syssi said. "It means the upholder of good."

"In what language?" Jacki asked.

"Old Persian. There were several Persian kings and princes with that name, and most people associate it with rich and kingly because of Emperor Darius the Great. It sounds very regal."

"I like it." Kalugal looked at Jacki. "How about you?"

"I like it too." Jacki caressed her son's back. "But it's such a big name for such a small boy."

Kian peered at the baby from the other side of the bed. "This little boy will one day be a big man."

"Amen to that." Kalugal grinned. "My son was born for greatness. He's going to be the next Darius the Great."

Jacki rolled her eyes. "Is there a nickname for Darius?"

"Rius, or Dar," Syssi said. "But they don't sound cute. How about just Ri? Or Riri?"

"We can come up with a nickname later." Kalugal leaned down to look at his son's little face. "What do you say, buddy? Do you want to be named after Persian kings?"

"Darius," Jacki said to taste the name on her lips. "Dary. That's what I'm going to call him." She chuckled. "I wonder how long he's going to let me call him that. If he's anything like his daddy, he'll demand to be called Darius the Great as soon as he understands what it means."

9

KAIA

*A*s morning arrived and Kaia's alarm blared, she was already awake despite spending most of the night thinking over her options.

She hadn't stayed at William's, not because she'd been worried about Kylie making nasty comments in the morning, but because she needed to distance herself from him to think things through without him distracting her.

Regrettably, though, she hadn't come up with any perfect solutions, and each permutation required compromises that were too painful.

Family came first, but in this case, she would be sacrificing her future family for the one she had now. Her mother was forty-seven, which according to William, was already too old to transition smoothly, so she couldn't wait for her grandchildren to arrive first.

Even if she got pregnant today, nine months was a long time.

But what if her mother was willing to get induced without waiting for Kaia to transition?

Right. As if she would have sex with some random

immortal for a hypothetical chance of immortality. If Kaia transitioned, though, it would be proof that her mother carried the immortal gene, and then she might consider doing that. But she wouldn't do it on a maybe.

Still, even if her mother agreed, which she most likely wouldn't, Kaia didn't want the father of her child to be some random sperm donor. She wanted him to be the man she would spend the rest of her life with. But since that man was William, they needed to figure out how to have sex without him biting her and inducing her transition instead of getting her pregnant.

Was it even possible?

Perhaps she could put a muzzle on him, but she wasn't sure he could ejaculate without biting her. Even if he could, though, his fertility was so low that he might not be able to impregnate her for years to come if ever, and in the meantime, she might get too old for induction.

The easiest course of action was to give up on her wish to have children. She could let William induce her right away, and if she transitioned, her mother would be a confirmed Dormant and could decide what she wanted to do.

But even that wasn't simple. Kaia didn't want to decide on a monumental thing like that without consulting with her mother and Gilbert, and she definitely didn't want to go through the transition without having them and Cheryl by her side.

With a sigh, she threw the blanket off and slid out of bed. Perhaps a cup of coffee or two would clear her mind enough so she could come up with a new angle.

When Kaia emerged from her bedroom, Kylie greeted her with a knowing smile. "Good morning. Coffee?" She put a pod into the machine.

"Yes, please." Kaia handed her a mug to put under the spout.

"I'm surprised that you came back last night." Kylie leaned

against the counter. "I was sure you were going to spend the night at William's."

Kaia shrugged.

She didn't owe her roommate an explanation. Even if the two of them were besties, she couldn't share with Kylie any of her dilemmas and ask for her advice.

"Are you two going to move in together?"

"Maybe." Kaia pulled out the mug from the machine, added cream and sugar, and stirred. "Let me ask you something." She leaned against the counter next to Kylie. "Do you think I'm too young to have a kid?"

Kylie gasped. "Are you pregnant? Oh my gosh. William will be in so much trouble."

She sounded disgustedly gleeful.

"Relax. I'm not pregnant. I was just thinking that people wait to have children later in life because they want to finish their studies, get a job, and get settled. But I've already done most of it, so why wait?"

Kylie eyed her suspiciously. "Getting pregnant to trap a guy is idiotic. You must know that. You're young and pretty, and you should spend the next ten years partying and sampling the selection. Don't settle for the first guy who shows interest in you."

Why were people so quick to judge, and why did they tend to gravitate toward the worst conclusions?

"William is not my first, I have no intention of trapping him, and he's certainly not someone to settle for. He's a rare find." Kaia pushed away from the counter. "I'm going to the dining hall."

She should have known better than to ask Kylie for advice. Darlene was a much better choice.

"Don't get all pissy at me." Kylie caught up to her. "Hearing the truth is not always pleasant, but I would be a shitty friend if I lied to you. William is smart and handsome, but he's too old for you, and I find it disturbing that he's taking advantage of an employee. Is it even legal for him to have sex with you?"

"I'm an adult. I can have sex with whomever I choose. And just so you know, he didn't initiate anything. It was all me, and he tried to resist me."

"And he has conveniently failed. You are so naive, Kaia."

WILLIAM

*T*he door to William's office banged open and Kaia walked in, slamming the door behind her.

"I've had it with them." She dropped into one of the chairs in front of his desk. "They are behaving like middle schoolers and giving me shit about us being together. Can you fire them? I don't need them to complete the project. You and I can do it by ourselves."

It was tempting, especially since he could just take Kaia to the village and close down the lab in Safe Haven, but it wasn't fair to the others. Besides, Kian would be upset about spending all that money on the new lab for nothing.

"I've gotten a few smirks and nasty looks as well." William swiveled his chair to the side. "Come here." He patted his knees.

Pouting, Kaia got to her feet, walked around the desk, and sat in his lap. "Are you going to fire them?" She wrapped her arms around his neck.

"No, but I'll have a talk with them." He kissed her lightly while rubbing soothing circles on her back.

William wasn't looking forward to having a talk with the team.

He didn't like confrontations, and if not for Kaia, he would have just pretended not to notice the looks and whispers. But for her, he would go to war and battle nasty attitudes with the ferocity of a dragon.

Her forehead furrowed. "Why not just get rid of them?"

"Because the contract obligates me to provide them employment as much as it obligates them to work for me."

"If you pay them what's in the contract, they wouldn't mind not having to work for the money."

"Come on, Kaia. They can't be that bad, and they are helpful. You give them all the tedious tasks that would be a waste of your time. Isn't that punishment enough?"

When she shrugged, he added, "I can also ask Maggie to make their lunches so nasty that they will beg to be released from their contract."

He didn't get the laugh he'd expected.

Resting her head on his chest, Kaia let out a breath. "Their help is marginal, and now that I know what I'm dealing with, I'm even more careful about what I let them work on. I don't want them to figure out the big picture. It would be so much less stressful if it were only the two of us."

"Let's give it another week. I'll take the team out for dinner in one of the neighboring towns, buy everyone drinks, and hopefully, that will do the trick. If not, I'll ask Eleanor to compel them to smile at you throughout the workday and say nothing about our relationship."

This time, he got the laugh he'd expected before. "They will figure out that they are under compulsion, but thanks for offering me the option." She straightened in his arms. "What do you think about me moving in with you?"

His heart skipped a beat. "That would be wonderful." He never would have dared to suggest it, but to have Kaia in his bed all night, every night, would make him tremendously happy. "When?"

"Today after work. I don't want to see Kylie's smirking face first thing in the morning."

"What about your family? They are coming to spend the weekend with you, and I'm sure Gilbert will not be happy about your new living arrangement."

Mirth dancing in her eyes, Kaia scrunched her nose. "He's probably going to punch you. Please, don't kill him."

That was an odd comment. He'd told her that immortals were stronger than humans, but he was no warrior.

"I'm not much of a fighter, so you should worry about me more than you should worry about your stepfather."

"You are very strong, though, right?"

He nodded. "Compared to a human."

"So, if you punch him back, it could be dangerous. Gilbert is not the young stud he thinks he is."

"I will not punch him back. I can seize his mind and make him believe that he's okay with us being together."

"Don't do that." Kaia cupped his cheeks. "I want my family to accept you and our relationship because they like you and see how happy you make me. I don't want them to be coerced, thralled, or compelled to give their approval."

"Are you sure? What if your mother and Gilbert throw a major tantrum?"

"They won't. I'll be subjected to some talking to, and probably you'll get the same treatment, but they will not make a scene. After all, I'm an adult, and I get to choose my own boyfriends."

William wasn't sure at all that there would be no scene. Gilbert liked stirring things up, and he enjoyed being the center of attention. He might do it just for kicks-and-giggles.

Perhaps he should have Max with him when he confronted the overprotective patriarch of Kaia's family. The Guardian could restrain the guy.

"Have you told your mother about us?"

Kaia shook her head. "Only Cheryl knows that there is something going on between us, and the secret is safe with her. She won't tell anyone."

"Good. So we have time to prepare a strategy. Any suggestions?"

Kaia chuckled. "We could throw an engagement party. If they know that you are serious about me and not just using me for your sexual needs, they would be more accepting."

He arched a brow. "I thought you were a very close-knit family. Don't they know you better? You would never let anyone take advantage of you, and so far, it's been more about your sexual needs than mine."

He regretted the words as soon as they left his mouth. It was true that she'd been the one to push for them to get together, but he wanted her just as much and probably more than she wanted him. And as for his needs not being fully fulfilled yet, it had been his choice to withdraw and not finish inside of her. He had done it to protect her, but he didn't want her to feel guilty about it.

Luckily for him, the comment didn't upset Kaia, probably because her mind was still focused on her family.

"That's all true," she agreed. "But Gilbert likes to pretend that I'm still a little girl. And speaking of needs, did you get condoms?"

Evidently, his comment hadn't flown over her head, but his Kaia was a pragmatic lady, and instead of playing games she thought of solutions, which he should have done instead of waiting for her to remind him.

William felt his cheeks warm up. "Not yet."

"I can get them at the nurse's office at the lodge," she offered.

He didn't even know that the nurse had them. "How do you know that you can get them there?"

"It makes sense. They preach free love in those retreats, and the community members practice that philosophy, so they must provide protection."

"I think that they demand proof of contraception from the females, and if they also screen everyone for sexually transmitted diseases, they might not have condoms. Perhaps I can get them when we take the team out for dinner."

"I don't want to wait that long." She clasped his cheeks and pulled his head down for a kiss.

MIA

*A*t five o'clock on the dot, Mia put away her journal and stored her coloring pencils in their box.

For the past week, she'd been writing down her ideas for Perfect Match adventures and sketching the environments she envisioned for them. Before meeting Toven, she'd done most of her storyboarding on the tablet, but he'd converted her to paper journals. The beauty of using them was that she could flip back and forth between the pages, and she would always have a physical copy of her journey. The downside was that making changes wasn't as easy, and her journals were messy.

How did he manage to keep his so neat and tidy?

Practice? Or did he have everything perfectly organized in his mind before putting it down on paper?

Mia sighed. He was a god with endless time to master every skill, and he was also brilliant. Why the heck had the Fates chosen her for him?

He deserved someone so much better, and she wasn't even thinking about her disability. Her heart was now perfectly healthy, and her legs were growing, and in a year, she would be physically whole. But she hadn't become any smarter or more talented, and he was still light-years out of her league.

Perhaps she would get an answer for that disparity today.

Amanda and Syssi were coming over to test her enhancing ability, and if they confirmed it, then perhaps what the Fates had in mind for her was to boost Toven's performance. Mia had no problem with being his supercharger and having no special talents of her own. It would at least make more sense to her as to why she'd been chosen for him.

Turning around, she drove her chair to the living room.

The motorized wheelchair was wonderful, allowing her to drive around the village and visit her neighbors, who happened to be part of her family. Well, Toven's family, but even though they weren't married yet, they regarded each other's relatives as their own.

Mia's life was so perfect that she was afraid of hoping for more things, like her legs to be done growing already and her friends to be able to move into the village, find mates of their own, and turn immortal.

If Frankie and Margo proved to be Dormants, plenty more members of their extended families could be Dormants too, join the ranks, and make more clan people happy. There were so many immortal bachelors and bachelorettes yearning for a meaningful, life-long partnership. If she could, Mia would find each and every one of them a mate so they could all be as happy as she was.

For now, though, her contribution could be enhancing some of their powers, provided that Syssi was right about her being a booster. She and Amanda were bringing along several immortals to test the hypothesis.

The original plan was for her to test her ability at the university, enhancing the performance of the people volunteering there, but Amanda had pointed out that her boosting ability would be most beneficial to the clan if she could enhance the skills of other immortals.

When the doorbell rang, her grandmother rushed out of the kitchen.

"I've got it." Mia zoomed over to the door and opened it. "Good afternoon, everyone."

Out of the four additional immortals accompanying Amanda and Syssi, Mia knew only two.

"You know Vivian and Ella." Syssi said.

"I do. Hello, ladies."

"Hi." Ella leaned down to give her a brief hug. "How are you doing?"

"Excellent, thank you." Mia moved her chair back to let everyone come in.

The tall, broad-shouldered female offered Mia her hand. "I'm Kri."

"And I'm Michael, Kri's mate." The only guy in the bunch offered her his hand.

"I've heard that you are both Guardians."

Michael smiled. "Kri is a Guardian. I'm still in training."

His mate patted his shoulder. "Michael is what we call a Guardian in training, but he's already gone on several missions with me."

When Mia's grandmother walked into the room, a few more minutes were spent on introductions, and then Amanda motioned for everyone to sit around the dining table. "Let's get to it, people. I've left Evie with Dalhu, and I want to be done as quickly as possible."

Syssi chuckled. "And I left Allegra with Kian. Both our daughters are perfectly fine with their daddies."

"Let's begin with Michael." Amanda motioned for him to get closer to Mia. "I also want to test if proximity has an effect."

"Michael is a telepath, but he can only read emotions and

intentions." Amanda waited for him to switch places with Vivian. "He can't read thoughts. I'm going to think something very specific, and he will try to read my mind."

"What do I need to do?" Mia asked.

"Nothing. You didn't do anything special when you were with Syssi, so we must assume that you do it involuntarily."

Amanda turned her gaze toward Michael, and for a long moment, no one said a word. When she was done thinking, she smiled at him. "What did you sense?"

He had a curious look on his face. "It was definitely stronger than usual, but I still couldn't hear your thoughts. You were thinking about a fashion show, with models going up and down the runway on impossibly high heels and sashaying their hips in an exaggerated way. I felt your yearning to be there in person, and a little sadness about not being able to attend."

"Excellent." Amanda clapped her hands. "It wasn't a verbal mind communication, but your visuals were much better than usual." She regarded Mia with appreciation in her incredibly blue eyes. "Let's see what you can do for Vivian. She can communicate mind-to-mind verbally, but only with her daughter. Ella and her mother can have a mind-to-mind conversation as if they were talking on the phone, and it's not affected by distance. They can be on different sides of the world and still be able to talk to each other."

"I'd rather Ella went first." Vivian motioned for her daughter to take the seat next to Mia. "You're the more powerful telepath."

"Can you hear the thoughts of people other than your mother?" Mia asked.

Ella shook her head as she took the seat Michael had vacated. "I have a little more control over the communication with my mother, but I still can't read the thoughts of others. Let's see if sitting next to you will enable me to hear Syssi's thoughts."

"Here it goes," Syssi said.

A long moment passed with the two staring into each other's eyes, and then Ella grinned.

"You were singing 'Itsy Bitsy Spider' in your head."

"Yes." Syssi clapped her hands. "Were you ever able to do that before?"

"Not with anyone other than my mother."

"I want to try." Vivian got to her feet and traded places with her daughter. "But this time, I want Kri to think something at me. She doesn't have a paranormal talent, and maybe that affects the results as well."

"I have a talent." Kri pouted. "How come no one knows about it?"

Michael chuckled. "Because no one expects you to be a calming influence. You are so intense."

"I'm not." She crossed her arms over her chest, her biceps bulging like a bodybuilder's. "I'm calm and collected."

"Can we go back to the experiment?" Amanda asked.

When everyone nodded, she waved her hand at Kri. "Think of something."

After a long moment, Vivian shook her head. "Nothing. I couldn't hear or sense anything."

Kri turned to her mate. "Michael. You give it a try."

It took only a couple of seconds for a grin to spread over Vivian's face. "Yellow, green, red, purple, and white. You were thinking about those colors. I could see them as if they were flashcards in my mind."

"That's exactly what I imagined." Michael lifted off the chair and high-fived Mia. "Congrats on the most awesome talent."

"Wow," Mia whispered. "I didn't believe it until now."

"You've got it, girl." Ella high-fived her as well. "I'm curious to see what you can do for Cassandra's talent. With you at her side, she might be able to blow up an entire building."

"I don't think so," Amanda said. "I think that Mia can

enhance only certain talents. We need to do further testing to dial it in, but that should be done at the university lab."

KAIA

*W*ith a frustrated sigh, Kaia glanced at the time displayed on her computer screen and willed it to be five-thirty already.

The underground lab felt stifling, her colleagues were annoying, and despite the fascinating research subject and the progress she was making, the day had been dragging on.

She couldn't wait to get topside.

But the truth was that it wasn't about her teammates or the tension in the lab. Halfway through the day, Corrine and Kylie had gotten tired of making comments about her and William, and Owen hadn't said anything to begin with. The cause of the antsy feeling was that she still didn't have clarity on what she was going to tell her family when she called home tonight.

When the clock finally announced that it was dinner time, Kaia let out a breath, collected her papers, and got to her feet.

"I can put everything in the safe," she offered to take her teammates' notes as well.

When they handed her their work without comment, and Corrine even smiled at her, Kaia wondered whether William had told them to back off. If he had, he'd done it by using a thrall, because she hadn't heard him talking with anyone about anything that didn't have to do with the project.

As she walked into his office, he took the papers from her and dropped them into the safe. "Ready for dinner?"

"Can we take it to go and eat at your place?"

He eyed her with a frown. "Are they still bugging you?"

She shook her head. "They either got tired of picking on me or you thralled them to stop."

"I didn't do anything." He wrapped his arm around her shoulders. "They must have realized that acting like idiots was unbecoming of scientists. Let's eat a quick dinner in the dining hall and then have coffee at my place."

"Yeah. You're right. I will not hide, and I will not cower."

"That's my girl." He kissed the top of her head. "On the way, you can update me on the progress you've made today."

She nodded.

When they were outside, she waited for the others to get ahead of them to tell William her findings. "We don't have the technology to grow skin, muscles, and the internal organs for the cyborgs. If we manage to build them, they are not going to look human."

He slowed down his steps. "Didn't they include instructions on how to make that happen?"

She shook her head. "The information I've deciphered provides molecular structure for some of the tissues, but so far, I found no reference to the equipment they used to actually produce them in mass quantities. We have the ability to make small quantities of skin by taking skin cells from patients and growing them into personalized artificial skin grafts. They are used to help burn victims. We can even genetically reprogram skin cells into their more primitive state, in which they have the potential to become almost any other type of cell in the body, including brain cells. But it's difficult to turn those cells into self-renewing stem cells for a particular organ. At this time, scientists are working on producing muscle stem cells as a treatment for muscle-wasting disorders like muscular dystrophy, but the research is still in its infancy. It will be decades before the research and the biotechnology reach the state where tissue and organs can be produced in quantity."

"Unless we discover how to make it happen faster with the help of Okidu's journals. So far, you've just seen part of one journal."

Kaia had known there were more than the one she'd been working on, but she underestimated the quantity of the remaining journals. No wonder William was reluctant to dismiss the rest of the team.

"I hope you don't intend to keep the team here until all the journals are deciphered. It will take years."

"I don't." He opened the door to the dining hall. "Once I have a grasp of what I'm looking at, I'll continue with my own team."

He meant the immortals working in his other laboratory.

With her family occupying whatever brain bandwidth was left over from her work, Kaia had neglected to ask more questions about William's people.

How many were there?

He'd said that the enemy had tens of thousands of immortal warriors and that his clan was tiny in comparison.

Had he meant a few thousand?

A few hundred?

Were there other immortals in Safe Haven apart from William, Eleanor, and Emmett?

The answer to that was probably yes. William had told her that he trusted the guys in security implicitly and that he'd worked with them for years, so they were probably immortal as well.

What about Darlene, though?

She looked to be in her forties, and that meant that she was human. Otherwise, she would look as young as the other immortals.

Well, Emmett's age was impossible to determine, but under his beard and long hair, and his flowing robes, he probably looked just as young as William and Eleanor.

As they collected their trays from the kitchen window and carried them to the table, Kaia looked around the dining room to check if anyone was paying them any attention. Her teammates were busy chatting with the paranormals, and only Darlene waved at them from where she was sitting with James and Mollie.

"Is Darlene like the others in your family?" Kaia asked in a whisper.

"Not yet, but we hope that she will soon join us."

So, Darlene was a potential Dormant. "Do you know that for sure?"

William nodded. "Her mother, sister, and son are all part of the family."

Interesting. So, they were all immortal except for her.

"How come she hasn't joined already?"

William sighed. "Up until very recently, she was married to a verbally abusive jerk. She wasn't ready to enter a new relationship."

Kaia snorted. "She seemed very ready to me. She and Eric hit it off right away."

"They did, but he's not what she needs."

Kaia's smile died on her lips. "Right. She needs one of yours to become a family member."

"Yeah. But she fancies your uncle. She knows he's not looking for a relationship, so he seems like a good choice for her first foray into the dating scene."

"That's a shame." Kaia lifted the lid off her plate. "They seemed to fit so well together, and I hoped that Eric had finally found a woman he could connect with. The guy needs to stop dating girls half his age."

William arched a brow. "Said the kettle about the pot?"

She laughed. "I'm not dating girls or guys half my age. That would be illegal."

WILLIAM

*A*fter dinner, William escorted Kaia to her bungalow. "Are you sure you don't need my help?"

He was thrilled about her moving in with him, and he didn't want to chance her changing her mind. If he helped pack her things and moved them into his place, she wouldn't have time to second-guess her decision.

"I have only one suitcase, and it has wheels." She smiled at him with understanding in her too-old eyes. "I'm perfectly capable of rolling it a hundred feet or so to your place." She put her hand on the door handle but hesitated before going in. "It might be a while before I come over, though, so I don't want you to worry if I don't show up in the next ten minutes. I didn't call my mom yesterday, and I'm sure she left at least ten messages on my phone demanding that I call her as soon as I can."

"Why didn't you call her last night?"

"I was overwhelmed, and I didn't know what to tell her. She always knows when I'm trying to hide things from her. She can hear it in my voice."

He took her hand. "What are you going to tell her?"

"I don't know yet, and that's why it might take a while. I need to figure out how to tell her about us without actually telling her that we are together. I don't want her freaking out and boarding a plane tonight, but I want to give her a hint, so she won't be totally shocked when she gets here and finds out that I moved in with you."

He didn't want her to get in trouble with her family, and as much as it pained him to admit it, the smart thing to do would be to wait until after they left. "Maybe we should wait. If you move in with me Sunday night, it will give you a whole month to drop hints and prepare them."

Kaia smiled. "That would be the prudent thing to do, but it would also be dishonest and cowardly, and that's not how I roll. I'd rather fess up and face the music than hide and lie. You are not a shameful secret, William." She rose on her toes and kissed his lips. "You are my Prince Charming."

Ducking into her bungalow, Kaia left him standing with a stupid smile stretching across his face.

He liked being her Prince Charming even though he hadn't earned the title yet. Kaia deserved to be courted properly, with flowers and chocolates and romantic candlelight dinners at fancy restaurants.

William hadn't done any of that, but he was going to.

First, though, he needed to stop by the nurse's office and get condoms, provided that she had them. It wouldn't be very Prince Charming of him to let Kaia pick them up.

Snorting a laugh, he turned on his heel and strode in the lodge's direction.

The girl was something else. She didn't have one shy bone in her body, and he loved that about her, but he had to man up and be just as fearless as she was, or she would lose respect for him.

Was it old-fashioned of him to think that? Did women still want their men to be brave and fearless?

"Hey." Darlene walked up to him. "Where are you going?"

Great. Now she would want to know why he was going to the lodge, and since he'd just made that speech in his head, he would have to tell her.

"To the lodge."

"I'm heading there too." She tilted her head. "Are you coming to watch the movie?"

It would have been so easy to lie and tell her that was the reason, but to be worthy of Kaia, he had to be brave.

Or not.

He could also be evasive.

"What movie are they playing tonight?"

"*The Runaway Bride*. I'm a sucker for silly romantic comedies. You should have brought your team with you." She smiled conspiratorially. "Or just one team member. Is Kaia joining you later?"

"She's not." He swallowed. "She's packing her things and moving into my bungalow."

"Yes!" Darlene pumped her fist in the air and then jumped to hug him. "I'm so happy for you."

"Thanks." He awkwardly patted her back. "Regrettably, the other teammates are not as happy about us getting together. They think of me as a cradle robber and of Kaia as an opportunistic girl who's sleeping with her boss to gain favor."

"Screw them." Darlene waved a dismissive hand. "They don't know what they are talking about, and their opinions are irrelevant."

He shook his head. "I need them to work with Kaia and not make her life miserable. I plan to take them all out to dinner and have a talk with them. Can you find a nice place in the area and make reservations?"

"I would gladly do that, but there is nothing in the area. The nearest town is an hour's drive away, and I doubt it has any decent restaurants."

"I know, and I don't mind the drive. I think the team is starting to develop cabin fever, and that's why they are being nasty to Kaia and me. A road trip would be good for them."

"Aye, aye, captain." Darlene gave him a two-fingered salute. "I'll take care of everything, and if you need me to talk some sense into them, I will gladly do that as well." She squared her shoulders. "Am I invited to the dinner as well?"

"Of course. And you should also allow for at least two Guardians. Kian will not approve an outing without a proper escort."

14

KAIA

*K*aia was done packing in minutes. She hadn't folded anything and had just emptied the dresser drawers into her suitcase, collected her toiletries, her laptop, her phone, and all the chargers, and dropped them in the suitcase as well.

If she hurried, she could be out of the bungalow before Kylie got back from dinner, but that would be a coward's move, and Kaia was no coward.

As she'd expected, her mother had left her several messages, and she needed to call her, but she could do that from William's place. Then again, if she was waiting for her roommate to return, she could do that now.

As Kaia sat down on the bed with the phone in her hand, she wondered whether she should launder the bedding. Supposedly, someone from the community had been hired to clean the place once a week, but she didn't know if that included changing the bedding and towels.

Probably.

The community ran the resort, and they did that for the guests of the lodge, so they probably did the same in the bungalows.

"Stop stalling." She bit down on her lower lip and called her mother.

She picked up before the first ringtone. "Kaia, I was worried about you. Why didn't you call me last night?"

It was on the tip of her tongue to say that she'd fallen asleep in front of the television, but her mother would sense the lie right away.

Was it her paranormal talent? Or just something every mother could do?

"I had a lot on my mind that I needed to sort through."

There was a long moment of silence, and then her mother sighed. "Are you still troubled by Anthony's disappearance?"

Kaia hadn't thought about Tony at all last night, but in a strange way, he was connected to everything she'd learned.

Coincidence?

Fate?

"Of course. It's not like he's been found."

"I don't want to sadden you, but you need to face the possibility that you're never going to see him again."

If her mother only knew how right she was.

"I know. I still hope he will get free somehow."

"Free from what?"

Kaia squeezed her eyes shut. "From whoever is keeping him. I refuse to believe that he's dead."

"I hope you are right. Let's move to a less depressing subject. How is the research going? Any breakthroughs since Tuesday?"

Kaia could only talk in generalities, but her mother knew that and was satisfied with what she could tell her.

"Nothing major. We are just chipping away at it one paragraph at a time."

"Do you still think that you will be done ahead of schedule?"

"I don't know. It's a massive project, but I don't think

William intends to decipher everything at one go. We might be done with the initial stage sooner than he expected."

"Good. I want you back home. The house feels empty without you."

Kaia chuckled. "I doubt it. How is Idina doing?"

"She's excited about visiting you. She packed her swimming suit in her backpack along with her teddy bear, and she was ready to go. She asks if you went swimming in the pool."

"I didn't but tell her that I will go swimming with her when she gets here."

"That will make her day. I have to go, sweetie. Ryan is screaming his head off. Evan probably took his favorite tiger away from him."

"Bye, Mom. Give everyone kisses from me."

"Will do."

As her mother ended the call, Kaia let out a breath. That had been easier than she'd expected. She had lied only by omission, which wasn't a big deal. Her relationship with William was the only thing she could have told her mother, and that could wait until Saturday. All the rest was locked down inside of her by compulsion, and she couldn't tell her about it even if she wanted to.

Given the sounds coming from the living room, Kylie was back, and she wasn't alone. Corrine and Owen were there as well, which was going to make moving out doubly awkward, but whatever.

Once it was done, it would be behind her.

Stalling for a few more minutes, Kaia opened every drawer, checked the bathroom, and even peeked under the bed to make sure she hadn't missed anything.

When there was nowhere else to look, she took a deep breath, extended the handle of her suitcase, and opened the bedroom door.

Kylie's eyes zeroed in on the suitcase. "Where are you going?"

"I'm moving in with William."

"Are you sure that's smart?" Corrine asked. "If you have a fight, it will be very awkward to work together."

Kaia looked pointedly at Owen and then back at Corrine. "We are not going to fight. William and I see eye to eye on most things." She pasted a sugary smile on her face. "We are a match made in heaven."

"Congratulations." Kylie rose to her feet and pulled Kaia into her arms. "It was fun rooming with you for a few days. I hope it works out between you and William, but if it doesn't, I'll happily share this bungalow with you again."

Surprisingly, she sounded sincere.

Maybe Kaia had been too quick to judge them all. "Thank you. It means a lot to me." She briefly hugged Kylie back. "I'll see you all tomorrow at breakfast."

As she opened the door and walked out, the crisp air dried off the sweat from her brow and cooled down her overheated skin.

It had gone much better than she'd expected, and she was glad to have that one hurdle behind her. But that had been the easy part. Her family would not be as accepting, and going by her teammates' initial response, Kaia would have one hell of a fight on her hands. It would have been so much easier if she could just tell them the entire story.

Or maybe not.

Perhaps it was better to pace the shocking revelations.

In a way, it was similar to her baby brothers' immunization shots. Instead of throwing everything at them at once, it was better to give them smaller shocks over an extended period of time.

15

WILLIAM

*W*illiam paced around the bungalow's living room. It was only fourteen feet across, and the pacing made him dizzy, but he couldn't stop. He was restless for reasons that had little to do with his daring expedition to get condoms.

Getting them from the nurse's office had been much easier than he'd expected. She hadn't been there, the door had been open, and he'd found a basket full of them on her desk with a note instructing guests to help themselves.

No one had seen him going in or leaving.

He'd filled up his pockets with an assortment without checking sizes or quality, so hopefully, at least some would work. His experience with using condoms was limited, and he hadn't bothered with them since Hannah had left. Even while they'd been dating, he'd been reluctant to thrall her, and had held off as long as he could. Eventually, though, she'd become impatient, and his resistance had crumbled. Still, they'd been intimate only a few times before she'd left.

Hannah must have thought that he had a low libido, and

compared to other immortals, that might be true, but not compared to human males. He'd done it to protect her, but as the saying went, no good deed went unpunished, and she'd left him.

Well, she'd left because she'd gotten a position in another lab that had been closer to her family, so it wasn't only about him, and if he'd cared about her enough, he would have followed, but he hadn't.

If a similar thing happened with Kaia, he would go after her to the ends of the earth and find a way to keep working for the clan remotely.

William didn't regret his time with Hannah. She'd gotten him started on a healthier lifestyle, and she'd given him a crash course in having a meaningful relationship with a woman. In a way, she'd prepared him for his truelove mate.

When the knock he'd been awaiting sounded at the door, he rushed to open it for Kaia and pulled her into his arms. "What took you so long?"

She chuckled. "It wasn't long at all. I thought that talking with my mother would take me much longer, but I was saved by Ryan demanding her attention."

He took the handle of her suitcase and rolled it toward his bedroom. "I made room in the closet for your things."

"I don't need much space." She followed him into the room. "One drawer for underwear and a second one for T-shirts and jeans, and I'm good."

"You didn't bring any dresses?"

"I don't even own any." She looked at the bed that he'd made while waiting for her. "Why are you asking?"

"I want to take you out on a proper date to a nice restaurant. I thought that you would want to wear something nice."

She sat on the bed and dropped her flip-flops on the floor. "I'm not the fancy restaurants kind of girl, and I don't need a nice dress to get a hamburger. Gilbert likes taking us to fancy places, and the truth is that I rarely enjoy the food." She smiled. "We are spoiled by Berta, who is an excellent cook."

"Who's Berta?"

"Our nanny and cook."

He sat next to her and draped an arm over her shoulders. "You said that you didn't know anything about me, but I don't know much about you either. What's your idea of a perfect date? What do you like to do for fun? What are your expectations from your guy?"

She leaned into him. "I love it that you want to please me, but I'm very easy to please. My idea of a perfect date is a walk on the beach with a smart guy who I can talk to about things that interest me. An ice cream cone for a snack, a hamburger with fries and an ice-cold Coke for lunch or dinner, great sex for dessert, and I'm as happy as can be." She put her head on his shoulder. "As for fun, I like all of the above, and as for expectations from my guy, all of the above plus honesty and kindness." She took his hand and brought it to her lips for a kiss. "So, as you can see, you meet all of my requirements, and the only thing you haven't done yet is treat me to an ice cream cone, a burger, and fries."

"I want to do so much more for you."

She lifted a finger. "I forgot one thing. Did you get condoms?"

William chuckled. "You are the least romantic female I've ever met, and I love that about you just as much as I love everything else. You're perfect."

Reaching into his pocket, he pulled out one of the packets he'd gotten earlier and handed it to her. "I grabbed a bunch. So, if this one is no good, I have plenty more."

She turned over the packet in her hand and then handed it back to him. "If you are counting on me to know what to do with one of these, don't. I've never put one on a guy."

"There is a first time for everything." He hooked a finger

under her chin and pressed a soft kiss to her lips. "Just thinking about you putting it on me got my fangs going."

Her eyes widened. "Let me see."

Smiling broadly, he gave her a full view of his elongating fangs. "Do they scare you?" The question came out slurred.

"Yeah, they do. They are huge." She lifted a finger. "Can I touch one?"

He nodded. "Just be careful. They are very sharp."

KAIA

$\mathcal{T}$he other time Kaia had seen William's fangs, they must have been only partially elongated, and looking at them now, they were monstrously long.

But even with the glowing eyes and the sharp fangs, William somehow still looked harmless. As her mother used to say, it wasn't about what gifts people were blessed with or disabilities they were burdened with, but what they chose to do with them. A good example of that was the guy with the highest IQ in the world who was bartending in a small town.

William might have the fangs of a saber-toothed tiger and the strength of a gorilla, but he would never harm anyone unless he was protecting those he loved.

As carefully as she could, Kaia touched one fang with her finger, not near the sharp point but higher up, and then gently smoothed it down.

When William closed his eyes and a groan escaped his throat, she realized that his fangs were sensitive and that having them touched turned him on.

"Can I touch the other one?"

His answer was another throaty groan, and as Kaia got emboldened and smoothed her finger down the other fang, she wasn't as careful and nicked it on the sharp tip.

"Ouch." She tried to pull it out, but William caught her hand and sucked the finger into his mouth.

As his tongue swiped over the small injury, the pain stopped, and when he released her finger, there was no trace of the nick.

"How did you do that?"

"My saliva has healing properties." He looked at her from under hooded eyes. "It can also do all kinds of other interesting things."

She remembered those things, and the memory had her core tighten in anticipation. "You have a very talented tongue, but today, I want to experience you coming inside of me."

"One does not negate the other." He slid down and kneeled at her feet. "Let me worship you, my princess."

"Well, if you ask so nicely." She whipped her T-shirt over her head. "Can you turn off the light?"

He looked at her with a smile tugging on his lips. "Are you being shy?"

She smirked. "I'm being romantic. Some things are better done in the dark."

"Indeed." William pushed to his feet, walked over to the light switch and flicked it off, plunging the room into nearly complete darkness.

Some moonlight filtrated through the semi-opaque window treatments, and William's glowing eyes provided additional illumination, but she could still barely make out his features.

"How come you can't turn the lights off with your mind?"

"I can't control inanimate objects." He kneeled before her again and tugged on her jeans. "I can only control the minds of sentient beings."

"No animals?" She lifted her bottom to help him take her pants off.

"Animals are sentient, but some have such limited brain capacity that they can only respond to the simplest suggestions." Chuckling, he shook his head. "Does this qualify as dirty talk?"

Kaia laughed. "For me, it's the dirtiest. And if you start talking about aliens hiding in the depths of the oceans, I might orgasm."

He arched a brow. "What about an alien underground base on the dark side of the moon?"

Kaia affected a moan. "Stop. You'll give me multiple orgasms before we even start."

He laughed. "You're funny."

"If you don't believe me, take off my panties and see for yourself."

Her offer turned the amusement in his eyes into raging desire. "Oh, I intend to." He nuzzled her over her panties, hooked his fingers in the elastic, and slowly tugged them down. "You smell delicious." He pressed a kiss to her folds. "And you taste delicious as well."

As it dawned on her that he had his fangs next to the most sensitive part of her, Kaia fought the urge to close her legs. "You're not going to nick me, are you?"

"Not by accident."

As he scraped his fangs over her inner thigh, she shivered in part from excitement and in part from fear.

"But don't worry." He lifted his glowing eyes to her. "I promise you that you'll know only pleasure from me."

Kaia wasn't averse to a little erotic pain, but she was still learning William's peculiarities, and if she was honest, those fangs still scared her.

Slow and gentle was the name of the game for now.

Letting out a breath, she lay back and braced on her fore-arms. "I trust you."

"Thank you." He kissed her folds again. "Your trust means a lot to me." He lifted her legs over his shoulders and pushed his hands under her bottom. "Gorgeous." He murmured for a moment before licking into her.

WILLIAM

When Kaia exploded all over William's tongue, throwing her head back and calling out his name, he fought the urge to bite into her inner thigh and release his venom right there and then. One day he would do exactly that, but since this would be her first time experiencing his bite, fully aware and also remembering it later, he wasn't willing to squander the delight of her offering him her neck.

He had never experienced a female's willing surrender, never had even thought of it as something that he desired, but now that he could have it, he craved it more than his next breath.

As Kaia's tremors subsided, he pressed one last kiss to her drenched folds, lowered her trembling legs to the bed, and with immortal speed, took off his clothes.

Pushing back to fully lie on the bed, Kaia chuckled softly. "I wondered if you could move so fast, or was it just my perception that was warped, but you really do have a vampire's speed."

Smiling to reveal his fangs, he grabbed the condom packet off the nightstand and tore it in half. "Let's see how fast I can do this."

She lifted her hand, the movement lethargic from her post-orgasmic bliss. "Take your time. I want to watch."

William didn't like anyone watching him undress, let alone put a condom on, and this was highly uncomfortable for him. But he was no longer a fat guy who never had sex with the lights on and always thralled the female's memory of him afterward. Even now, after the weight loss and the training, he was still far from a sexy Adonis, but he was okay to look at, and Kaia accepted him the way he was and didn't want him to change.

"I hope I remember how to do it." He tried to roll the condom on his shaft, but the thing was either too small, or he was doing it wrong, and it tore. "Damn."

"Let me do it." Kaia shifted on the bed and rose to her knees. "I've never done it before, but it's not rocket science." She snorted. "Or maybe it is." She looked at his shaft and licked her lips.

As his manhood swelled even more in response, William doubted Kaia would have better luck putting the condom on him than he'd had.

For a long moment, he just stared at her gorgeous body, transfixed by the sight of her breasts.

She was so unabashed, so free with her body that it was enviable. But then she was perfect, and he wasn't.

Kaia smirked. "Not so fast now, big boy, are you?"

Was she referring to his overall size or to the size of his manhood?

Hoping it was the latter, William leaned down, picked his pants off the floor, and pulled out a new packet.

"I hope this one is the right size." He handed it to her.

Kaia looked at it for a moment before tearing it with her blunt front teeth. "This one is an extra large. It should fit." She beckoned him to get closer.

As her palm wrapped over his shaft, the grin her comment

had put on his face was replaced with a hiss, and when she leaned down and kissed the tip, he nearly climaxed.

"If you don't want me to come all over your face, don't play with me."

"Who said I don't want that?" She rolled the condom on his staff with deft fingers. "But we should save that for later." She let go, lay back down, and cupped her breasts. "Come to me."

He was on top of her before the last word had left her mouth, and as she spread her legs to cradle him between them, his shaft found her entrance like a heat-guided missile.

Kaia moaned as he gently pushed just the tip into her, arching to take more of him inside her. She was slick from orgasming only moments earlier, but she was tight, and he wanted this to be the best sexual experience she'd ever had, even before the venom made it so.

Wrapping her arms around him, Kaia lifted her head and licked at the seam of his lips, demanding that he let her in, and although his first instinct was to deny her entry and take over the kiss, he wrestled it down and opened for her.

Her tongue darted in, and as she swirled it around his right fang, his restraint was shot, and he surged the rest of the way inside of her.

She gasped into his mouth, but he detected no distress in the sound, and as he pulled nearly all the way out and surged back in, the throaty moan she emitted was all about pleasure and need and not about pain.

"William," she whispered against his lips. "You fill me up so perfectly."

He couldn't agree more.

The need to go fast and hard was so strong that it threatened to overwhelm his resolve to go slow, but he was still mindful of Kaia's human fragility and wrestled the animal threatening to take over.

It had never risen so close to the surface before. When

William had heard other immortal males talking about it, he assumed that they didn't have enough control over themselves, but now he understood how difficult it was to keep the beast subdued when the sexual encounter was as explosive as this one.

Letting go of Kaia's mouth, he continued controlling the force of his thrusts until he felt her nearing another climax. With only seconds to go, she turned her head, offering her neck, and he had no choice but to let the beast take over. Somehow, he still retained enough reason to lick the spot before biting down and ejecting his venom along with his seed into her.

Kaia exploded again, her climax nearly as violent as his, and as another one hit her a moment later, her eyes rolled back in her head, and she blacked out.

Panting, William remained suspended over her for long minutes, the blissed-out expression on her beautiful face soothing his worry and assuring him that she was perfectly fine.

Even if he'd been a tad too rough, no trace of it would remain by the time she floated back to earth, and there would be no ache in her body to indicate otherwise.

JADE

*T*wo months had passed since the last time Jade had been summoned to Igor's bedchamber. Two blessed months to mentally recuperate from the humiliation.

But she was in her fertile cycle again, and the bastard either kept a calendar to keep track of his breeders' cycles or he had sniffed out her fertile state despite the strong soap she cleaned herself with and the fragrant oils she used to rub all over her skin to throw him off.

The worst part, the most humiliating, was that her body responded to that murderer. She had no control over it. Kra-ell females were programmed to challenge their males and allow only the strongest the chance to impregnate them, and Igor was no doubt the strongest and most ruthless she'd ever been with.

Except, nothing about coupling with Igor was according to Kra-ell traditions. The females were the ones who were supposed to summon the males and not the other way around. On top of that, the females in Igor's compound couldn't refuse a summons, while according to Kra-ell customs, the males were not obligated to accept the invitation and could refuse it. It rarely happened, and only when the male's station was far above the female's or if her leader objected. To receive a summons was considered a great honor for a male, and to refuse it was considered a great offense to the female.

The system was perfect for their society and given to them by the Mother of all Life. To turn it on its head the way Igor had done was a great affront to the Mother and to their customs, and since he and his men didn't allow the females the right of refusal, the correct term for sex in the compound was rampant rape.

It didn't matter that once Igor overpowered her, Jade's traitorous body welcomed him inside of her. She hadn't invited him, and she didn't want to be with him. They weren't animals, and nonconsensual sex couldn't be defined as anything other than a violation.

Jade's one ray of hope was her discovery of Veskar's whereabouts, or Emmett as he called himself these days.

For the past two days, she'd been trying to come up with a plan for contacting him without getting caught or alerting Igor and his cronies to his existence, but so far, she had only a seed of an idea. She needed to phrase her email to Veskar in a way that would let him know it was from her, but to anyone else, it would seem like an innocent inquiry about some random crap she needed for her teaching.

She was known for her parables and her twisting of human fairytales, so if she were to write the email in such a way, Igor might not catch on to the secret message hidden within it.

Veskar might not be able to help her or want to get involved, but hopefully, he didn't harbor that much resentment against her that he would betray her trust or ignore her plea for help. At the very least, he would know that she and the other females were still alive and their general whereabouts. She couldn't give him an exact location, but she could give him broad coordinates. It was a tall order to hide all that between the words of a parable or a fairytale, but she'd figure it out.

When Jade reached Igor's chambers, the guards posted at his door opened it for her, and she gave them a haughty look as she walked in. She wouldn't give them the satisfaction of looking distraught or reluctant. If they thought she was willing, she could retain at least some scraps of her dignity.

Igor knew how much she hated him and that she would kill him on the spot if she could, but the sick bastard enjoyed her hatred and used it against her.

As usual, she found him sitting in his favorite throne-like chair in front of the fire.

"You summoned me." She remained standing at the doorway.

He demanded of her and all the other females to call him master, but she didn't unless he forced the issue.

"I did." Igor turned in his chair and regarded her with a frown. "Why are you dressed in your work clothes?"

"I didn't have time to change. Your summons was to come right now, and as you know, I have no choice but to obey your commands."

"One of those commands is for you to change into traditional formal robes, and yet you find ways to defy me time and again."

Jade stifled a smirk. It was a tiny and insignificant rebellion, but to defy him in any way felt like a victory, and she needed those small wins.

Dipping her head in mock respect, she hid the twitch of her mouth. "When you command me to show up right away, it overrules your previous command to change for the occasion."

For a long moment he regarded her with his cruel eyes, and despite her bravado, Jade could barely control the trembling of her limbs. He'd whipped her several times during her years of imprisonment, and he'd reveled in her pain. She was careful not to cross the line and give him an excuse to punish her so severely, but the truth was that he could do whatever he wanted to her whenever he felt like it.

"Get in the shower," he commanded.

Jade released a covert breath and dipped her head. "Yes, master."

19

KAIA

"*I*'m going to work in the main room." Kaia rose to her feet, walked over to the other side of the desk, and kissed William's cheek.

He pulled her down on his lap. "Why? Don't you like being all alone with me in here?"

"I like it too much, which makes it hard to concentrate."

Sitting in front of William was distracting. Her mind kept wandering to last night, and she'd caught herself daydreaming about the bite, the explosive orgasms it had triggered, the euphoria, and the incredible trip through alien worlds.

Kaia had never experimented with drugs, not even weed, but she doubted any hallucinogen could rival that experience. She could easily get addicted to that and turn into a nymphomaniac.

William nuzzled her neck. "I have a solution for that. I can lock the door and do naughty things to you on my desk."

She laughed. "How is that going to solve the problem of my inability to concentrate for more than five minutes? Every time I look at you, I'm reminded of last night, and I start daydreaming."

His smile was all smug male satisfaction. "If we do as I offered, you will no longer have to daydream." His hand snaked under her T-shirt, rubbing gentle circles on her belly.

Yeah, as if blacking out for several hours would help with her workflow. After William had bitten her, Kaia had been out for at least three hours, and when she'd floated back down from the clouds, she'd felt so refreshed that she'd woken William up and had her way with him again.

He hadn't bitten her the second time, though. Evidently, immortal males had no limit to the number of times they could make love, but their venom glands weren't as randy.

As his hand inched up to her rib cage, she put her hand over his to stop him. "I'm trying to downplay our relationship for the sake of teamwork. This is not helping."

Grimacing, he pulled his hand out from under her T-shirt. "Yeah, you're right. Which reminds me that I need to check with Darlene about our outing this evening."

"What outing?"

"Did I forget to tell you? I asked her to find a nice restaurant in one of the nearby towns and make a reservation for eight."

Kaia frowned. "Eight in the evening? Isn't that late for dinner?"

"The reservation is for five-thirty in the evening for eight people."

Her frown deepened. "Did you hire more people and didn't tell me?"

Talk about absentminded. Most times it was adorable, but sometimes it got annoying.

"Of course not. I wouldn't forget a thing like that. There are five of us on the research team, Darlene is coming with us as well, and I need to take at least two Guardians along."

"Oh." She pushed out of his arms and got to her feet. "Since the nearest town is an hour's drive away, you will need to cut the day short. We have to leave Safe Haven around four o'clock to get there on time."

"Right." He rubbed a hand over the back of his neck. "I didn't think of that."

Kaia put a hand on her hip. "In fact, you should let everyone go at two, so they can get ready. Especially if it's a nice restaurant. If it's a burger joint or a pub, we can go straight from here."

William chuckled. "A pub is not an option. You can't order alcohol."

That was so ridiculous. She was a damn PhD, could vote, get married, and have kids, but she couldn't order beer in a pub.

"Can't you get me a fake ID? I'm sure you and your people make them in-house."

Being immortal and living in hiding probably required them to have multiple serial fake IDs. Their faces didn't age, so every ten years or so they needed to get a new ID with a different name.

That must be so confusing.

Was William using his first name in all of them and just changing his last name?

Someone someday might notice that there were several Williams who looked identical and had different last names.

"We have a guy," William said. "He does an excellent job of producing fake documents for us, but he won't be able to make it and ship it here before we go out this evening. If I order it now, I can get it in a few days." He pulled out his phone and typed something on the screen faster than humanly possible.

"Seriously?" She gaped at him. "You are getting me one? I was just joking."

He stopped typing. "Do you want one or not?"

"Of course I do." She sat back in her chair and leaned her elbows on William's desk.

Her mother and Gilbert wouldn't be happy about it, but she didn't have to tell them everything. It wasn't as if they didn't approve of her having the occasional beer or a glass of wine at home. And she didn't plan to get drunk or do something outrageous with the help of her fake ID. She just wanted to order one measly beer with her meal.

"All done," William said as he finished typing the text.

20

WILLIAM

"Thank you." Kaia smiled.

She was so beautiful, but when she smiled, she was breathtaking.

"You're most welcome."

William couldn't take his eyes off her. In fact, he hadn't been able to wipe the smile off his face since waking up this morning with her in his arms. It had been almost as good as the two bouts of lovemaking last night, and if they hadn't overslept, he would have treated her to another round before work.

Thankfully, Darlene had given up on him showing up for their morning swim and hadn't called him at four-thirty in the morning to wake him up.

Kaia crossed her arms over her chest. "When you're done staring at me, call Darlene and ask her how fancy the restaurant is where she made the reservation. I don't have anything to wear other than jeans and leggings."

He stared at her for a moment longer. "You are so stunningly beautiful that it doesn't matter what you wear."

Her smile was brilliant. "Thank you, but some of the fancier

DARK WHISPERS FROM AFAR

places frown upon customers showing up in flip-flops and T-shirts."

"I can always thrall them to think that you are wearing an evening gown and stilettos."

Kaia laughed. "I thought that it was against clan law to thrall humans for frivolous reasons."

"It is, and it's also against the law to thrall people to gain an unfair advantage. But it's not strictly enforced, and I'm not a lawman, but I am a council member, so I guess I need to hold myself to higher law-abiding standards."

Kaia lifted a brow. "You didn't tell me that you are a council member."

William shrugged. "Sometimes I forget. I'm first and foremost an engineer and an inventor, and my domain is the tech lab. I leave the politics to others."

Kaia nodded. "I get it. I hate politics too. Most people are in it for the money and not because they want to serve the public. The whole system is built on companies financing candidates who will look after their interests when elected." She chuckled. "The United States is probably the only country in the world where corruption is part of the system and perfectly legal."

"It's not like that in the clan. The goddess's children who manage the clan affairs as regents, dedicate their lives to protecting our people and providing for them. Their share in the clan's profits is significantly larger than that of members who don't contribute their work to the clan, but it is in no way proportional to what they've had to sacrifice over the years nor to the amount of work they still put in to this day."

Kaia unfolded her arms. "I want to know more about the clan and how it's run, but you'll have to tell me about it later. Right now, you need to call Darlene and find out about the reservation."

"Right." He picked up his phone and dialed Darlene's number.

She answered right away. "Hello, boss. Did you sleep well this morning?"

"Kaia and I slept splendidly." Switching to the speaker so Kaia could hear, he smiled. "Thank you for not calling to wake us up."

"Yeah, thanks for that," Kaia said.

Darlene laughed. "I value my life. Despite how sweet you usually are, I didn't want to push my luck."

"Thank you. Did you find a restaurant in the area?"

"I found a seafood restaurant with decent reviews, but it's nearly a two-hour drive from here. All the ones that are closer are simple eateries. Do you still want me to make a reservation?"

He looked at Kaia, who was shaking her head. "Simple is good. I won't need to change into anything fancy, which I don't have."

"I can lend you something," Darlene said. "You're taller than me, but I'm wider, so the difference should even out."

William wasn't sure how that could work, but what did he know about women's clothing?

"Are you sure you have stuff to spare?" Kaia asked.

Darlene chuckled. "I brought two full suitcases with me, and they are filled with new stuff. After being kept on a strict budget most of my life, I went a little wild with mail order. You'll have a lot of never-before-worn items to choose from."

Kaia pouted. "Is that seafood restaurant really so highly rated?"

"It looks promising," Darlene said. "After what we've had to eat here all week, I can't wait to order a plate of succulent shrimp."

Kaia's eyes lit up. "Okay, I'm sold. When can I come over to borrow something?"

"Right now, if you want. It's not like I have to drive from the office. It's a five-minute walk."

William didn't want to point out that she was supposed to stay in the office, but the truth was that she didn't have much to do now that the team was settled and Kaia and Corrine were keeping the lab organized. But Darlene was still remotely taking care of his stuff in the main lab back home.

Kaia looked at him. "When are you letting everyone out of here today?"

"If we make reservations for six in the evening, I think two o'clock dismissal should do it."

"Can I come over then?" Kaia asked Darlene.

"I'm looking forward to it. I always wanted to have a daughter I could go clothes shopping with. I had a couple of shopping trips with my mother and sister, and those were fun, but it's not the same."

Kaia leaned over the phone. "I hate to spoil your fun, but I'm going to be the only one shopping, and it's going to be from your closet."

"It's as close as I'm going to get unless my son gives me a granddaughter."

KAIA

*K*aia stared at her computer screen, the symbols blurring into a shadowy, incoherent mass. Focusing on her work hadn't been any easier in the main room than it had been in William's office, but for a different reason.

No longer being exposed to his male magnetism didn't mean that her imagination couldn't provide the missing stimuli or that she could push the memories of last night's passion aside. Besides, her mind had found more issues to obsess about.

How could she reconcile being with William and having children in the foreseeable future?

Could she have both?

Should she try to have children before attempting to transition?

Or should she transition first and let fate decide when to gift her with a child?

Could she have a child from a sperm donor for William to raise as his own?

That was the best compromise she could think of. William would be a wonderful father even if the child or children weren't biologically his, and one day, in a few centuries, they might be blessed with a child who would be.

Her family was doing wonderfully despite her and Cheryl not belonging to Gilbert biologically and not referring to him as their father. That wasn't because they didn't love him or didn't accept him as a father figure, but because calling him Dad would have felt like a betrayal of their biological father's memory.

Nevertheless, their family worked great, and it was proof that her idea of using a sperm donor could work.

But then there was the issue of her mother's age. She didn't have the luxury of time to wait for Kaia to have a couple of kids if she were to successfully attempt transition.

Why did it have to be so complicated?

Kaia really needed to talk to someone, but she couldn't because all of this was a secret, and she'd been compelled not to share it with anyone but William.

Once two o'clock finally arrived and William's office door opened, she turned her computer off, pulled out her fob, and collected her papers.

After everyone's work was locked in the safe and William opened the lab's door, Corrine put her hand on Kaia's arm. "Do we have you to thank for this outing?"

"It was William's idea, but my complaining about the food might have inspired him."

"Good job." Corrine patted her arm. "Keep complaining."

"Yeah," Owen said. "I've already started developing cabin fever. Isn't that odd?"

"It's too soon." William climbed the stairs. "It's the idea of being isolated rather than the isolation itself that gets to you."

"I know." Owen was right behind him. "It's not like I get out a lot when I'm back in the Bay Area. I'm either working or in my apartment."

"We only see each other and the paranormals," Kylie said.

"That's not enough. I want to see new faces. Let's make an outing to a restaurant a once-a-week treat."

William looked at her over his shoulder. "I'll see what I can do."

When they were out of the building and the others headed to their bungalows, William took Kaia's hand. "They seem to be getting used to the idea of us being together."

She nodded. "It was a good decision to just flaunt it instead of trying to hide it."

He wrapped his other arm around her. "I'll escort you to Darlene's place."

It was only a few minutes' walk away, but she wasn't complaining.

"Can I talk with her about the stuff you told me?"

"I don't see why not. She knows most of it. The only thing she doesn't know is what we are working on, and I would like to keep it that way."

"Why? Don't you trust her?"

"I do, and I also trust many others who have no idea what I'm working on out here. But the fewer people who know about it, the better. Not everyone is good at keeping secrets, and this is important." He sighed. "There is still so much I need to tell you, but whenever we are alone, we get distracted by other things."

Kaia lifted a brow. "Is that bad?"

"No, it's good." He stopped in front of one of the bungalows in the paranormals' section. "Have fun with Darlene." He leaned and kissed her cheek.

"Wait." She held on to his hand. "How are you going to release me from Eleanor and Emmett's compulsions so I can talk to Darlene?"

"Easy. You need to keep everything I told you a secret from everyone except Darlene. Just don't tell her about the project or about the informant we have on the Doomer's island. That's classified information as well."

Kaia frowned. "I don't think this will work. You can't pick and choose which part of the secret I can reveal and which I cannot."

"I can't. But I trust you not to reveal things I asked you not to."

"I'm glad." She leaned up and kissed him on the lips. "I'll see you in a bit."

"Take your time." He squeezed her hand. "I'm jealous about every moment you spend with someone else, but you need someone who is not me to talk to, and Darlene is a great listener."

DARLENE

"Welcome to my humble abode." Darlene pulled Kaia into a quick hug. "We are going to have so much fun."

Kaia seemed a little taken aback by the exuberant display of affection, but Darlene didn't care. She was in a great mood today and dressing up a doll-like Kaia was going to be super fun.

"Thank you for inviting me." Kaia looked around the messy living room. "Who are you rooming with?"

"No one." Darlene led her to the bedroom. "I asked for a bungalow all to myself, and William graciously provided one for me. Don't mind the mess. It's part of my therapy." She opened the closet door. "Pick whatever you want."

Kaia thumbed through the selection of outfits hanging in the closet. Most were brand new with the tags still attached, and some Darlene hadn't even tried on yet. She was waiting until she lost a few more pounds before she dared to get into the size eight dresses she'd ordered.

"Forgive me for asking, but how is mess therapeutic?" Kaia pulled out a black dress and looked it over. "My mother drilled it into my head that a well-organized room is a reflection of a well-organized mind." She hung the dress back in the closet.

"She isn't wrong." Darlene pulled out a pink one that she knew would look lovely on Kaia. "It's just that I lived with a neat freak who terrorized me for over two decades to the point that I got an anxiety attack if something was out of place. I'm curing myself of that by ignoring the mess."

"Good for you." Kaia eyed the dress as if it was indecent. "You want me to try this on?"

"It's going to look lovely on you. I don't know what possessed me to order it for myself. It doesn't go with my coloring, and it's too tight in the hips." She gave Kaia a once-over. "You have slim hips and large breasts, which is the perfect shape for this dress."

"If you say so." Kaia took the hanger from her. "Well, it doesn't hurt to try, right?" She put it on the bed. "It's what I tell Idina when she doesn't want to eat something." She whipped her T-shirt over her head and dropped it on the bed as well. "I tell her to take one small bite, and if she doesn't like it to spit it out." She kicked her flip-flops off and pushed her jeans down.

The girl had a killer body, which was so unfair given that she also had a beautiful face and a brilliant mind. Darlene was a god's granddaughter, but her gifts were much more modest than Kaia's.

"I hate you," she said jokingly. "How can you be so perfect?"

Snorting a laugh, Kaia took the dress off the hanger and pulled it over her head. "Thank you for the compliment, but I'm far from perfect." She shimmied into the tight dress, trying to pull it down to cover more of her thighs. "Isn't that too short for me?"

"A little," Darlene admitted. "And the pink color is too light for you. You look like an albino." She reached into the closet and pulled out another black dress that was slightly longer than the one Kaia had looked at before. "Try this one on."

"Thank you." Kaia looked relieved to take off the pink one. "Maybe you should return it. It still has the tags on."

"I might do that when I get back to the village." Darlene took the dress from her, put it on the hanger, and returned it to the closet.

"Do you like it there?" Kaia unzipped the black dress and pulled it on.

"I love it." Darlene zipped it up for her. "I've never been happier. But then, I'm finally free, and I get to spend time with my son, so that might be the reason. I also found out that my mother wasn't dead, that I have a sister, and that my grandfather is a god."

"Wow." Kaia's eyes widened. "William didn't tell me any of that. Heck, he didn't tell me much at all." She smirked. "We often get distracted."

Darlene laughed. "I bet." She looked Kaia over. "There is a mirror in the bathroom. Go take a look."

"I want to hear all about your grandfather and the mother that you thought was dead but wasn't."

"First, choose what you want to wear tonight, and then I'll make us coffee and tell you my story." She narrowed her eyes at the girl. "You know that you can't reveal any of the things I'm about to tell you?"

Kaia put her hand over her heart. "Your secrets are safe with me. Can I tell William?"

"He already knows everything there is to know about me." She gave Kaia a slight push into the bathroom and followed her inside.

"I love it." Kaia smoothed her hand over the side of the dress. "It's not too tight or too revealing, but it's still sexy." She turned to look at herself in profile. "Do you think I can wear it with flip-flops? I have a black pair."

Darlene grimaced. "You need nice pumps with a dress like that."

"I don't have any with me. I only have one pair of sneakers and three pairs of flip-flops."

"What's your shoe size?"

"Nine and a half." Kaia wiggled her toes. "I have big feet. My sister calls me Frodo."

"That's mean. You have very nicely shaped feet." Darlene sighed. "Regrettably, my shoes won't fit you, so you are stuck with the flip-flops."

Kaia grinned. "I'll rock that look." She pulled off her glasses, put them on the vanity, and then tugged on the elastic holding her long hair and shook it out.

When Kaia let her hair down, she looked like a supermodel. It was long, wavy, and full, and it framed her face in a gold halo.

"Wow." Darlene took a step back. "Why the hell do you keep that hair in a ponytail? It's gorgeous."

"It gets in the way." Kaia flipped it over her shoulder. "So, what do you think? Can I get away with wearing flip-flops?"

"You can, but can you see without your glasses?"

"I'm farsighted, so yeah, I can see, but it's not going to be comfortable." She lifted the glasses off the vanity and put them back on. "That's much better."

"You know that you won't need them after your transition."

Kaia nodded. "I'm not going to miss them, that's for sure. I tried contact lenses, but they irritated my eyes, and I figured looking good wasn't worth the pain."

Darlene laughed. "You're a rare breed, Kaia. Most women are willing to suffer a lot to look good. Take stilettos for example. In my opinion, they are torture devices that some sadist designer invented to torment women with, and yet, they are not only willing to wear them but also to pay a lot of money for the privilege."

"Or corsets." Kaia stepped out of the bathroom. "Why would anyone subject herself willingly to that?"

KAIA

"*L*eave it on," Darlene said as Kaia reached behind herself to unzip the dress. "Is there a chance you will let me do your makeup?"

Normally, Kaia would have said no, but Darlene seemed so happy to play dress-up with her that she didn't have the heart to refuse.

"You can if you want to, but I don't look good with a lot on. A little mascara and some lip gloss are the most I can get away with. Anything more, and I look like a clown."

With her fair skin, even the lightest blush and a smidgen of color on her lips looked fake.

"I will just line your beautiful eyes with some shadow and add mascara. You don't need any more than that." Darlene pulled out a chair and motioned for Kaia to sit down. "So, how are you taking the whole thing? William said that you weren't overly surprised when he told you about the shadow world of immortals no one knows about."

"I was surprised, just not shocked. I have always believed that humans are not the only intelligent species in the universe, and I also believe that we have had many alien visitors throughout our history. The one thing I never imagined was that I might be part of that as well." She wanted to say immortal but couldn't.

Evidently, the compulsion still prevented her from repeating what William had told her, but she could work around it. None of what she'd said was sharing what he'd told her. Those had been her thoughts and beliefs long before she'd met him.

"I assume that you already started working on it?" Darlene opened a makeup bag and pulled out a brush and a shadow palette.

"Not yet. I need time to think things through."

"What is there to think about?" She opened the palette and swirled the brush in the powder.

"You didn't do it right away either. Is it because of your age? Are you afraid of attempting it?"

"That's not it." Darlene hooked a finger under Kaia's chin and tilted her head up. "I'm a god's granddaughter, which means that I am close to the source, therefore I have better odds of transitioning successfully, so I'm not worried about being too old, and I'm taking my time. It's just that I'm recently divorced, and I'm still healing from the scars caused by my marriage. I need to re-enter the dating scene gradually, and jumping into bed with a hunky immortal who looks my son's age is intimidating." She swiped the brush over Kaia's eyelid.

So that was why Darlene had been flirting with Eric. He was her chosen training-wheels lover, not someone she wanted long-term. That would be her immortal inducer.

"I guess Eric is not as intimidating."

Darlene nodded. "I know that he's a player and that he's not looking for a relationship, and that makes him perfect for my re-entry."

"I understand, but I'm disappointed that nothing can come out of it. It's time for him to stop chasing women who are too young for him and settle down with someone closer to his age, but you need one of your own people to do that thing for you."

Darlene took a step back and regarded her with a frown. "Are you still under compulsion not to talk about what William told you?"

"He tried to remove it, but it didn't work." Kaia smiled. "But I'm managing to work around it."

"Clever girl." Darlene dropped the shadow palette into her makeup bag and pulled out mascara. "Now that you know why I'm still human tell me why you are not jumping on the immortal bandwagon with both feet."

"It's the fertility thing. I've always wanted a big family, and I didn't want to wait long before having it. If I accept William's proposal, I will have to give up that dream, so I'm trying to figure out a way around it."

"There is no way around it." Darlene brushed mascara over Kaia's lower lashes. "That's the way it is with immortals. But you might get lucky and not have to wait for centuries to have a child. Kian and his wife have a little girl, and they met only four or five years ago."

"Is Kian's wife like me?"

Darlene nodded. "She was the first Dormant the clan discovered, and that's also a great story, but I will tell you about it some other time. We need to talk about you and what's keeping you from immortality."

"It's good to hear that Kian and his wife got lucky, but I can't count on it. I even considered having a kid or two before changing, but William said that he probably couldn't get me pregnant so quickly, so I thought about getting artificially inseminated, but that doesn't solve all of my problems either. If I'm a carrier, my mother is a carrier as well, and since the only way to prove it is to go for it, I have to do it quickly because she's not getting any younger."

Darlene finished applying the mascara, dropped it in the

makeup bag, and sat on the bed facing Kaia. "When you dreamt of a big family, you didn't know that you were a Dormant and that you had all the time in the world to have a child. Now that your circumstances have changed, you need to adapt your dreams to your new reality. Besides, what if you are not a Dormant? Do you want to have some random stranger's children and then discover that you did that for nothing?"

She hadn't thought of that, but while it was a chilling thought, it wasn't a deal-breaker. "I come from a blended family, and it's great. I would prefer to raise my children with their father, but it's not as important as having them in the first place."

Darlene shook her head. "I had Roni with a guy I met at work while I was separated from my ex, and he had no idea that Roni was his. I went back to my ex-husband and convinced him that he was the father. My ex must have suspected that it wasn't true, and even though he never demanded a paternity test, he was a shitty father. But at least I knew who the real father was and that he was a good guy with a great brain that Roni has been lucky enough to inherit. When you get pregnant from a sperm donation, you don't know anything about the other half of your child's genetics. They can tell you all kinds of stories at the clinic, but you will never know for sure. And let's face it, genetics determine at least half of a person's character. Don't you want to know that your child is not going to have murderous tendencies?"

Kaia rolled her eyes. That's a bit far fetched, don't you think?" Nevertheless, her conviction was starting to falter. "Artificial insemination is just one of the ideas floating around in my head. Given my mother's situation, it's not likely that I'll go that route, but it makes the decision to attempt this thing right now even harder. Perhaps my mother should attempt it first, and in the meantime, William might get me pregnant."

She shook her head. "I can't believe I'm considering any of this. I'm nineteen. I'm not ready to become a mother."

Darlene leaned forward. "Do you love William?"

Kaia swallowed.

They'd known each other for a week, and it was stupid to think that she was in love with a man she barely knew, but the thing was that she did know him, and he was the best man she'd ever met. Even if he wasn't immortal, and she wasn't a Dormant, she would have wanted a future with him.

"I do."

Darlene smiled. "Then that's your answer. You need to rearrange your priorities accordingly. I would never tell you to abandon your dreams for a man, but in this situation, it's a no-brainer. Regardless of your mother, you need to find out whether you are a Dormant before you make any other decisions about your future, and that means going for the transition now with the knowledge that you might have to wait much longer to fulfill your dream of having a large family."

24

WILLIAM

*A*s Kaia opened the door, William's breath caught in his throat.

She had been beautiful before, with her hair gathered in a ponytail and in loose-fitting jeans, but she was absolutely stunning in a black mini dress with her wild hair cascading down her back and shoulders.

"We are not going anywhere." He pulled her into his arms. "I don't want any men to see you looking like that and ogle you."

She laughed. "Those who ogle would do that no matter what I wear. Besides, I'm yours." She kissed his lips. "So all they can do is be jealous."

Kaia's words made William's heart soar with emotion. She'd told him that she was falling for him, and she'd even told him that she couldn't fathom a future without him in it, which was as good as saying that she loved him, but she hadn't said those words to him, and she'd never said that she was his before.

He hadn't told her that either, not because he didn't feel it but because he didn't want to spook her. For the same reason, he also hadn't told her about the powerful bond immortal couples formed or about the addiction that, in time, would prevent her from desiring anyone but him.

How could they talk about spending eternity together and having a family without going through those important steps? Those affirming words needed to be said, and he also needed to tell her what she should expect.

Kaia wasn't a coward, and she wasn't rash either. She could handle him telling her that he loved her, and she might be okay with the bond, but the addiction might scare her.

"I like to hear you say that you're mine." He took her hand and led her to the couch. "You know that I'm yours, right?"

She smiled nervously. "It's still nice to hear."

"Does that scare you? Are we going too fast?"

Kaia barked out a laugh. "I should be the one asking you that question. I was the one pushing for us to get together."

"So why are you nervous?" He clasped her hand.

She closed her eyes and let out a slow breath through her nose. "I need to tell you something, but I don't know how to do it right." She opened her eyes. "So, I'll just say it. I love you."

When William opened his mouth to tell Kaia that he loved her too, she lifted a hand to stop him. "I know that you're going to say it's not possible to fall in love after knowing a person for only one week, but we are perfect for each other. I will never find another man like you, and I'm not talking about the immortality part. I would have felt the same if you were human. In fact, I would have been less conflicted about our future together if you were not an immortal with sucky fertility because I want kids."

Even her comment about his fertility couldn't wipe the smile off his face. "Are you done?"

She nodded.

"What I wanted to say was that I love you too. I fell in love with you on the doorstep of your house back in California. And you are right about us being perfect for each other. You might be young and haven't met a lot of people to compare me with, but I have been around for a long time, and I've never felt for anyone anything even remotely close to what I feel for you. I'm looking forward to spending eternity with you, and that's a very long time."

"I feel the same." She gave his hand a light squeeze. "Do immortals adopt children?"

"We can't adopt human children for obvious reasons, but if an immortal couple gets married and the lady has children, her partner can adopt them." He lifted her hand to his lips. "If you decide to have kids before your transition, I'm fine with that." He narrowed his eyes at her. "I can't get you pregnant in time, so your only alternative is artificial insemination because I can't think of you with another man. Once you transition, I will adopt your children and raise them as my own."

"Thank you for being so considerate." She slumped back against the couch pillows. "But I'm not going to do that. Even if I was willing to get pregnant right away, which after giving it a little more thought, I've decided that I am not ready for that, my mother doesn't have the time to wait nine months or eighteen months until I have the minimum two kids that I want. Besides, it will really suck if, after having those kids and attempting transition, I find out that I'm not a Dormant and that we don't have a future together. I would have rushed for nothing while giving up on raising my children together with their father."

It pained William that he couldn't give Kaia everything she wanted, but there was always a chance that the Fates would bless them with children sooner rather than later.

25

KAIA

*W*illiam didn't look as relieved as Kaia had hoped he would be. In fact, he looked pained.

"What's the matter? I thought you would be happy that I'd given up on the idea of having kids before transitioning."

Wrapping his arms around her, he lifted her into his lap. "I'm sorry that I can't give you everything you want."

She cupped his cheek. "You've given me more than I ever expected from a guy, and you might also give me immortality. All I'm giving up on is my impatience. I will just have to wait until we are blessed with a child, no matter how long it takes. Darlene helped me realize that I need to change my perspective on things and adjust to my new reality."

"I'm glad that you have someone to talk to about all this. Most Dormants don't have that luxury."

"I know, and it helped a lot. But just so you know, the compulsion still holds. I had to talk around it, but luckily, Darlene had no problem figuring out what I was talking about."

"I'm sorry about that. I was concerned that the only ones who could change it were Emmett and Eleanor."

"Yeah, I suspected the same, but it was worth a try. It was

also good practice before my family arrives tomorrow." She winked at him. "I can tell them everything despite the compulsion."

The panicked expression on his handsome face made her laugh.

"Don't worry. I won't tell them anything." She sighed. "It will be difficult enough to tell them about us being together. Gilbert is going to flip."

"How about your mother? Will she be more accepting of us?"

Kaia chuckled. "She's going to flip on the inside and try to appear reasonable on the outside. She will try to convince me very calmly and logically why I should not be with a man thirteen years my senior, especially after knowing him for just one week. Even Cheryl tried to talk me out of it."

He arched a brow. "You told your sister?"

"I told her that I've managed to break through your defenses and that you've given in to my advances. She said that you were the smart one and that I probably pursued you so incessantly only because you were resisting, and I always have to win. Then she added that my stubbornness would one day bite me in the ass."

"Was she right about any of it?"

"Totally wrong." Kaia lifted her face to him and kissed the corner of his lips. "I pursued you because you were awesome, and I wanted you, and you wanted me back. Your reasons for resisting me were nonsensical."

"Not really." He let out a breath. "If you are not a Dormant, we are both in for a lot of pain. I convinced myself and you that you must be a carrier of the immortal genes because of the insane attraction between us, but it would have been a lot smarter if I had kept my heart protected until I knew for sure."

"The heart wants what the heart wants." Kaia shifted so she

could put her head on his chest. "That's what I'm going to tell my family, and I hope that they accept it."

He rubbed small circles on her back. "Would it help them accept us if we got engaged?"

She chuckled. "Are you proposing?"

"I've already told you that I want to spend eternity with you. Our clan doesn't require a legal document to accept a couple's union, and marriage is optional. Some have a party to celebrate their joining, and the goddess is more than happy to preside over the ceremony, but it's not legally binding."

She lifted her head to look at him. "Can we have a human wedding with a marriage certificate and all?"

"Sure. But it, too, won't be legally binding because I don't really exist in the human records. I have a fake last name and fake documents."

That should have occurred to her. "Will those fake documents pass inspection for the purpose of obtaining a marriage certificate?"

He nodded. "We are very good at altering official records."

"Then it's good enough for me." She lifted her hands. "We can't be officially engaged without a ring."

"Then I'll get one when we go out tonight."

She laughed. "I was just joking."

"But I'm serious. I want to get you a ring."

"Good luck with that. By the time we get there, all the stores will be closed."

"Let me worry about that." He kissed the top of her head. "I'll find something. But it's only going to be a placeholder until I can buy you a proper ring."

"I don't need anything fancy."

"You might not need it, but I want to give you a ring that reflects my adoration of you. The problem with that might be that it would be too heavy a ring to wear."

Kaia laughed. "What's the largest diamond in the world?"

"I have no clue."

"I remember reading somewhere that it weighs over a pound. I need to start exercising my finger muscles." She wiggled her ring finger. "I wonder how much it's worth."

He kissed the top of her head again. "Not nearly as much as you."

"And to think that I'm worth that much despite being a diamond in the rough. Once I get refined, I'll be worth much more."

William's chest shook with suppressed laughter. "You can't be worth more. There is no larger number than infinity."

"Not true. In cardinal and ordinal numbers, there are other bigger infinities which are surreal numbers."

He laughed. "You are such a gorgeous geek."

WILLIAM

*I*t was a shame to ruin Kaia's good mood with the things William still needed to tell her, but she needed to know.

"There are a couple of things I failed to mention."

She lifted one blond brow. "More caveats? I thought we were done with those."

William rubbed the back of his head. "I should have made a list. I keep forgetting about aspects of my people's physiology that you have no way of knowing, but that's not an excuse."

Kaia waved a hand. "Just tell me and get it over with. The preamble is scaring me."

He swallowed. "The first thing is the bond. Immortal couples who are truelove mates form an unbreakable bond. That's why marriage is optional. Once that bond snaps into place, it's good for life and beyond."

Smiling, Kaia cupped his cheek. "That's very romantic, but I doubt it's true in this life or the one beyond. It's most likely a myth."

"It's as much of a myth as gods and immortals are. Trust me, it's real. If we are each other's truelove mates, neither of us will ever even look at anyone else with desire."

"Fine." She shrugged. "I hope that's true because once I commit, it's forever."

"Even if I annoy you and you can't stand to be around me?"

"Not going to happen, and I don't like to indulge in what-ifs." She narrowed her eyes at him. "Just to be on the safe side, though. Do you have any annoying habits that I should be aware of?"

"I talk too fast, I'm obsessed with my work, I don't like going out much, and I love to eat."

"That's it?"

"Isn't it enough?"

She laughed. "You don't talk too fast for me. I'm also obsessed with my work, but I like going out, especially if it's to get something good to eat, so I think we can compromise on that."

"You've got yourself a deal." He took her hand and shook it.

"Don't you want to hear about my annoying habits?"

"Nope. Nothing you can do would ever annoy me."

Her eyes were full of mirth. "Remember you said that when I blast music in our house and dance in my underwear."

"Is that supposed to be a deterrent?" He moved his hips to let her feel the erection that had sprung up beneath her bottom. "I'm looking forward to seeing you dancing in your underwear."

"Don't forget the blasting music. Gilbert hates it when I do that."

The guy fulfilled the role of her father, but he wasn't, and it bothered William to think that she had done that.

"Do you dance in your underwear in front of him?"

"Not anymore. I did that when I was little, but now I do it in my room."

"Good to know." He let out a breath. "The next thing I'm

going to tell you is connected to the first, but it's a little more difficult to accept."

She rolled her eyes. "Just spit it out already."

"My venom is addictive. Well, not just mine. All immortal males' venom is. If a female is repeatedly bitten by just one male, she becomes addicted to his venom. She craves only him and is sexually repulsed by others. Also, her scent changes, so the other immortal males know that she's taken, and they can't feel attraction toward her either."

Kaia pursed her lips. "That's one hell of a nifty trick to ensure fidelity. What about the males? Do they get addicted to the females?"

"They do, but it takes a little longer."

"Why is that?"

"I don't know. It's just the way it works. In the days of the gods, they used to frequently switch partners to avoid getting addicted."

She frowned. "Do any of your people still do that?"

He shook his head. "So far, all the clan matings have been truelove matches, and the couples welcomed the bond along with the addiction."

"Then I welcome it too." She tilted her head. "What happens when one of the mates dies? I know that it almost never happens, but you said that immortals can be killed, so I assume some have fallen in battle. What happened to their mates?"

"Withdrawal is long and difficult, but eventually, the effects of the addiction diminish, and the living partner can find love with someone new, but they won't be truelove mates. You get only one."

KIAN

*K*ian had sensed Syssi approaching a moment before a soft knock sounded at his office door, and as he rose to his feet to open it for her, she walked in with Allegra strapped to her chest in a baby carrier.

"Is everything all right?" He kissed his wife and daughter.

It was only ten minutes after three o'clock, and Syssi usually wasn't back from the lab until five.

"Everything is fine." She kissed his cheek. "Allegra kept going Baba all day long, so I figured she missed you and cut my day short."

"Baba," Allegra agreed while flailing her legs and arms.

"Say Dada, sweetheart." He unstrapped her from the carrier and lifted her into his arms.

Bridget said that Allegra was just babbling and that it was too early for her to mean Daddy by that, but he and Syssi disagreed. Her Baba and Dada babbles were very obviously directed at him.

"Dada." She smiled at him with a challenge in her big blue eyes.

"That's right." He kissed both her cheeks. "I'm your Dada."

He turned to Syssi. "She knows exactly what she's trying to say, and she understands when we are talking about her."

"I know." Syssi sat on one of the chairs in front of his desk. "I had an idea on the way home. What do you think about spending this weekend at Safe Haven? I met Gavin this morning at the café, and he kept boasting about the bungalows and how perfectly they'd turned out. It made me curious to see the completed project."

Syssi wasn't the spontaneous type, and informing him on a Friday afternoon that she wanted to go to Safe Haven the next day was atypical of her.

"Are you sure you want to do it this weekend? If we go next week, we will have more time to plan."

"Dada." Allegra's little hand closed over a strand of his hair, and she gave it a mighty pull.

Kian winced. "Don't pull on Daddy's hair, sweetie. It hurts." He tried to gently dislodge her tiny fingers, but she got a stubborn expression on her little face and refused to cooperate.

"What's to plan?" Syssi leaned over and tapped on their daughter's fist. "Let go, Allegra."

She released his hair immediately but kept staring defiantly into his eyes.

"Sometimes this girl scares me." He stared back. "It's like she's trying to communicate things with her eyes and daring me to understand her meaning."

"She wants to go on a trip." Syssi smiled at Allegra. "Right, sweetie?"

"Baba." Allegra smiled sweetly back as if to say, "You finally got it."

"I guess that's a yes." Kian let out a breath. "I'll tell Shai to make the arrangements."

"We can stay at Emmett's bunker," Syssi said. "I talked with Anastasia, and she said that Emmett and Eleanor are staying in one of the bungalows in the paranormal enclosure. Eleanor wanted a fresh start in a structure that wasn't contaminated by Emmett's past shenanigans."

"You mean orgies."

"Shhh." Syssi looked at Allegra. "Watch what you say in front of her."

"Right." He leaned and kissed her soft cheek. "Sugar and spice and everything nice. That's what little girls are made of."

Syssi laughed. "Boys are made from the same things until they reach puberty and can think of nothing but sex. Anyway, don't dismiss Eleanor's preference as superstition. If Mey can hear echoes left in the walls then Eleanor is right to not want to live there."

"And you don't mind staying there with our daughter despite that?"

"Not really. What's the difference between that and any hotel room?"

Kian grimaced. "Thanks for planting that thought in my head. From now on, we are only staying in rooms that were never occupied before."

She laughed. "Thankfully, neither of us is sensitive to echoes. I want to bring Okidu along, though, and have him change all the bedding with the stuff we will bring with us, including mattress toppers. Anastasia promised to send a cleaning crew to the cottage to make it ready for us, but the mattresses there were not as comfortable as what we have at home, and the bedding was not as soft."

Kian smiled. His wife wasn't picky in most things, but she was choosy about her coffee and her bed, and he loved indulging both.

"I see that you have everything planned already. Is there anything else you want me to take care of?"

She nodded. "If you don't mind, I would like you to allow Brundar and Anandur to bring their mates along. I feel bad about taking the guys away for the weekend, and I know you can't travel without them."

Kian pursed his lips. "Technically, I can. There are guardians posted in Safe Haven, and if they pick us up from the airport, I don't need to drag the brothers with me."

"Baba," Allegra said in a demanding tone. "Baba."

Syssi smiled. "I think I know what she's trying to say. She wants Anandur, Brundar, Wonder, and Callie to come with us."

"Baba," Allegra said in an affirmative tone and followed it with a smile.

Kian shook his head. "I'm officially stunned."

"Why? Just because your six-month-old daughter can communicate her desires so expressively? We know that she's special."

"That she is." He hoisted Allegra higher on his chest so he could kiss her sweet cheeks. "She's Daddy's brilliant little girl."

KAIA

"*I*s that the place?" Darlene asked as the bus driver stopped in front of the restaurant.

"That's the one." He opened the door.

"It doesn't look as fancy as it purports to be." Darlene rose to her feet. "I hope the food is good."

Max followed her up. "Don't judge a book by its cover."

She turned to look at him over her shoulder. "That's what I usually do, and more often than not, I'm right."

"Whatever works for you, darling." He put his hand on her shoulder.

Kaia smiled.

The two had been engaged in flirtatious banter throughout the nearly two hours it had taken to get to the restaurant.

During the ride, William had kept his arm wrapped around Kaia's shoulders, held her hand, and kissed her cheek or her temple every five minutes or so, and at first, there had been some quiet snickers, but as time had gone by, her teammates had found Max and Darlene's shameless flirting more interesting.

If not for the fact that Eric was arriving the next day, she would have been all for Darlene and Max getting it on tonight, but Eric would be disappointed.

After spending the weekend with Darlene, he would probably lose interest like he was known to have done with all of his other conquests, and after he was gone, Darlene could move on to Max with renewed confidence in her sexuality.

Should she have a talk with Eric and warn him to show Darlene a good time? He was used to women half her age that weren't interested in long-term relationships any more than he was, so he might not know what to do with a woman who had a wounded soul that needed mending.

As the bus stopped next to the restaurant's front door, her teammates and the two Guardians accompanying them disembarked and followed William and Kaia inside.

Only a few tables were occupied, which wasn't a very promising sign. If the food was good, the place should be packed.

"Hello." The hostess smiled at William. "McLean party of eight?"

"That's us."

"Follow me." She collected a bunch of menus and led them to a long table on the far side of the restaurant.

"What about the bus driver?" Kaia asked. "We should invite him to eat with us."

"I did." William pulled out a chair for her. "He doesn't want to hang out with us. He wants to go to a local pub." He leaned closer. "Look over the menu and order for me whatever you want. I have a quick errand to run."

He probably meant the ring, but she didn't want to ask him in front of everyone. "Is there anything you don't like to eat?"

He chuckled. "Do I look like a picky eater? I'll eat anything that's put in front of me."

"Lucky you." Corrine nudged her. "When the two of you get

married, you won't have to work hard to prepare meals for him. Picky husbands are a drag."

Kaia was ready to answer that she loved to cook and that it wouldn't be a problem even if William was picky, but he stopped her with a hand on her shoulder. "When we move in together, I'll cook for Kaia. My princess will not have to do anything other than use her brilliant mind to solve genetic puzzles." He winked at her. "I'll be back as soon as I can."

When he left, Corrine put a hand on her heart. "I take back every negative word I've ever said about William. He's a treasure. My ex expected me to do all the cleaning and cooking as if we were in the fifties. Finally, I got sick of waiting on him hand and foot, and I left his sorry ass."

"Good for you," Darlene said. "My ex was like that as well. Did yours come from a rich family?"

Corrine nodded. "Yours too?"

"Yeah. Guys like that grow up with a maid doing all the housework, and when they get married, they expect their wife to do everything for them as if she's the new maid."

Kaia wondered how William had grown up. Shame on her that she hadn't asked him about his mother, who was probably still around and looking like she was his sister.

Did he even have siblings?

With how low the immortals' fertility was, that was probably a no.

Was his family rich?

He'd said something about a share in the clan's profits. As a council member and his clan's tech authority, he was probably paid well. Did he have a maid cooking for him back home?

Kaia lifted the menu. "I don't know how good of a cook William is, but even if he's great, I'm not going to let him hog the kitchen. My family has a nanny who also cooks for us, but from time to time, I like to unwind by preparing something special for dinner. I'm not just a brain."

Owen gave her a meaningful look. "You definitely are not just a brain."

As Corrine cast him a glare, the restaurant's front door opened, and a family with four kids entered. The three boys looked like they were about two years apart, with the oldest being about eight and the youngest four, and their sister was about a year old.

Compared to her younger siblings, they were very well-behaved, and as the father doted on his daughter, Kaia's heart squeezed with envy.

She wanted that.

She wanted to have a little girl with William and watch him go crazy about her. And she wanted to have a bunch of sons who would be as handsome and as sweet as their father and who would adore their mother.

For a human, it was such a simple thing to wish for, but she was something more and at the same time, something less.

Evidently the saying about balance was right, and when fate bestowed a gift, it usually took away something in return.

WILLIAM

"*I*'ll take this one." William pointed to a diamond ring with a simple platinum band.

"Excellent choice, sir." The jeweler pulled it out of the display case and placed it on the counter. "If the lady needs it adjusted, come back with her, and we can have it done in a week."

"It will fit her just fine." William handed the guy his credit card.

"Nice ring," Max said. "Kaia is going to love it."

"It's just a placeholder until I can get her something nicer."

The store owner looked aghast. "This is a very fine ring, and the diamond is top quality."

"I don't doubt it for a moment." He gave the guy a tight smile. "And knowing my fiancée, she will not want it replaced by a bigger diamond, but half a carat is just not enough for her."

It was the largest the store had.

The guy looked as if he'd taken a bite out of a lemon. "I'll wrap it up for you."

"Thank you."

Max chuckled. "Are you trying to compete with Kian? The

117

ring he gave Syssi requires a security guard to accompany her whenever she leaves the house with it on."

"Didn't she have a fake made?"

Max shrugged. "What's the point of owning a ring like that if she has to exchange it for a lookalike?"

"True. But I'm not going to buy Kaia an extravagant ring like that. Not because I can't afford it but because it will look strange on a nineteen-year-old girl who's most comfortable in jeans and flip-flops."

Come to think of it, Kaia might not like diamonds at all. Maybe he should get her a sapphire?

Moving to the next display over, he looked at the non-diamond rings, but none of them caught his eye. The diamond ring he'd chosen was simple and modern looking, and Kaia was going to like it. If not, he would know what she preferred when he replaced it.

"Here you go, Mr. McLean." The jeweler handed him a small bag with the ring box inside of it. "Here is the receipt and your credit card back."

"Thank you. I appreciate you staying open late for me."

The guy smiled. "I'm glad to help a young man in love. Congratulations on your engagement, and the best of luck to you and your bride."

"Thank you."

When they were outside the store, Max clapped William on the back. "I don't know whether I should congratulate you or not. You said that you were doing it to appease Kaia's family, but since you think she's your one and only, perhaps congratulations are in order?"

Max's words sent a spear of fear through William's heart.

He was taking it for granted that Kaia was a Dormant when all he had to base it on was their intense attraction to each other. She was incredibly smart, and her ability to decipher the journals bordered on paranormal, but it was far from proof.

The Fates supposedly rewarded those who had suffered greatly or had sacrificed a lot for others with a truelove mate, but he hadn't suffered, and he doubted his work for the clan qualified as a sacrifice. William loved what he did, and his work fulfilled him and satisfied him.

Kaia had suffered, though. She'd lost her father at a young age, but then the Fates had provided her family with a good man who cared for them. He was no substitute for the father they'd lost, but he made their lives better.

William let out a breath. "Let's hope that she transitions. You can congratulate me then."

When his phone rang, William reached into his pocket to pull it out, expecting it to be Kaia calling to tell him that the food had arrived, but the number on the screen was Kian's.

"Hello, boss."

"I hope I'm not interrupting your dinner."

"You're not. I left the team at the restaurant to run a quick errand. What can I do for you?"

"I wanted to give you a heads up that Syssi and I are coming to Safe Haven for the weekend. Naturally, Anandur and Brundar are coming with us, and they are bringing their mates along. We will stay in Emmett's old bunker, and Anastasia is taking care of the arrangements, so there is nothing you need to do, but I thought you would want to know."

William shook his head. "That's really bad timing. Can you come next weekend?"

"Why?"

"Kaia's family is arriving tomorrow as well, and I will have my hands full with them. Kaia thinks that they will not be happy about her dating a man thirteen years her senior."

Kian chuckled. "Imagine what they would do if they knew you were three hundred and thirteen years older than her."

William grimaced. "Frankly, I don't think it would make a difference. Can I persuade you to postpone your visit?"

"Syssi and I are not going to bother you. She wants to see the completed development, but we don't need you to show us around. Eleanor and Emmett can do that. Naturally, we would like to meet Kaia, but if that doesn't work out because you have a war on your hands, so be it. We will meet her when you bring her to the village."

William let out a breath. "We don't know for sure that will ever happen, but I hope it will. When are you arriving?"

"We are leaving here at around eleven, so we should land at around two o'clock and arrive at Safe Haven at around four in the afternoon. Does that work for you?"

"Kaia's family will get here a little earlier. The lodge's dining hall closes at two and opens again at five for dinner, but I spoke with the kitchen's manager about keeping the dining hall open for them. I hope they'll be done by the time you get there."

"If not, we will stop by to say hello and continue to the other side of the dining hall. Don't worry about it. I don't expect you to drop everything to spend time with us."

"I want you to meet Kaia, and I'll try to work it out. If her family is not as incensed about our relationship as we expect them to be, would you be averse to having dinner with them?"

Kian groaned. "You know how much I dislike spending time with humans, but Syssi would want to meet them, so I guess I will have to suffer through it."

"Thank you. I appreciate your sacrifice."

"Yeah, yeah. I'm not doing it for you. I'm doing it for my wife."

William chuckled. "The things we do for love."

KAIA

*T*he food arrived a couple of minutes before William and Max walked back into the restaurant, but given William's expression, his mission to get her a ring hadn't been successful.

"What happened?" Kaia whispered as he sat down next to her. "Was the store closed?"

"It was open." He lifted his fork and stabbed it into one of the prawns.

For a guy that usually talked a mile a minute, he was strangely tight-lipped.

"They didn't have what you were looking for?"

He put the fork down and turned to her. "I got what I wanted." He leaned closer to whisper in her ear. "I got a phone call from the big boss. He and his wife are coming to Safe Haven tomorrow. I asked him if they could move their visit to next week, but he said no."

Kaia's gut clenched. "Is he coming because of me?"

William shook his head. "Let's talk about it on the way back."

After that intro, Kaia couldn't wait for the meal to be over. What could the clan's leader possibly want with her?

Maybe he was worried that she was taking advantage of William? Their whirlwind romance probably seemed as suspicious to him as it would no doubt seem to her family, and maybe he assumed that she had an ulterior motive the same way her family would assume William had. Well, in William's case, the suspected ulterior motive would be simple lechery, but in her case, it would be something more nefarious.

Romeo and Juliet, anyone?

Except, her Romeo wasn't a teenage boy, and he didn't answer to his family.

Or did he?

What if his boss told him to leave her? Would William do as he was told?

When they were finally done with the meal and got on the bus, she took William's hand and led him all the way to the back, hoping that the others would stay up front, but Corrine and Owen followed them and took the seat in front of them.

Whatever. Kaia could wait no longer to find out what William's boss wanted with her.

"Why is Kian coming to Safe Haven?" she whispered.

"His wife wants to see the completed project. They were here in the planning stages, and she's curious to see how it turned out."

She narrowed her eyes at him. "Are you sure it has nothing to do with me?"

He took her hand. "They want to meet you, but after I told him that your family is coming and that we expect them to raise hell over our relationship, he said that they could wait to meet you when you come to the village."

Relief washing over her, Kaia slumped in the seat. "I was afraid that they wanted to check out the temptress who snagged their genius tech guy."

He chuckled. "I'm sure that they do, but that's not the reason for their visit." He wrapped his arm around her shoulders. "On the upside, you might get your wish to meet an Odu sooner than later. Kian is bringing his butler along."

Her mood instantly brightened and Kaia straightened up. "That's fantastic. I'm so excited."

Smiling, William leaned over and kissed her cheek. "You are a strange girl, Kaia. You're about to meet a demigod, but you're more excited about meeting his butler."

"Okidu is much more interesting to me than your boss."

"Okidu?" Corrine turned around. "Do you mean Enkidu?"

Damn, Kaia hadn't bothered to whisper her last sentence, so maybe that was all Corrine had heard, but what if she had overheard more of their conversation?

When in doubt, it was always better to get the other party talking. "What about Enkidu?"

Corrine looked confused, which was precisely what Kaia had intended. "I heard you say Okidu, and I thought that you confused it with Enkidu. Enkidu was King Gilgamesh's companion in a famous story from Assyrian mythology."

Kaia remembered something about a legendary Mesopotamian figure called Gilgamesh who had sought immortality, but she didn't remember the details.

"Yeah, I was trying to remember that legend. Wasn't Gilgamesh the guy who claimed to be three-quarters god and searched for the secret to immortality?"

If Corrine had heard William talk about a demigod, that would cover it.

"That's the one." Corrine grinned. "But his friend's name was Enkidu, not Okidu."

"Gilgamesh was the king of Uruk," William said. "Enkidu was created to be his servant, and he was described as a wild man, someone who was strong enough to stand up to Gilgamesh. Later, he became the king's friend and companion.

When Enkidu died, Gilgamesh was heartbroken and grieved his loss."

"What do you mean by created?" Kaia asked. "By whom?"

"The gods, I guess."

"Interesting." Kaia leaned back.

What if Enkidu was an Odu? The similarities were too much to be a coincidence. A created servant whose name was almost identical to Okidu and who was very strong. The main difference was that Enkidu had died, while the Odus were supposed to be indestructible.

"I want to refresh my memory." Kaia pulled out her phone and typed the inquiry, but the cellular signal was too weak, and Wikipedia refused to load. "It's no use. The reception is just too bad. I'll have to wait until we get back home."

"Home?" William asked softly.

She smiled. "Yeah. Our temporary little home."

DARLENE

There was plenty of available seating on the bus, but Max chose to crowd Darlene with his bulk.

His legs were so long that he had to sit sideways for his knees to clear the seat in front of them, and his shoulders were so broad that Darlene had to squeeze herself against the window to avoid touching them.

It would have been semi-tolerable if the guy wasn't so damn attractive.

She found it impossible not to react to his proximity, but since she was waiting for Eric to arrive the next day, she didn't want to encourage Max.

Was it William's doing?

Up until now, the Guardian had been giving her charming smiles whenever their paths crossed, but their interactions had been limited to brief greetings and a few polite words. Why was he suddenly laying on the charm so thick?

Her hunch was that William had told him about her interest in Eric, and Max had taken it upon himself to seduce her before the guy's arrival.

Wasn't going to happen.

Darlene had a plan, and she was going to stick to it. She would have a short fling with Eric as a test run, and once she regained her confidence, she would give Max or one of his fellow Guardians a chance.

Maybe that was what he was after? To secure his spot at the top of her list once she was ready?

"Am I making you uncomfortable?" He smiled as if he knew the answer to that.

"The seats on this bus are ridiculously narrow. I have to scoot all the way to the window to avoid touching you."

"You can touch me." His smile turned lascivious. "You can even put your head on my shoulder and take a nap if you want." He patted his bulging bicep. "Right here."

"Thank you for the offer, but I'm not sleepy."

"Good, then we can talk."

He'd asked her a thousand questions on the way to the restaurant, and she had nothing more to tell him. "It's your turn to tell me about yourself. I've already told you everything there is to know about me."

"Not true. What is your favorite ice cream flavor?"

"Pistachio. What's yours?"

"Cookies and cream. What's your favorite drink?"

She rolled her eyes. "Please, can we stop with the endless questions? Tell me about your life in Scotland and what you did after retiring from the Guardian force."

He tilted his head to look at her. "How do you know that I retired?" A smile bloomed on his handsome face. "Did you ask about me?"

"It was just a guess. Roni told me that most of the Guardians were recruited from retirement by Bridget's impassioned speech about all the good they could do."

He looked disappointed. "Yeah, I was one of those Guardians." He dipped his head to whisper in her ear. "I joined the force a little over five hundred years ago, and I retired after serving for seventy-two years."

"How old are you?"

"I'm five hundred and twenty-three years old."

"That's ancient," she whispered back. "What did you do after retiring?"

"Many things. I was even a stage actor for a few years." He cast her one of his charming smiles. "I have a good singing voice, and I also joined the opera, but I wasn't getting any leading roles, so I quit."

That piqued her interest. "How come I've never heard you sing?"

He waggled his brows. "Would you like me to give you a private performance?"

She was willing to bet that his idea was to perform for her in the nude, and the truth was that she wasn't averse to that.

"I would love to hear you sing," she skirted around the trap he'd set up for her. "What did you do other than that? Four centuries is a long time to dabble in acting and opera singing."

"For most of my life, I was a stonemason. I love building things, but eventually I got tired of doing that as well. Rescuing victims of trafficking and getting their handlers arrested is a much more fulfilling job." He sighed. "But it's stressful and emotionally charged. Sometimes I miss the quiet of masonry. It's relaxing."

"I get it." Tired of fighting for space, Darlene relaxed and let her thigh press against his. "In my opinion, creating something is much more fulfilling than dealing with mystery and corruption. On the other hand, I'm sure that helping others who have no one else to fight for them is fulfilling as well."

Max nodded. "It would be easier if I had a mate to come home to at the end of the day or the night as it may be. Most of the missions are at night."

Great. Now he was pulling out the guilt card to persuade her to give him a chance.

"It's up to the Fates." She patted his bicep. "Your one and only is waiting for you somewhere out there."

That was not a subtle way to communicate that this was not what she was looking for at present, but it was effective and clear.

"I hope so." He looked into her eyes. "It would be so nice to have someone welcome me when I get back from a mission, ask me how it went, and tell me how proud she is of me for rescuing innocents."

WILLIAM

*W*hen the bus entered the outer security ring surrounding Safe Haven, everyone's phones started buzzing with incoming messages.

"After that long drive through the countryside with no reception anywhere, I feel like we are back in civilization." Kaia read over her texts.

Kaia and her teammates didn't know that their lines were tapped, and William felt bad about that, but it was either that or not allowing them to have phones at all.

"Cheryl is asking what she should pack and if it's cold here at night." Kaia typed up a quick answer. "I told her that a hoodie should do it."

Corrine turned around. "Now that you have reception, you can read up on the epic of Gilgamesh."

"Right." Kaia typed the search term into the box and started scrolling through the endless selection of articles. "This is going to take a while." She leaned against William's side.

He'd read the poems in their original Sumerian, or rather the parts that had survived, but it had been a long time ago, and he didn't remember much.

Kaia kept reading until the driver eased the bus into its parking spot by the main lodge.

"Did you find anything interesting?" William asked as they stepped out.

"Plenty. But I'll tell you about it at home."

That was enough to put a grin on his face. "I have a little something to give you when we get there."

"I almost forgot." She reached into his pocket and palmed the small box. "I can't wait to see it."

Kaia didn't sound as excited as he'd hoped she would be, but perhaps that was because she was treating their engagement as a ruse, or maybe she just wasn't the type of girl who got excited about things like that. She seemed more interested in the Gilgamesh legend than she was in the ring.

When they said goodbye to the others, William asked, "So, what did you find out that's so fascinating?"

She glanced over her shoulder at Kylie and waited until her former roommate entered her bungalow and closed the door behind her. "Did it ever occur to you that Enkidu could have been an Odu?"

"The name is similar, but Enkidu was created as a wild man, not a cyborg."

"That's true, but the whole story is about gods and immortals and legendary monsters. Gilgamesh was a harsh king who abused his power and behaved amorally, so the goddess of creation made Enkidu in order to teach Gilgamesh a lesson." Kaia followed him inside. "At first, Enkidu was a mighty wild man who lived like an animal, which could be a metaphor for him having to learn even the most basic things about acting like a human." She put her wallet-size purse on the coffee table and sat down on the couch. "You said that the Odus learned by mimicking human behaviors, so that could be what the legend was trying to show."

"That's an interesting hypothesis." William walked over to

the kitchenette. "But they sent him a temple prostitute to teach him about being human, which an Odu wouldn't have known what to do with. They don't have sexual urges or even the appropriate organs."

He loaded the coffeemaker, wishing that he'd thought ahead and gotten wine for the occasion, but all he had was a bottle of whiskey, and he doubted Kaia would want that.

"That could be an allegory as well. I don't know for what, but I'm sure that if I give it some thought, I'll figure it out. Maybe it was meant to show that women were morally superior to men. After all, they chose a sacred prostitute to teach him about morality and not some old sage. When she brings Enkidu to the city, he's nice and helpful to the shepherds and trappers he'd terrorized before, and when he sees Gilgamesh on his way to take a bride on her wedding day, as was the king's nasty custom, he stops him. Meaning that Enkidu internalized what he had learned from the prostitute and became morally superior to the king."

"Coffee?" William asked.

"Yeah, sure. It helps me think. After engaging in an epic fight, Gilgamesh and Enkidu become good friends. In the next chapter of his life, Gilgamesh is bored and decides to journey to the gods' forest and kill the guardian who keeps mortals from entering the gods' realm. Enkidu is the voice of reason, advising against such a foolish quest, and he ends up being punished by the gods for killing their guardian, and dies."

William handed Kaia the coffee mug and sat down next to her. "The Odus are practically indestructible. They can't die."

She took a sip of coffee. "I might be wrong, but I think it's an allegory for what happened to the Odus in their home world. They were created to be servants and companions and to mimic all the good behaviors of the gods. But an ambitious ruler with crazy ideas decided to use them in warfare. The ruler won, but the Odus paid the ultimate price for the victory.

In the legend, Enkidu's death is portrayed as a descent to the underworld. I think Enkidu was an eighth Odu who got separated from his brothers and sent to Earth."

"Where is he now?" William put his mug on the coffee table and pulled the small ring box out of his pocket.

Kaia pouted. "That's the one part I don't have a theory for."

He laughed. "Just that one?"

"Yeah." She eyed the box in the palm of his hand. "It's just a fun mental experiment with what-ifs, but you must agree that there might be something to it."

"It's possible."

She seemed satisfied with his answer. "Can I see the ring now?"

KAIA

*K*aia stifled a chuckle when William slid off the couch and went down on one knee before her.

"Will you marry me, Kaia Locke?" He opened the box.

She gave the ring a cursory glance and was about to act out a scene, pretending that the proposal was real and making some comic remarks about it, but William's hopeful expression gave her pause.

He wasn't a good actor, and he seemed serious.

Was she ready to commit to him?

Before seeing the family in the restaurant, her answer might have been yes, but with her heart yearning for what they had, her resolve was shaken.

Looking into his eyes, she chewed on her lower lip. "I thought that this would only be a placeholder until you get me a real engagement ring."

"It is a placeholder, but I hope that our commitment to each other is not dependent on the size of the diamond."

That was such an offensive thing to say. Did he really think that she'd hesitated because she didn't like the ring?

"It's not about the diamond, and you know it. The ring is

lovely, and I would be more than happy with it being my permanent engagement symbol. I just need a few more days before I can say 'yes'." She folded her arms over her chest. "Keep the ring until then."

William frowned. "I thought that you already gave me your answer. You said that Darlene helped you rethink your priorities."

It was true. She had said that, but she'd just shared with him her deliberations. She hadn't made a steadfast commitment to him yet.

Besides, she still hadn't told William her secret, and accepting his marriage proposal before fessing up to that wouldn't be right.

With a sigh, she unfolded her arms and leaned over to close the box. "There is something you need to know before you propose to me for real. I thought that I had more time to tell you my secret, but if you are serious about this proposal, then you should know who the girl you plan to spend the rest of your very long life with really is."

William remained on the floor, his hand extended with the box resting on his palm. "There is nothing you can tell me that will alter the way I feel about you."

She lifted a brow. "What if I'm a murderer?"

He smiled. "You're not, and if you were, you would have had a good reason for committing murder."

It was good to know that he had such faith in her. But then, who would suspect a nineteen-year-old professor of murder?

"Let's hit a pause button on the proposal." She patted the spot next to her. "Come sit with me."

William turned to put the box on the coffee table and then pushed up and sat next to her. "So, what's your big, scary secret?" He reached for her hand.

Kaia swallowed. "Do you remember what the aura guy said he saw?"

His eyes widened. "About the parasitic spirit?"

She nodded. "Only it's not a parasite. It's all me. I remember pieces of my previous life as a man who was a gifted mathematician. The mathematics is what I remember best from that life. That's what made me a prodigy. But I also remember other things." She lifted her hand and wiggled her fingers. "I was a big guy, and I hated my sausage-like fingers. I lusted after women, but I was too shy to pursue them, and I lived a lonely life."

William looked perturbed but not repulsed, so that was a relief.

"How do you know that those memories are yours from a past life and not those of an invading spirit?"

Kaia pursed her lips. "I think I would have known if those weren't my own memories but someone else's. Are you asking because of what the aura guy said?"

He nodded. "If those are just memories of your past life, you shouldn't have two auras."

She waved a dismissive hand. "How reliable is that guy anyway? Did he ever make an observation about a strange aura that was proven correct?"

"I don't know. I will have to ask Eleanor. You should also talk with Nathalie. She had a parasitic spirit living in her head for many years, but she's always known that he was a separate entity. Then that spirit passed on and made room for a much nicer spirit." He smiled sadly. "The spirit of someone very dear to me. Mark was a gifted programmer who was murdered by our enemies."

Kaia felt the blood drain from her face. William had told her about the immortals splitting into two opposing camps, but he hadn't told her that the others were murdering his people.

"Is that why you have such formidable security around Safe Haven? Are you afraid they will find out about the research and attack us?"

As her mind processed the information and its implications, her fear ratcheted up several notches.

William's enemies were also immortal, which meant that they were as strong and as fast as the Guardians in his security detail. But there were many more of the others, and they could easily overpower the small unit assigned to their lab.

What if an attack happened when her family was visiting? Should she call them and tell them to cancel their visit? But what would she tell them? If she told them about the danger to the lab, they would demand that she return home right away, and if she refused, Gilbert and Eric would come right over and make a scene.

WILLIAM

*K*aia looked apprehensive, and William couldn't blame her. He hadn't told her anything about the clan's war with the followers of Mortdh, or rather Navuh, and he could see that mentioning Mark's murder had her imagination filling in the blanks.

"You have nothing to worry about." He gave her hand a reassuring squeeze. "At this time, our enemies are not planning any attacks on us. They are busy breeding their new smart army, so we have a couple of decades of reprieve. Besides, their mode of operation is not to attack us directly but to ally themselves with countries that don't aspire to the ideals that our clan promotes, like democracy and equal opportunity for all. The Doomers do their best to undermine our work."

Kaia chuckled. "Doomers? Is it a nickname?"

"Doom is their acronym. They are the Brotherhood of the Devout Order of Mortdh. It just works out nicely in English."

"So, if they are not a clear and present danger, why the insane security around Safe Haven?"

He sighed. "First of all, we can never know when or why the Doomers will change tactics. They haven't attacked us directly because they can't find us, but if they ever do, they will strike against us. The likelihood of that is marginal, but on the remote chance that it will happen, we prefer to err on the side of caution."

The truth was that he was no longer sure that Navuh sought the clan's destruction. The clan did a great job of hiding, but it wasn't impossible to find, and Navuh wasn't dumb. It had occurred to William that the despot was content with using Annani and her clan as a means to unify his people, and annihilating that unifying factor didn't serve his best interest.

Finding an enemy to vilify was a common tactic that was successfully employed by despots and tyrants throughout history as a means aimed at rallying their troops behind a cause. But once that enemy was no more, a new enemy had to be found, or the entire underpinning of the rotten structure collapsed.

"And what's the second reason?" Kaia asked.

"Humans are no less of a threat, especially when something as valuable as the secret to eternal life could be attained."

She let out a breath. "Since the only two people who know what we are working on are you and me, I'm not worried about humans."

"We are not the only ones," William admitted. "I suspected that we might find answers in Okidu's journals from the moment Kian had told me about them, and I shared my suspicions with him and the clan council."

"But no humans other than me know about it, right?"

He nodded.

She waved her hand at the box on the table. "Then you'd better give me that ring and marry me as soon as possible."

William tilted his head. "Why the sudden change of heart?"

"I just realized that once the project is completed and you no longer need me, your best option to keep it a secret is to eliminate the only human who knows about it. I'd better turn immortal as soon as I can."

Was Kaia joking? Or was she serious?

It was hard to tell with her, not because she didn't emit emotional scents, like Turner, but because she emitted such a smorgasbord of them that it was impossible to isolate just one.

"I would never harm even one hair on your head. If by the end of the project you haven't transitioned, I will thrall you to forget what you've learned."

She narrowed her eyes at him. "So once my job is done, my mind will no longer be precious to you?"

"Of course, it will. But a one-time thrall is not dangerous, not even when it involves eliminating many memories."

That wasn't entirely true, but William was positive that Kaia was a Dormant and that she would transition successfully.

She shook her head. "I don't know why we are arguing about hypotheticals."

"I'm not arguing." William took the box and opened it again. "I love you, Kaia. And even a hundred spirits living in your head won't change that. If you feel the same about me, say yes. But if you don't, or you're not sure that you do, there is no rush. You can wear the ring with no obligation attached."

Looking at the ring, Kaia chewed on her lower lip. "I'm sorry for ruining your romantic proposal."

His heart sank. "I understand." He handed her the box.

She lifted her hand to stop him. "No, you don't. I want to say yes, but I can't. What if I don't transition? If I'm just a regular human, you can't marry me. You will need to erase my memories not just of the project but of everything that you told me and probably of our relationship as well."

"I know in my gut that you are my one and only, and I'm willing to put my heart on the line and commit to you as if you have already transitioned. Are you willing to do the same?"

She hesitated for a moment longer and then nodded. "But I

want a do-over. I don't want our engagement to come on the heels of an argument."

William's heart floated up from his gut back into his rib cage and flapped its wings in excitement.

Hooking his finger under her chin, he dipped his head and sucked on that luscious lower lip that she'd been nibbling on. When she was breathless and panting from the kiss, he let go of her lips and leaned back.

"I love you, Kaia. Will you be mine? Will you marry me?"

She smiled. "Yes, William. I love you, and I will marry you provided that I transition." She wound her arms around his neck. "Now take me to bed."

JADE

o you know what day it is today?" Jade asked the eight little ones gazing at her with adoring eyes.

"It's Saturday," Gaycha said.

She was an intelligent three-year-old, and she wasn't afraid to speak up. She showed potential as a future prime.

"And what happens on Saturdays?" Jade asked.

"Story time." Rikon clapped his hands.

"That's right." Sitting on a large pillow, with the little ones sitting on smaller ones in a semi-circle facing her, Jade put her hands on her knees. "Which story would you like to hear today?"

"Can you please tell the one about the prince and the princess?" Gaycha asked.

It was the kids' favorite story, and Jade had told it hundreds of times before, at least fifteen times to this group alone. She'd changed the story over the years, creating many variations but maintaining the core principles she wanted to convey.

She was treading on dangerous ground.

Through her stories, Jade tried to teach the young ones the true way of the Kra-ell, but that's not how Igor's compound operated, and she had to be careful how she worded it. If Igor didn't like her teaching methods, he would not allow her anywhere near the kids.

"Aren't you tired of hearing that story over and over again?" she asked.

All eight kids shook their heads as one.

"Please," Rikon pleaded.

"Okay." Jade folded her legs into the lotus position, which was a signal for the kids to do the same. Not all had mastered the pose yet, but they were doing their best, and one day soon, they would all sit with their backs straight and their legs folded in the proper position.

"Since you've heard the story so many times, you can help me tell it. Who wants to go first?"

As always, Gaycha lifted her hand. "I do."

"Go ahead."

"A very long time ago, in a land far, far away, lived a strong and just queen."

"Excellent opening." Jade motioned for Radina to continue.

The girl swallowed, her big eyes growing even larger. She was a timid little thing, and if she didn't grow some backbone soon, the others would eat her alive.

"The queen set her eyes on a king from a strange faraway land," Radina said so quietly that it was almost a whisper.

"Speak up, Radina. You are a strong Kra-ell female. We do not speak in whispers."

"I'm sorry."

Jade lifted a brow. "Don't be sorry. Just continue the story in a louder voice."

The girl squared her shoulders and thrust her chin out. "The king saw the queen, and he thought that she was beautiful and strong, and he desired her."

"Very good." Jade looked at Moshun. "Continue."

"The king didn't know the Kra-ell way, and he offended the queen, but he didn't mean to. It was an accident."

"What did the queen do?" Mondy asked.

Jade smiled. That was as far as the kids could recite the story. From that point on, they would start messing it up. "The queen told the foreign king that he could not be hers because he was not of her people, and the law prohibited her from mating him."

"But she liked him," Mondy said.

"Yes, she did. And then what happened?"

"War." Moshun pumped his fist in the air.

"Not yet." Jade lifted her hand. "The queen and king started to meet in secret, hiding their relationship from both their peoples. But when their secret was discovered, and their people got angry, demanding that they never meet again, the king left his people and went to live with the queen."

Jade paused when Kagra entered the room and leaned against the wall.

Kagra waved a hand. "Please, don't let me interrupt the story."

She'd heard it many times before, in at least ten different versions.

"The king's people thought that the queen had bewitched him," Jade continued. "So, they declared war on her lands, demanding that she release the king from her snare. The queen refused because she was proud and selfish and wanted to keep the handsome king. The war was long and bloody, and many good people died needlessly, all because the queen and king cared more about each other than about their duty to their people."

"Your story is depressing." Kagra walked over to the semi-circle of kids and sat between Moshun and Radina. "We want a story with a happy ending. Right, kids?"

They were raising Kra-ell, not humans, and Kra-ell didn't

believe in happy endings and love and all that other nonsense that humans drugged themselves with.

The best ending a Kra-ell could hope for was to die honorably in battle.

"If you want a happy story, you will need to ask Kagra to tell it." Jade unfolded her legs and got up. "My stories don't have happy endings. We are Kra-ell, and we live for the glory of battle and the honor of serving the Mother of All Life."

KAIA

As the bus neared the airport, Kaia took the ring off and put it in her purse.

Next to her, William tensed. "Why did you do that? The engagement was meant to placate your family. Did you change your mind about it?"

"No, I still think that it will help, but if I show up with the ring on my finger, it will be immediately obvious, and things will get ugly fast. It will be better if I ease them into it."

He let out a breath. "You know your family. I trust your instincts on that."

"I wish I was as confident in myself as you are in me. I don't know if the engagement will make our relationship more palatable to them or the other way around. Without a ring, they can dismiss it as a fleeting infatuation. The ring might act as a call to battle."

"By them, I assume you mean Gilbert."

Kaia shook her head. "Gilbert makes a lot of waves, but he's harmless. My mother is the one I'm worried about. She is extremely protective of Cheryl and me, and she's always suspicious of boys." Calling William a boy was just wrong. "I mean men. My mother is not the trusting kind."

William chuckled. "Your mother is a smart woman. Men have one thing on their minds when it comes to desirable women, and it usually isn't platonic love."

She shrugged. "Nature ensures the propagation of the species. Imagine a world in which men were content to sit around and wait for women to come to them." She lifted a pair of mock innocent eyes to him. "Oh, wait. That's what you did."

"I guess I'm lucky my lady didn't forget her past life as a man and took the initiative."

"Gah." She elbowed his side. "It's not cool to bring that up in that context. My past memories had nothing to do with it." She scrunched her nose. "Well, that's not entirely true. My assertiveness has nothing to do with it, but my understanding of how men think does. I don't get offended by comments that I know were not meant to offend, and I also understand the male sexual drive on the one hand and the inhibitions on the other. It's not easy to be a guy."

That was especially true of big guys who took up too much space. She remembered Edgar trying to make himself look smaller so as not to intimidate people. He'd hunched his shoulders, tried to get out of people's way, and smiled a lot even when he hadn't felt like it.

"Does your family know about those memories?" William asked.

"I told my mother about it when I was younger, but she thought that I'd invented an imaginary male friend as a result of the trauma of losing my father. She wanted to take me to a shrink, so I told her that I had just imagined it and that was it. I told my sister, and she said that she believed me, but it was a long time ago, and we haven't talked about it recently. Other than that, I didn't tell anyone else."

He leaned toward her and kissed her lips. "Thank you for trusting me with your big secret."

"You trusted me with yours, so I trusted you with mine."

"I ensured mine would remain a secret with compulsion, and I feel bad about it."

She patted his knee. "Don't. You had no choice because your boss demanded it. Besides, if my secret gets out, I might get threatened with visits to a shrink, while if your secrets get out, your life and the lives of all your clan members would be in danger."

William glanced at the Guardian sitting at the front of the bus, then shifted his eyes back to her. "I forgot about him." He motioned with his head to the guy and then dipped his head to whisper in her ear, "Immortals have exceptionally good hearing."

Damn. So now three people knew about her past life.

Kaia whispered back. "Can you ask him to keep it to himself?"

"I'm not sure that he heard anything, and even if he did, it wouldn't make him think any less of you. Paranormal phenomena are common among immortals and Dormants."

"Yeah, you told me that. I wonder how Eleanor's group would feel about my past life. They would probably be more open than others to accept it as real." She chuckled. "What do the paranormals call regular people, mundanes?"

"I don't know. I don't think they have a special term for non-paranormals. You should talk to Eleanor first, though."

It could be an interesting experience to talk openly about remembering her past life, and maybe even get some feedback. The aura guy would be the first one she would approach.

The problem was that Kaia usually met the paranormals during meals in the dining hall, and most of the time, her team-mates were there as well. The last thing she needed was to give them more ammunition against her.

As the driver parked the bus and opened the door, the three of them got out, and Kaia cast a quick look at the Guardian, checking to see if he regarded her differently than before, but the guy just smiled politely and said nothing.

Taking a fortifying breath, Kaia released it slowly through her nose and took William's hand. "Let's get this show on the road, shall we?"

WILLIAM

$\mathcal{W}$illiam stood with the Guardian who'd accompanied him and Kaia to the airport, and watched her hugging and kissing her mother, her sisters, Gilbert, and Eric.

"Lots of love in that family." Conrad crossed his arms over his chest. "Should I offer to help with their luggage?"

"Thank you for the offer, but I would wait until they are done."

"Roger that."

The Guardian's words tugged on William's heart strings. Once Kaia's family learned of their engagement, that happy reunion would be over, and he hated being the cause of strife between them.

Kaia scooped one of her baby brothers into her arms and peppered his smiling face with kisses. "I missed you so much." She hugged him tightly to her, which he didn't seem to mind at all.

Winding his little arms around her neck, he gave her a sloppy kiss.

Kaia laughed. "I even missed your slobbery kisses."

The other twin didn't like being left out, wiggling in his mother's grip and flailing his arms toward his sister.

"Wait your turn, you little monster." She walked over to William and handed him the baby. "Hold him while I get Ryan."

The boy didn't protest as William held him suspended in front of him, debating whether he should hug him like Kaia had done, or put him over his shoulders the way Idina demanded to be carried around.

The boy looked at him with curiosity in his eyes, lifted his little fist and stuck it in his mouth.

"Hold him against your chest," Cheryl advised. "But don't squash him. Do it gently."

"Have you never held a baby in your arms?" Gilbert asked.

"I haven't," William admitted. "They are so small and fragile." He offered the boy to his father. "I'm afraid I'll hurt him."

Gilbert didn't make a move to take his son from William. "You can carry Evan for a little bit. He seems to like you."

William frowned. "He does?"

"Yeah. He didn't kick you in the nuts yet, so he must like you."

William looked down at the boy's feet, which were dangling right in front of his crotch, and lifted him higher, putting him against his chest.

Gilbert grinned. "You see? It's not that difficult."

The baby wiggled, wanting to turn around and look at his father.

"What do I do now?"

Gilbert sighed and reached for his son, but the boy refused to leave William, clinging to his shirt and making an angry face at his father.

"I guess you're stuck with him. Just turn him sideways and make sure that you don't drop him."

"I won't drop him." William did as the guy had instructed,

and Evan calmed down. Settling in his arms, he chewed on his fist, covering it in slobber.

Idina tugged on her father's sleeve. "I want William to carry me."

Gilbert made a pouty face at her. "You don't want your daddy to give you a ride?"

She sighed dramatically. "Okay, you can carry me," she said like she was doing him a favor.

William would have preferred to carry the girl, who looked sturdy enough, but her brother had claimed the spot and wasn't willing to give it up.

"Can I help you with the luggage?" Conrad asked Kaia's mother.

"Thank you." Karen pointed him to the pile that Eric had taken out of the small executive jet. "Eric can't handle all of that, and the rest of us have our hands full."

"No problem." Conrad squared his impressive shoulders. "That's what I'm here for."

He was there to provide Guardian escort, but that answer was better.

As William led the procession toward the bus with the baby in his arms, he felt everyone's eyes on him, and it was unnerving. Well not everyone's. Cheryl was typing on her phone while walking.

Kaia and her mother looked at him with amusement in their eyes, Gilbert cast him suspicious glances and exchanged silent looks with his brother, and Conrad was stifling laughter while carrying most of the family's luggage.

When they were all seated in the bus, Evan finally agreed to let go of William and sit in his father's lap, and Idina immediately jumped on the opportunity to take his place.

"My children seem to like you," Gilbert said. "Do you get that a lot from kids?"

There weren't that many children in the village for him to

be exposed to, and William hadn't had many opportunities to be around them.

"I don't get to interact with kids much," he admitted. "I spend most of my day in the lab, and sometimes I even sleep there. I don't have much of a life outside of it."

"That's no way to live," Eric said. "When I was still in the Air Force, I had no life either. I retired as soon as I could and never looked back."

"And now you live the merry life of a bachelor." Gilbert bounced his son on his knee.

"Perhaps those days are coming to an end." Eric looked at William. "I hoped Darlene would come along to pick us up."

"I'm sure that she wanted to come, but she had to stay behind and take care of a few things for me." William adjusted Idina in an attempt to make her stop swinging her leg and banging it against the seat in front of them. "I wanted her to keep an eye on the kitchen staff in the lodge so they wouldn't close the dining room like they normally do. I asked them to have a late lunch waiting for you when you arrive." He looked at Eric. "We will have the entire dining hall to ourselves, and Darlene is going to join us there."

Karen gave him a grateful smile. "I didn't know that they closed the kitchen between lunch and dinner; if I did, I would have timed our arrival better."

"That's okay. My boss is arriving at Safe Haven an hour later, so I need the place to stay open for him and his party as well."

"Where is he coming from?" Eric asked.

"He's flying in from Los Angeles."

It was a big city, so telling them that was pretty meaningless.

Gilbert arched a brow. "I'm surprised that you came with Kaia to collect us from the airport when your boss is arriving today as well. Won't you get in trouble for not picking him up?"

William shouldn't have mentioned Kian, and it was no wonder that Gilbert was suspicious.

Groaning internally, he assumed an impassive expression.

"I offered, but he preferred to rent a van. He's not one of those bosses who enjoys his people groveling."

Gilbert still looked suspicious. "Tell me about him. Is he a scientist like you?"

"He's a businessman. My lab and the things we work on are just a small fraction of the holdings he manages."

"Like what?" Gilbert pressed.

"Developing and building, among other things. Mostly office buildings and hotels." Again, it was just a small part of the clan's investments, but he didn't need to list them all.

That got a smile out of the guy. "A fellow builder. I would like to have a chat with him."

"I don't know if he will have time." William swallowed another groan. "He's also a bit of a recluse."

Kian had said that he would agree to have dinner with Kaia's family because Syssi would want to meet them, but if they became hostile after learning about the engagement, dinner with them would not be a good idea.

DARLENE

*N*ervous butterflies fluttered in Darlene's belly as she waited for Kaia's family to arrive at the dining hall.

She'd spent the morning getting ready, shaving what needed to be shaved, exfoliating, putting a moisturizing mask on, doing her hair, and obsessing over which outfit to wear. Darlene had wanted to accompany Kaia and William to the airport and greet Eric, maybe even have him show her his jet, but William had been right to put her in charge of making sure they had a proper meal waiting for them upon their arrival.

If she hadn't been there to intervene with the kitchen staff, they would be eating lunch leftovers that they had to reheat themselves.

She had to remind the chef that the new owners of the resorts were arriving soon after Kaia's family, and if the big boss didn't like the service, he might hire a new chef and new kitchen staff.

That had worked like a charm, and the kitchen had gone into a frenzy of preparing vegan dishes for Kian. When she'd pointed out that he was the only vegan of the bunch, the chef shrugged her shoulders.

The others would have to make do with the vegan fare as well, but Darlene had a feeling that it would be an improvement over the parboiled fish and dry chicken breasts that they usually served for lunch and dinner.

Blah.

Safe Haven was a beautiful place, and Kian's renovation had turned it into a luxurious resort, but she needed to have a talk with him about the food, especially if he wanted the guests to return.

Or maybe he didn't want repeat customers, and the bland food was intentional?

After all, the idea was to attract people with paranormal abilities, so if they didn't have what the clan was looking for, the only reason to tempt them to return would be financial.

Nah. Kian probably didn't know that the fancy chef he'd hired was not all that she'd claimed to be. Though given the smells coming out of the kitchen now, she'd made a special effort to impress him.

When the doors to the dining hall finally opened, and William ushered Kaia and her family in, Darlene's eyes met Eric's, and when he smiled at her, her heart did a happy little flip.

Max might be more handsome and pack double the muscle, but there was a certain cocky charm to Eric that Max didn't have and that Darlene found irresistible.

He also was more age appropriate for her, but that was an illusion. Max only looked like he'd just turned thirty. The Guardian was ancient.

She should remember that when the thing with Eric ended and she moved to the next stage of her plan. Not that she wanted to, but she had no choice.

Eric wasn't long-term material. He was human, and he was a player who was not interested in settling down.

"Hello, Darlene." He walked over and took her hand. "You look even lovelier than I remembered."

"It's funny, but I wanted to say the same thing to you."

"Oh, thank you." He put his other hand over his heart. "Do I look lovely today?" He batted his eyelashes.

"You look even more handsome than I remembered and cockier as well."

"Cocky is my middle name." He wrapped his arm around her shoulders. "How have you been?"

"Great. And you?"

"Wonderful." She leaned closer and whispered in his ear, "I couldn't stop thinking about you."

His hand squeezed her shoulder. "Same here," he whispered back.

"Can we sit down anywhere?" Karen asked.

"Yes." Darlene ducked out from under Eric's arm. "The entire dining hall is ours for the next hour and a half."

"Did you hear anything from the boss?" William asked.

"Not since they boarded the plane. But I estimate that they will get here around four in the afternoon."

"We should hurry." William walked over to one of the tables and pulled out a chair for Karen.

"I would like to meet your boss." Gilbert sat next to Karen.

"William already told you that he doesn't like to interact with the plebs." Eric pulled a chair out for Darlene.

"It's not that," William said. "It's just that he's a very private person, and he doesn't like attention."

It was precisely that.

Hiding a smile, Darlene unfurled a napkin and draped it over her knees. Perhaps it was just her impression, but Kian was a snob. He might tout democracy and champion humanity, but he regarded most humans as plebs, and so did Kalugal. Her grandfather wasn't any better, and Annani was on a whole different level of haughty.

Toven and Annani were gods, so they were entitled to their feelings of superiority, and maybe as demigods, Kian and Kalugal were entitled to that as well. But Orion and Geraldine were also demigods, and yet they didn't flaunt it, weren't stuck up, and were comfortable pretending to be human.

It was probably a matter of personality.

Eric wasn't a god or a demigod, but he certainly acted like one.

KAIA

*T*he ride to Safe Haven had gone well, with Gilbert and William talking about his boss's building projects and the rest of them listening to the conversation. When Gilbert found out that Kian had used 3D printing technology to have the bungalows built in record time, he had a thousand questions for William that, thankfully, her guy knew how to answer.

Evidently, William was involved in the clan's projects and was well-informed about the tech that went into all of them. Kaia's area of expertise was much narrower, and she made a promise to herself to expand her horizons once she transitioned and joined the clan. There was so much she could learn from William, and she would have limitless time to learn as much as she wanted.

Provided that she transitioned.

But first, she had to deal with her family and get them to accept William as her fiancé.

To hide her frayed nerves, Kaia held Ryan on her knees, bouncing him up and down and eliciting happy giggles from him even after the food had been served.

There were no highchairs in the lodge's dining hall, but her mother had come prepared with boosters for the little ones that attached to regular chairs.

"Put him in his seat, Kaia," her mother said. "He needs to eat."

Reluctant to let go of her shield, Kaia lifted her baby brother and strapped him into the booster.

"This is not bad," Eric said to Darlene. "After your preamble about the vegan meal, I was afraid we would be served the same slosh as last time, but this is actually better."

"It's like what the grumpy food critic ate in *Ratatouille*," Cheryl said.

"I think it is actually ratatouille," Karen said.

There was also creamy mushroom pasta, which Kaia assumed was made with coconut cream, and two bowls of family-sized salads for them to share.

"Do you like it?" William asked Idina.

She nodded. "I like vegetables."

For the next few moments, everyone got busy eating and commenting about how tasty everything was, but Kaia could barely taste anything.

She'd spent half the night trying to come up with a clever way to ease into announcing her and William's engagement, but dancing around a subject had never been her forte. She was the direct type who liked to shoot first and deal with the consequences later.

Maybe she should do just that and stop agonizing over it. The problem was that she knew her shot would backfire, and she wasn't sure she could deal with a combined attack from Gilbert and her mother.

Maybe talking with Eric first and getting him on her side was a better plan?

It could have been if not for Darlene.

Kaia suspected that the two would disappear right after

dinner and not emerge until Sunday afternoon, when it was time for Eric to take everyone back home.

"So, Kaia." Gilbert pushed his empty plate aside and gave her a penetrating look. "Is there something that you want to tell us?" He shifted his eyes to William, then back to her.

Damn. He'd guessed it.

The challenge in his tone was a call to battle, evaporating Kaia's resolve to ease her family into the news. Gilbert had fired the first shot, giving her the ammunition she needed to fire hers.

"Your nose is infallible, Gilbert." She gave him a bright smile while opening her purse and pulling out the ring. "William and I are engaged." She slipped the ring over her finger.

A stunned moment of silence followed, but it didn't last long.

"Are you out of your effing mind?" Gilbert threw his napkin over his plate as if he was throwing down a gauntlet. "You've known the guy for a week."

She shrugged. "When you meet your one and only, you know it. William and I are perfect for each other."

"You're nineteen, Kaia," her mother said. "You shouldn't be engaged to anyone." She looked at William. "No offense, William. You are a nice guy, and if Kaia were twenty-five and you had dated for a couple of years prior to getting engaged, I would have congratulated you and started working on the wedding plans. But Kaia is nineteen, you are thirty-two, and you've known each other for a week. That's a hard no."

"Did you knock her up?" Gilbert spat.

"I'm on the pill," Kaia spat back.

Gilbert didn't even shift his gaze to her and was still glaring at William. "Accidents happen. Otherwise, I can see no reason for two intelligent people to rush into getting married."

Evidently, the engagement had been a mistake. It was making things worse, not better.

"We are not rushing," Kaia said. "And we are not planning a wedding yet. The only reason we got engaged so quickly was to show you that we are serious about each other, and this is not a fling. William and I are in love, and we want to be together. That's all."

Her mother let out a relieved breath but then shook her head. "I'm glad that you are not running off to Vegas to get married, but you need to think of your future and whether what you feel now can endure." She cast an apologetic glance at William. "Right now, the thirteen years difference might not seem like much to you, but when you are forty and William is fifty-three, the difference will become more problematic."

Gilbert was still engaged in a glaring battle with William, who was glaring back but saying nothing.

It was a good tactic to let them vent out all of their objections before responding to them and escalating things into a shouting match, but it required patience that Kaia didn't have.

"What I want to know is how you coerced Kaia into sleeping with you," Gilbert snarled at William. "What power do you wield over her?"

"He didn't coerce me into anything." Kaia folded her arms over her chest. "I was the one who initiated everything, and William tried to resist me."

"You didn't resist hard enough." Gilbert was starting to get red in the face. "You should have realized that Kaia is a young girl, who's away from home for the first time in her life, alone, vulnerable, and latching on to the only person available to her. But you took advantage of her infatuation, and that's deplorable." He turned to look at Kaia. "We are taking you home."

WILLIAM

*G*ilbert's words hit William in the chest like a volley of daggers. He was right, and William was deplorable for not realizing why Kaia had pursued him with such determination.

He'd seen how she'd fallen apart saying goodbye to her family and how she couldn't stop crying. How could he have overlooked all that?

The answer was simple. He wanted her, and it had been easy to just accept that she'd wanted him back for the same reasons and not because she needed to fill the hole in her heart that her family's absence had created.

"I'm sorry," he murmured. "I've acted despicably."

"What?" Kaia's head whipped around, and she looked at him as if he had lost his mind. "You haven't done anything wrong, and neither have I. We fell in love because we found in each other our other half." She turned to Gilbert. "Do you really have so little faith in me? Am I the kind of girl who is so desperate for love that she clings to the first guy who shows interest in her?"

Gilbert's eyes softened as he gazed at her, but his expression remained determined. "At home, you are surrounded by love. Out here, you find yourself alone and away from the protective cocoon of your family, so it's not surprising that you sought someone to fill that void. If you were older and more aware of your feelings, you would have understood that and would have proceeded with more caution. But you are young and impulsive, and you think that you are smarter than everyone. That might be true in regard to science, but it's not true for relationships. Nothing can replace life experience when it comes to feelings, and I'm telling you that what you feel for William is not the mature love that makes a marriage work."

She snorted. "Look who's talking. You and Mom have three kids together, and you are still not married. Maybe you are the one who's not mature enough."

"Kaia," her mother admonished in a stern tone. "We are talking about you, not us. Gilbert and I are in a committed, mature relationship, and we don't need a document to bind us."

"You can't seriously compare us to you," Gilbert said. "Your mother and I met as mature adults, we are only two years apart in age, and neither of us took advantage of the other's vulnerability."

"Oh yeah? Mom was a young widow with two little girls. Maybe you took advantage of her?"

"Pfft." Gilbert waved a dismissive hand. "You're just proving my point about you being immature and impulsive by hurtling accusations at me that you know perfectly well are untrue."

"You're too quick to judge," Eric told Gilbert. "Kaia is very mature for her age, and she's not impulsive. Besides, you would not have been so opposed to their relationship if William was a few years younger. Would you have been foaming at the mouth if he were twenty-three?"

"I'm not foaming at the mouth, and a twenty-three-year-old

boyfriend would have been borderline acceptable, provided that they were just starting to date and taking it slowly."

Eric glared at his brother. "Age is not important, and thirteen years is not that much. Why can't you just accept that they are in love?"

Gilbert snorted. "You are guilty of the same thing, so of course, you would come to his defense. Dating twenty-something-year-olds is only slightly better than dating teenagers. Frankly, you are an embarrassment to the family."

"Is that so?" Eric pushed to his feet. "Then maybe I'll remove my embarrassing presence from here, and you can find yourself another way to get back home?" He turned to Darlene. "How about you and I fly to Miami for the weekend? I have good friends out there."

"Please, Eric." She tugged on his hand. "Sit down. Both you and Gilbert need to calm down. You are scaring the kids."

No one had paid any attention to the little ones, but now that Darlene had brought it up, William looked at Kaia's four siblings.

Idina seemed fascinated by the argument and didn't look scared at all. Cheryl seemed worried and was holding Kaia's hand under the table, but the twins were on the verge of tears, their eyes wide and the corners of their mouths turned down in identical mournful expressions.

"I'm perfectly calm," Eric said with a fake smile on his face and sat back down. "Gilbert just needs to stop being an asshole."

Idina gasped. "Uncle Eric said a bad word."

"I meant asshat." Eric patted her head.

"You said asshole. I heard it."

Gilbert smiled at her. "Your Uncle Eric made a mistake, sweetie. One of many."

"That's it." Eric threw his chair back. "I'm out of here." He offered Darlene a hand up. "Are you coming?"

She cast William an apologetic glance before taking Eric's hand. "I think everyone needs some space to cool down. Let's take a walk on the beach."

SYSSI

*E*mmett's underground bunker had undergone an interior design transformation since the last time Syssi had stayed there with Kian and Allegra. Eleanor must have used Ingrid's services to get rid of everything that reminded her of what Emmett had been up to in those rooms. The interior designer's signature look was evident not only in the transformed guest suites but also in the common rooms, making Syssi feel at home. The only things that remained almost unchanged were the kitchen and the bathrooms. Those rooms had gotten a fresh coat of paint, but none of the fixtures or the cabinetry had been replaced.

Okidu bowed. "I shall put everything in the closets, mistress."

"Thank you." Syssi handed Allegra to Wonder, folded the stroller, and gave it to Kian. "I can't wait to see the bungalows."

"We can go there now," Eleanor offered.

"I'm starving," Anandur said. "Let's eat first."

"That's a good idea." Syssi followed Kian up the stairs. "If we go now, we will have the place to ourselves. At five, the dining hall opens to the lodge's guests."

"Then we definitely need to go now," Kian said. "I'd rather avoid having to smile at random humans. I just hope that Kaia's family is out of there already. I promised William that we would stay out of their way."

"Why?" Anandur asked.

"Kaia expects opposition to her and William's relationship, and he expects a fight." Kian opened the cottage's front door. "I'd rather not be there and get dragged into the argument. If they say anything offensive about William, I might overreact."

"I'm curious to see the girl who has stolen our William's heart." Anandur closed the door behind them. "But right now, all I can think about is food. What do they serve in the lodge?"

"We hired a new chef," Kian said. "She came highly recommended, but I haven't sampled her cuisine yet. I hope she's good."

"Where did you find her?" Callie asked. "Is she a famous chef?"

Kian shrugged. "She's not famous, but she's a graduate of the Culinary Institute, and I stole her from a competitor hotel chain. I can't remember her name, though. I think it's Jasmine something, but I will have to check with Shai."

Syssi laughed. "You never take notes because you have him next to you. But what about the times you don't?"

"I remember what's important."

Callie threaded her arm through Brundar's. "I can't wait to sample her cooking. It's probably excellent."

"How is your restaurant coming along?" Syssi asked. "You have a village of anxious customers awaiting the opening night."

"I know." Callie grimaced. "That's what is keeping me from opening right away. I don't have enough staff to serve all the tables, and I know the demand will be high." She looked at Wonder. "Any chance that I can steal you away from the café? Now that Aliya is working there, you can leave."

"Not really. Wendy is starting college this fall. She said she would work as many hours as possible, but it would depend on her class schedule."

As they were about to enter the lodge, the door opened, and Darlene stepped out with a handsome guy by her side.

"Good afternoon." She looked perturbed. "How was your flight?"

"Excellent." Syssi looked at the man standing next to Darlene. "I'm Syssi." She offered him her hand.

"Eric, Gilbert's brother." He shook hers and then turned to Kian. "I guess you're the reclusive boss William told us about?"

Gilbert was Kaia's stepfather, and Eric was her uncle. Syssi connected the dots. What was he doing with Darlene?

"That's me." Kian shook Eric's offered hand. "This is Brundar, his lovely partner Callie, and that's Anandur and his much better half, Wonder."

Eric shook everyone's hand and then knelt next to Allegra's stroller. "And who is this beautiful girl?"

"Ba." She reached with her hand and patted his cheek.

"Is your name Ba?"

"Her name is Allegra," Syssi said.

"A beautiful name for a beautiful little girl." Eric pushed up to his feet. "It was nice to meet you all. Darlene and I are going for a walk on the beach. Would you like to join us?"

"Thank you," Anandur said. "But we are hungry."

Darlene winced. "I can ask the kitchen staff to deliver your meal to the cottage. It is World War III in there."

Eric nodded. "My brother is unhappy about Kaia dating a guy thirteen years older than her, and he's not bashful about expressing his opinion."

"Yeah," Darlene concurred. "He's threatening to take Kaia back home with them."

"He can't do that," Kian said. "She has a contractual obligation to stay until the end of the project."

Eric nodded his agreement. "Not to mention that Kaia is an adult, and he can't force her to leave. He's just making her and William miserable for no good reason. William seems like a very nice guy, but he's too mellow and polite to stand up to Gilbert."

"We should go in and help William," Syssi said. "We will introduce ourselves and sit at the next table over. Your brother will not be nasty in front of strangers, and he will have to back off William."

Eric snorted. "You don't know how pig-headed my brother can be."

KAIA

A long moment of awkward silence stretched over the table after Eric and Darlene's departure.

Kaia had never heard Gilbert talk like that about Eric, not to his face and not behind his back. He'd joked about his brother's dating habits, but it had always sounded good-natured. He must be really riled up to lash out at him like that.

"You shouldn't have said that." Her mother glared at Gilbert. "What has gotten into you?"

"I don't know." He let out a sigh. "I lost it for a moment there. The only thing that bothers me about Eric's penchant for women who are too young for him is that he's not looking for someone suitable to settle down with. I don't want him to be one of those guys who are still alone and childless in their late fifties, wearing a damn toupee and baking their skin in tanning salons to look younger. That's the image I had in my mind when I said that he's an embarrassment to the family. I was thinking of him in the not-so-distant future."

Kaia had to admit that the picture Gilbert had painted of future Eric was depressing. It was good that Darlene viewed him only as a step in her journey of self-discovery and not as a possible partner. She was too old to have children, and Eric deserved to be a father.

He'd had a shitty experience, getting married young to a person who turned out to be a control freak with rage issues. It had soured him for future relationships, but his marriage had ended four years ago, and it was about time for him to get over it.

As the dining hall's door opened, everyone shifted toward it, expecting to see Eric and Darlene returning, but it wasn't them.

Kaia knew immediately that the guy pushing a stroller with a baby girl in it was William's boss. Kian was the most stunning male Kaia had ever seen. A god, or rather a demigod. No human was that perfect, and neither were the immortals she'd met so far.

How did he manage to go unnoticed? Did he thrall everyone he encountered to forget him? Or did he just live the life of a recluse as William had told them, and avoid being seen in public?

The two men walking right behind him were unnaturally gorgeous as well, and given how their eyes scoped the dining hall and her family, it was pretty obvious that they were Guardians. They were both wearing light jackets even though it wasn't cold, and Kaia was willing to bet that they were hiding weapons under them.

The three women and the baby in the stroller were all beautiful, but they could at least pass for humans. The blond with the kind face was no doubt Kian's wife, the tall brunette who looked like an Amazonian warrior woman was with the redhead, and the one with the penetrating green eyes was with the blond Guardian with the stoic expression.

Out of the three males, he seemed the most dangerous despite his angelic features. With his stick-straight blond hair that was even a lighter shade than Kaia's and longer as well, his beauty bordered on feminine, but she knew it for the illusion it was. The guy was deadly, and she would never want to get on the wrong side of him.

"Hello, everyone," Kian's wife smiled brightly. "I hope you don't mind us joining you." She walked over to Kaia's mother and offered her hand. "I'm Syssi."

"I'm Karen." Her mother rose to her feet and shook Syssi's hand.

Gilbert followed her example, pushing to his feet and offering the newcomers one of his charming smiles.

"This is my husband, Kian," Syssi continued the introduction. "And those are his cousins, Anandur and Brundar, and their partners, Wonder and Callie."

As her mother and Gilbert shook hands with everyone, Kaia stood next to Cheryl, anxiously awaiting her turn.

William's boss was intimidating as hell, and so was one of his so-called cousins, but the tall redhead and the ladies seemed friendly.

Kian and the Guardians joined William in the back, and a nearly silent conversation started that Kaia would have loved to be privy to.

"Wonder?" Gilbert shook the statuesque brunette's hand. "Is it a nickname, or is it your given name?"

She smiled brightly. "It started as a nickname, and I decided to adopt it as my legal name."

"I get it." Gilbert nodded. "You look like Wonder Woman." He turned to look at the baby. "And who's the beauty in the stroller?"

"This is Allegra," Syssi said. "Our daughter."

"Enchanted." He leaned down, took the girl's little hand, and kissed the back of it.

"Ba." She smiled, her big blue eyes assessing him with a smart, penetrating gaze.

"I'm Idina." Her sister crouched next to the stroller. "I have two baby brothers. I wanted a baby sister, but I got two boys instead."

"Da." Allegra reached for a lock of Idina's hair and gave it a tug.

"Ouch. Don't do that." Idina glared at the baby.

Kaia tensed, but for once, Idina didn't retaliate.

Syssi laughed. "She'll let go. It's her way to say hello."

The baby did that a moment later and offered Idina the plush toy she'd been clutching in her other hand.

"Thank you." Idina accepted the plush tiger graciously. "What's his name?"

"Da."

Standing behind her mother and Syssi, Kaia cleared her throat, reminding them that she hadn't been introduced yet.

Her mother whirled around and smiled apologetically. "These are my older daughters, Kaia and Cheryl."

Instead of taking Kaia's extended hand, Syssi pulled her into a quick hug and whispered into her ear, "Thank you for making William happy."

43

WILLIAM

*W*illiam thanked the Fates for Kian and Syssi's timely arrival.

Gilbert had worked himself into a frenzy of anger, and there had been no chance of reasoning with him without using a thrall, but Syssi had managed to press the reset button with just the calming effect of her presence.

The guy was back to his usual charming self, working on getting on Kian and Syssi's good side. Perhaps now that they were there, Gilbert would be willing to listen to someone other than himself.

When all the introductions were done, and another table had been added to make room for everyone, the twelve of them took their seats.

Unlike before, when the kitchen staff had served everything buffet style, they tripped over themselves to serve Kian and his retinue in person.

"You have a lovely family," Syssi said.

Karen beamed proudly. "Thank you."

"If I may ask, how old were you when you had Idina?"

"I was forty-three. After my husband died, I never imagined I would have three more kids, but then I met Gilbert, and he worked diligently to convince me to have another one." Karen looked at her partner and smiled. "I finally agreed, and Idina brought so much joy to our family that I decided to have one more and ended up with twins." She turned to look lovingly at the boys. "My two cherries on top."

"They are adorable," Syssi agreed. "How did you and Gilbert meet?"

"A mutual friend introduced us. I wasn't ready to date, and when my friend told me about Gilbert, I told her that I wasn't interested. But she tricked us both, inviting us for dinner at her house without telling either of us that the other one would be there."

"It was love at first sight," Gilbert said.

Karen shook her head. "We were both still hurting from the loss of our spouses, and we found comfort in each other's company."

Syssi shifted her gaze to Gilbert. "Were you a widower as well?"

"I was the victim of a nasty divorce, and I'd lost my faith in humanity, not just the female half of it. Karen was incredible, patient, and kind, and she restored my faith in people."

Karen chuckled. "He was so cocky, trying to play the part of a newly released bachelor who was ready to plow his way through scores of women, but I saw the pain in his eyes. He evoked my motherly instincts to comfort and heal, and we became inseparable from that day on."

Gilbert cleared his throat. "There was nothing motherly about what you felt for me." He cast a quick glance at Kaia and Cheryl. "Karen told you the PG version." He leaned closer to Kian and whispered, "The truth was that we couldn't keep our hands off each other."

His stepdaughters couldn't have heard him from the other

side of the table, but Kaia must have guessed what he'd told Kian.

"How long after you met Gilbert did it take you to tell Cheryl and me about him?" she asked.

"A week later."

Kaia snorted. "So, you two fell in love in one week, and you have the nerve to doubt my relationship with William because we've known each other for the same length of time?"

"It's not the same," Gilbert said. "Your mother and I were both mature adults, and we were close in age. I'm only two years older than Karen."

Kaia rolled her eyes. "Can you even hear what you're saying? The differences in circumstances are so small that they are negligible. The biggest difference is that William put a ring on my finger as a symbol of his intent to spend the rest of his life with me, while you haven't given my mother one yet."

"I don't want one," Karen said. "I was married once, and I loved your father very much. I love Gilbert no less, but it's important to me to make this relationship different. I'm perfectly happy with our partnership the way it is, and I don't like you and Cheryl pushing us to get married. It has nothing to do with you."

"Huh." Kaia folded her arms over her chest. "William and I have nothing to do with you either, and yet you feel entitled to try to push us apart."

Gilbert's face twisted in a grimace. "I should have known he was trouble the moment he let his Scottish accent come out. The age of consent in Scotland is sixteen. No wonder he sees nothing wrong with seducing a nineteen-year-old. To him, she's a mature woman."

"It is?" Cheryl asked. "So, if I go to Scotland, I can have sex?"

"You can have sex whenever you want," Kaia said. "It's a legal offense for whoever has sex with you, not for you."

Gilbert pointed a finger at Cheryl. "You're not having sex until you are twenty-one."

"Or married," Cheryl chuckled. "I know. You've said it many times before."

She hadn't added that it was hypocritical of him, but William could practically read it in her expression.

How could Gilbert preach abstinence until marriage when he hadn't practiced it himself? Even a bachelor like William knew that do-as-I-say-and-not-as-I-do never worked with kids.

The only way to lead was by personal example.

44

SYSSI

*T*hings were about to get out of hand again, and since the subject was ancestry, Syssi decided to follow the thread and divert the conversation away from William and back to Gilbert and Karen.

"I'm curious. What about your origins, Gilbert?" She asked. "Do you know where your ancestors came from? Perhaps you are part Scot as well."

The guy straightened in his chair and grinned. "I know a lot about my ancestry because I've done quite a bit of research on it, and I'm proud to be a mutt. I'm part Norwegian, part Pole, part Austrian, and part Portuguese."

"The age of consent in Norway is also sixteen," Anandur said. "So, it's not just us randy Scots."

If he had been sitting next to her, she would have kicked him under the table. She was trying to steer the conversation away from William and Kaia.

"What prompted you to research your ancestry?" she asked Gilbert, to keep him talking about himself.

He sighed. "All that's left of our family is Eric, our sister Gabi, and me. Our grandparents and parents passed away, and we didn't have any uncles or aunts. I wanted to find out whether we had any extended family in the countries our grandparents came from."

"Did you find any?"

He was about to answer when one of his sons let out a wail and was soon joined by his brother.

"I'm afraid it's way past their nap time." Karen unstrapped one boy and handed him to Gilbert, and then freed the other one. "We will have to continue this conversation at another time."

The boys stopped crying as soon as they were in their parents' arms, but given the way Evan put his head on Gilbert's shoulder and Ryan rubbed his eyes, it was obvious that the little ones were exhausted.

"We can meet for dinner." Syssi rose to her feet. "I'll have the kitchen deliver it to where we are staying." She smiled at Karen. "You'll have an opportunity to visit the leader's underground facility and hear about all the naughty things that happened in there."

That got Gilbert excited. "What time?"

"Since it's already after four, no one will be hungry until eight."

"That's late for the little ones." Karen turned to Cheryl. "Can you babysit?"

"I don't want to be left out. I want to come and hear about those naughty things."

"You're too young for that," Gilbert said.

She rolled her eyes. "We live in the era of the internet. Do you really think there is anything that can still shock me?"

He shook his head. "I guess not, and it's a shame. Your generation was robbed of the precious few years of innocence our generation had. The world seemed like a kinder place back then."

"It was an illusion," Kian said. "The world was never kind."

He didn't look happy about having Kaia's family over for dinner, but thankfully, he didn't object. Syssi needed time to come up with a strategy to bring Gilbert and Karen around to supporting their daughter's relationship with William, and she hoped to come up with something by dinnertime.

"We can bring their travel crib," Karen said. "Is there a bedroom down there we can use?"

Syssi nodded. "There is one spare bedroom where you can put the boys and Idina to sleep."

"Good luck with that." Kaia took Idina's hand. "She will not want to miss out on the fun." She leaned closer to Syssi and whispered in her ear, "When you tell us about the bunker's history, I'll have her watch a movie on her tablet with the earphones on."

"That's a good idea."

Overhearing her sister, Cheryl grinned. "Count on me not being on my phone for a change."

Gilbert frowned at the two of them. "You two are incorrigible."

Stifling a chuckle, Syssi turned to Karen. "I can tell Darlene that she and Eric are invited, but just in case I can't get hold of her, you should tell Eric about our plans for tonight as well."

Karen nodded. "I will."

"You should invite Emmett and Eleanor," Anandur suggested. "I want to see Eleanor's face when Emmett tells us about the things he did in that place."

"That's not a good idea." Kian lifted Allegra onto his lap. "I need them both alive and well to run this place. It would be difficult to find a replacement for Emmett if Eleanor murdered him."

"That sounds like an interesting story," Karen said. "But we really need to go before the boys get overtired. When they get like that, they cry for hours and can't fall asleep." She looked down at Idina. "She was such an easy baby. I've never had problems like that with her."

Kaia chuckled. "She compensates for it now. Right, Idina?"

The little girl looked up at her sister. "I don't understand what you're talking about."

As all the adults either chuckled or laughed, Idina stomped her foot on the floor. "Stop laughing at me!"

"We are not laughing at you, sweetie." Kaia lifted her into her arms. "You just sounded so grown up when you said that."

"I'm a big girl."

"Yes, you are."

45

KIAN

*A*fter William left with Kaia's family, Kian signaled for the server. "Can we please get coffee?"

"Of course, sir."

When the guy rushed into the kitchen, Kian turned to Syssi. "You were uncharacteristically engaged today."

Usually, she was shy around strangers, and he'd enjoyed seeing her leading the conversation and striking up such a quick friendship with Kaia's mother.

"William needed help, so I overcame my natural tendency to sit back and listen while others talk. Besides, I like Karen. She seems like such a sensible person, and she's a great mother."

"It's the affinity at work," Anandur said. "Regrettably, her mate is a buffoon."

Wonder nodded in agreement. "I don't know why William didn't say anything in his defense."

Kian shook his head. "William was wise to stay silent. Anything he said would have been held against him. And as for Gilbert, the guy is protective of his stepdaughter, and that's admirable. If Allegra got engaged to someone much older than her, who she had known for only one week and who Syssi and

I had never met, I would be just as angry as Gilbert if not more."

Syssi chuckled. "Did you forget how quickly we fell in love? I imagine my dad reacted the same when I told him I was getting married to a guy I met just a few weeks ago, but he trusted my judgment."

"He had Andrew to vouch for me, and both your father and brother warned me that if I ever did anything to upset you, they would cut off my balls and then chop me into little pieces."

Her eyes widened. "They didn't. I can imagine Andrew saying something like that, but not my father."

"Your dad was a little less graphic, but his intent was the same."

"That's kind of sweet," Anandur said. "In a gruesome way." He wrapped his arm around Wonder's shoulders. "If your father was still around, he would have nothing to fear. If I ever deserve my balls to be chopped off, you are perfectly capable of doing that yourself."

Despite how proud Anandur sounded saying that, Wonder winced. "Thanks for reminding me that I'm a freak."

"You're not a freak." He leaned toward her and kissed her cheek. "You are the original Amazonian warrior."

That seemed to placate her, and she leaned her head on his shoulder. "Somehow, you always know what to say."

He clapped his hand over his chest. "That's because it comes from the heart."

After the server brought them coffee and a vegan dessert, Syssi took a few sips and put her cup down. "The fact remains that all of us here fell hard and fast for each other. It's the special connection between truelove mates. The problem is that Gilbert doesn't know about it, and we can't tell him, so he can't understand that a powerful bond already exists between Kaia and William."

Callie nodded. "It was so evident that I could actually feel it.

I'm happy that William finally found the right woman to complete him."

"Kaia is perfect for him," Wonder said. "She's brilliant, beautiful, and assertive."

"Dada." Allegra lifted her face to him.

"What, sweetie?"

She stuck her thumb in her mouth and put her head on his chest.

"She's telling you that she's tired." Syssi finished the last of her coffee and pushed to her feet. "We should get back and put her down for a nap."

As the brothers and their mates followed them out, Wonder took in a deep breath. "I can smell the ocean. The breeze here is so much stronger than what we get in Malibu."

"Let's take a walk on the beach," Callie suggested.

"We can't." Brundar wrapped his arm around her waist. "We need to stay with Kian and Syssi."

"No, you don't." Syssi turned to Kian. "Do we need them with us twenty-four-seven?"

"That's my mother's protocol for whenever I'm out of the village, but I can ask for two of the Guardians stationed here to trade places with Anandur and Brundar."

"That's a good solution." Syssi stroked Allegra's head. "Who's in charge of the Guardians here?"

"Leon." Kian pulled out his phone and called the guy.

"Good afternoon," Leon answered. "What can I do for you, boss?"

"Can you send two Guardians to Emmett's cottage? Anandur and Brundar want to take their mates for a walk on the beach."

"I'll do better than that. Anastasia and I will come over to say hello, and we'll bring Emmett and Eleanor with us along with two Guardians who will remain outside."

"Sounds like a plan. We are heading back to the cottage right now."

"We will meet you there."

"Very well." Kian ended the call and put the phone back in his pocket.

"We will walk with you to the cottage," Anandur said.

Kian was disappointed to have his plans for an afternoon delight with Syssi ruined. With the brothers and their mates gone and Allegra napping, it could have been a perfect opportunity, but he couldn't have said no to the visit without sounding rude.

"What's the matter?" Syssi asked. "Don't you want to see them?"

"I do." He put his arm around her while holding Allegra with the other. "I just hoped for some time alone with my wife while our daughter takes a nap."

46

WILLIAM

*O*utside the lodge, William parted ways with Kaia. "Enjoy your time with your family. I will come to escort you to the cottage at quarter to eight." He gave her a quick peck on the cheek.

Gilbert pretended like he wasn't there, Karen gave him a tight smile, and only Cheryl smiled at him with fondness. "See you later."

Kaia mouthed, "Wish me luck."

William nodded, pivoted on his heel, and headed toward the lab.

It wasn't unusual for him to work on Saturdays, but that wasn't why he was going there. He needed a few moments of solitude to collect his thoughts and decompress.

He'd gotten no more than fifteen minutes of sitting in his chair and staring at the wall before his phone buzzed with an incoming text.

Hoping it was from Kaia, he pulled it out and looked at the screen but was disappointed to see that it was from Kian.

Leon and Anastasia are coming over with Eleanor and Emmett. If you're not busy, come over.

William hesitated before answering.

He needed some time alone, but being among friends would also be therapeutic. After being under attack from Kaia's mother and stepfather, it would be a welcome change to be with people who had his back.

He typed, *on my way.*

When he got to the cottage, he found Max and Conrad sitting on a couple of rocks near the front door.

"What are you doing here?"

"Anandur and Brundar went on a walk with their mates," Max said. "We are just waiting for them to come back, and then we are out of here. Leon and Anastasia are already down there."

"What about Emmett and Eleanor?"

"On their way," Conrad said.

Max eyed William with a frown. "You look like you've been through the wringer. Was it that bad?"

William nodded. "Worse than I expected. Syssi smoothed things over, but I have a feeling that it was just a temporary reprieve and that the battle will resume when we meet again for dinner."

Max nodded. "I'm here for you, buddy. If you need to get drunk with someone, I'm your man."

"Thanks." William gave him and Conrad a thankful smile before heading inside.

Max was a good guy, and he appreciated the words of encouragement even if he had no intention of taking him up on the offer. He'd never gotten drunk, and he didn't intend to start today.

Once he was inside, he pressed the intercom button, and when the door opened, he took the stairs down.

"Hi, William." Anastasia rose to her feet when he entered. "I heard that you had a difficult time with Kaia's family."

Kian handed him a glass of whiskey. "I'm sure you need this."

Leon lifted his glass in a salute. "To truelove mates." He threw the whiskey down his throat. "They are worth every difficulty."

"Amen to that." Kian grabbed the bottle, walked over to Leon, and refilled his glass.

William sat down and put the glass on the coffee table. "We are not sure that Kaia is a Dormant, let alone my truelove mate."

"She is." Syssi walked into the living room. "I'd be very much surprised if she isn't."

"I hope you are right."

"Did you see Darlene on your way here?" Anastasia asked. "Syssi told me that she and Eric went on a walk."

"Eric got angry at Gilbert." William lifted the glass and took a sip. "Darlene offered to take him out on a walk to calm him down. I guess they are still on the beach. She can't take him to her bungalow, so there aren't many places they can go."

"Eric has a room in the lodge," Leon said. "They can be there."

"Right." He finished the rest of the whiskey. "I hope they are not too affected by the family drama."

"What are you going to do?" Anastasia asked.

"You could thrall the guy," Kian offered. "Since Kaia is a potential Dormant, and so are her mother and siblings, his opposition to your relationship is harmful to the clan, and therefore thralling him is justified."

"It won't be necessary," Syssi said. "Gilbert just needs to get over the initial shock. Besides, William can't thrall him into liking him. He will have to do it the old-fashioned way."

"I'm open to suggestions." William rose to his feet, walked to the bar where Kian had left the whiskey bottle, and refilled his glass.

"Just be yourself." Syssi smiled at him. "You are one of the nicest people I know, and Gilbert will realize that sooner or later. The rest is up to us." She looked at Kian. "When they come over for dinner, we will talk about William's position in the clan and his contribution to our safety and prosperity, and also mention that he's a council member."

Kian shook his head. "That will reveal too much about the clan."

Syssi smiled at him indulgently. "We will talk in terms of an organization or a family run business, not a clan, and instead of calling it a council, we can call it the board of directors."

47

KAIA

"*C*ome see my room." Idina pulled on Kaia's hand.

Kaia looked at her mother. "Will you join us after you put Evan and Ryan down for their nap?"

"Of course." Her mother kissed her cheek and followed Gilbert into their room.

Cheryl opened the door. "It's not large, but it's nice."

Two single beds were tucked against the walls with a small chest of drawers between them. The one that was Idina's had a lineup of Barbie dolls propped against the pillow, and Cheryl's tablet was on the chest.

It was such a familiar sight that it tugged at her heartstrings.

Kaia missed home, and her dual nature pulled her in two opposite directions. On the one hand, she was an old soul who'd lived for a long time and was primed and ready to live on her own. But on the other hand, she was a nineteen-year-old girl who wasn't prepared to fly the nest to William's village and only see her family on holidays.

Kaia had thought she had years until she would find a guy she wanted to settle down with. But fate had other ideas. Her guy was a member of a clan of immortals, he believed that she could turn immortal too, and if he was correct, then her mother and her siblings could also turn immortal. But that left Gilbert out, and that along with the risk involved would most likely be a deal-breaker for her mother. She had three little kids that needed their parents, and Kaia wouldn't be surprised if her mother gave up on the chance of immortality to keep what she had now.

If Kaia were in her mother's shoes, she would probably say no to immortality, but she had the advantage of having proof that the soul was immortal, so perhaps gaining physical immortality was not the be-all and end-all that others might view it as.

The problem was that the vast majority of people didn't retain their memories of past lives, so in a way, their previous personas died along with their bodies, and they were reborn to start anew.

On the one hand a fresh start was preferable, but on the other hand, knowing that their essence lived on would alleviate people's fear of death.

But was that a good thing?

Not necessarily.

To appreciate life, people needed to treat it as the precious gift it was.

Idina took off her shoes, climbed on the bed, and took a Barbie doll in each hand.

"You are an embarrassment to the family, Emily," she said in a deep voice. Lifting the other doll, she shook her from side to side. "You are a mean sister, Rebekah."

Smiling at Kaia, Cheryl patted her bed. "You can sit here."

For a few moments, they watched their little sister re-enacting the earlier argument with her dolls.

"Are you really in love with William?" Cheryl asked quietly.

"I am. He's wonderful." Kaia dropped her flip-flops, lifted her feet on the bed, and leaned against the wall. "I suspected that Mom and Gilbert would think that I didn't know what I was doing, but I didn't expect them to put up such a fight. Poor William. I will need to make it up to him."

"William is so nice," Idina mimicked Kaia's voice. She picked up two different dolls, one male and one female. "You are so mean to him. You should be ashamed of yourselves."

Cheryl chuckled. "With Idina on your side, you have nothing to fear. She'll fight for you and William. Right, Idina?"

Their sister treated them to one of her dark looks. "I don't want Kaia to marry William."

"Why not?" Cheryl asked. "They love each other."

"Because she will not come home."

"What if I bring him home with me? Would you be okay with me marrying him then?"

Idina shrugged. "Daddy doesn't like William."

"He will change his mind once he gets to know him. He's the nicest guy I've ever met."

"Really?" Cheryl asked. "Or are you just saying that?"

"No, I mean it. William is smart and sweet."

"What about sexy?"

"He's that too."

A knock sounded at the door, and her mother ducked into the room a moment later. "They were out in two minutes flat. I left Gilbert to watch over them." She sat on Idina's bed. "What did I miss so far?"

"Kaia told me how William is smart, sweet, and sexy, and that she loves him."

"Are you sure?" Her mother leveled her intense gaze at her. "I hope it's not some kind of delayed rebellion against the parents."

Kaia snorted. "You know me better than that. I love my family, and I love our home."

"So maybe Gilbert was right about you feeling sad and

lonely and needing someone to fill the void of being away from home?"

"It's not that either." Kaia grabbed a pillow and pushed it behind her back. "If you two weren't so focused on the age difference and on how little time we've known each other, you would have seen how perfect William and I are for each other. I will never find anyone like him again. So, if you force us apart, I will become a cat lady because I could never fall in love with anyone who is less perfect for me than him."

She wasn't hyperbolizing, and she wasn't being overly dramatic. Every word was true, and it filled her with anxiety. If she wasn't a Dormant, William would have to let her go, and becoming a cat lady wouldn't be a joke.

If he erased himself from her memories, it would be a mercy. Otherwise, she would compare every guy she met with the one who'd been perfect for her, and would choose cats instead.

"Oh, sweetie." Her mother shifted to Cheryl's bed and pulled Kaia into her arms. "I want what's best for you, and so does Gilbert. We just don't want you to make a mistake." She kissed Kaia's temple. "I was lucky. I've never had a relationship go bad. Your father loved me very much, and I loved him just as much back. Then I found love again with Gilbert. But Gilbert and Eric weren't that lucky. They didn't choose the right woman the first time around, and they suffered dearly for it. Gilbert doesn't want you to suffer a similar fate."

Kaia hadn't thought of it from that angle. Hearing her mother explain it, she understood where Gilbert was coming from and why he was so strongly opposed to what he thought was her whirlwind romance with an older man.

"What you said helps me understand Gilbert better and makes me less mad at him for making William and me feel bad, but my love for William is not a mistake. I want your approval, but I will not leave William if I can't convince you to approve of my choice. He's not only the man I love and the one I want to spend the rest of my life with. He's important to my future and to the future of our entire family."

Her mother frowned. "In what way is he important to our family?"

"I can't say. Not yet."

"Do you sense it?" Cheryl asked.

Her family was used to her making cryptic comments about the future based on hunches she couldn't explain, and they had learned not to dismiss them. Maybe her subconscious mind collected bits and pieces of random data, and her ability to solve complicated puzzles helped her see patterns that others couldn't. Although, this time, it wasn't a hunch but information she wasn't allowed to share with them yet.

"I don't sense it. I know it."

48

DARLENE

*E*ric held Darlene's hand as they walked on the beach, the contact sending delicious shivers through her body, and as she imagined that rough, callused hand caressing her skin, she nearly moaned from how turned on she got.

The molten looks he was sending her way weren't helping either. His brown eyes were full of lust, the long black lashes framing them evoking thoughts of a boudoir's curtains.

Heck, with Eric so near, every thought she had was carnal. Mostly, she felt aroused and excited, but some insidious doubt still managed to infiltrate all those sexy feelings.

Years of being told she wasn't exciting in bed had left their mark on her. She'd been too timid, hadn't initiated enough, and her blowjobs had been mediocre at best.

Was it true? Was she a lousy lover? Or was it just part of Leo's campaign to keep her from raising her head?

"What are you thinking about?" Eric asked.

She averted her gaze. "Something I shouldn't."

"Talk to me." He gave her hand an encouraging squeeze. "I'm a good listener."

It was humiliating enough to tell those things to a therapist, which was why Darlene hadn't availed herself of Vanessa's services, let alone a hunky guy that was probably a god in bed.

She smiled up at him. "Sharing those thoughts with a man I plan to seduce tonight would be counterproductive."

A lascivious grin spread over his handsome face. "Why wait for tonight?" He stopped and looked around. "See that outcropping?" He pointed at a rock formation a hundred feet or so in front of them. "I bet I can find us a cave in there."

Darlene laughed. "Even if there was one, which I know there isn't, I'm not keen on the sand getting in my privates."

"Then let's go to your place." He started turning around.

"I'm afraid that's not possible either. I'm not allowed to bring visitors into the secure inner zone."

He frowned. "So, how did Kaia show Karen and Gilbert her bungalow?"

"William made an exception for her and notified the guys in security. If they didn't have cameras all over the place, I would sneak you in, but they would stop us as soon as we crossed the gate."

"We can go to my room at the lodge," Eric offered.

"That would be awkward. Your family is staying next door and might be going between rooms or leaving their doors open."

He shrugged. "I don't care. They should be happy that I'm finally hooking up with a woman my age."

She winced, the reminder of who he usually hooked up withsending a spear of apprehension through her.

"I didn't mean it that way." Eric stopped walking and turned to face her. "You're more than just a hookup to me."

He must have noticed her wince and misinterpreted it.

"I don't need you to pretend that I'm more than a casual fling, and I don't mind being just that. We are both adults, and we are after the same thing." She lifted on her toes to plant a kiss on his lips.

Eric didn't take over like she'd expected. Instead, he waited for her to drop down to her heels, and his expression remained serious.

"If you were just another hookup, I wouldn't have reorganized my entire schedule so I could fly the family over here this weekend. Since the moment we met a week ago, I haven't been able to stop thinking about you. Do you know how many times I've jacked off imagining all the things I'm going to do to you?"

Did that mean he hadn't been with anyone else during that week? And why was he so fascinated with her? She was no great beauty, and her flirting skills were rusty.

Heat creeping up her cheeks, Darlene shook her head. "Why? What's special about me?"

"Everything." He cupped her cheek. "I feel a connection to you that I haven't felt for any other woman. Not even for my ex, whom I was madly in love with, or so I thought." He raked his fingers through his hair, pushing back the wavy bangs. "I can't explain it, but when I look into your eyes, I see a real person. I see a woman who thinks and feels and who has a great sense of humor."

She narrowed her eyes at him. "Everyone thinks and feels, Eric. What makes me more real to you than others?"

"It's something in your eyes. I wish I could explain myself better. But the bottom line is that I'm not planning for this to be a weekend thing and then to never see you again. I'll be back without the family, and I will take you out on a proper date. I can fly you anywhere you want to go."

He sounded serious, and that was a problem. If he were an immortal, she would be elated to find someone she liked so much and who was interested in a long-term relationship with her. But he was human, and she couldn't lead him on with promises of a potential future.

Lowering her eyes, Darlene forced a smile. "Let's take it one day at a time and see where that leads us."

ERIC

*E*ric didn't know what had possessed him to say those things to Darlene. First of all, he didn't plan on settling down anytime soon. Secondly, telling a woman that he was interested in a long-term relationship right from the start was a rookie mistake he hadn't made since junior year in high school.

Women were less predatory than men, but they needed to feel that they had to work for it too. A fish easily caught was just as quickly thrown back into the sea.

Was there something in the sea breeze that had addled his brain? Or was it really something about Darlene?

Given the guilty expression on her beautiful face, she didn't feel the same. If he wanted to salvage the situation and get her naked today, he had to think fast.

"Gilbert's lecture about settling down must have affected me more than I realized. I'm not ready for anything serious." He wrapped his arm around Darlene's waist and pulled her against his body. "So, beautiful, where can I do to you all those dastardly things I've been dreaming about?"

A conspiratorial smile bloomed on her face. "We have two

options. We can try to sneak into your room in the lodge without your family seeing us and then make very quiet love, or we can sneak into the bus and go as wild as we want."

He arched a brow. "The bus?"

"Yeah. No one is coming or going today, and the driver parked it in the shade. If you wait for me in the lodge, I can go to my bungalow and pack a couple of blankets to make it more comfortable."

He hadn't made love on a bus before, and he doubted the novelty could compensate for the discomfort, but given the blush coloring Darlene's cheeks, she was excited about it, so why not?

Eric was an adventurous sort, and he was willing to try everything once.

"Sounds like a plan to me." He pulled her against his body, letting her feel how hard he was for her.

She kissed him on the lips. "I can take a shortcut through there." She pointed. "You just need to walk back the way we came to find the lodge."

"Don't worry about me." He turned her around and smacked her bottom to send her on her way. "Don't make me wait too long."

"I won't." Darlene cast him a smile before rushing off.

He loved that her cheeks had pinked when she'd suggested the bus, and when he smacked her ass, they turned flaming red.

There was a level of innocence and expectancy in Darlene that made his heart beat faster with anticipation and desire. Today's young women were more brazen than those of his generation, and it had been a long time since he'd made a girl blush. It excited him more than if she'd stripped naked in front of him and offered to suck him off.

What did it say about him that offers like that no longer excited him?

Was he so damn jaded, or had he gotten too many offers of

that lately? Not that he didn't appreciate being treated to an enthusiastic blowjob, but it was somewhat of a turnoff when the offer came after the first date. It became as common as a kiss goodnight on the cheek and just as meaningless.

The last time Eric had been so excited about the prospect of having sex with a new partner had been when he'd met his ex. She'd played the game expertly, pretending she wasn't interested and making him work hard for her, then pretending finally to succumb to his charms.

She'd told him she'd only had two boyfriends before him, and since she'd been only twenty, he'd believed her. Not that it would have deterred him if he'd known that she'd had five or ten or fifteen. All he'd asked for was honesty, and he'd expected loyalty while they were together. When he'd told her that, she'd pretended offense that he could even think she would ever cheat on her man.

He'd eaten up all the crap she'd fed him, discovering years later that she'd kept her bed warm with multiple partners while he'd been gone on missions.

When rumors of her infidelity had reached him, and he'd confronted her, she'd reacted with such a tantrum that he'd once again been fooled into believing that the rumors had been false—a malicious attempt that had been born of envy and meant to besmirch the reputation of a beautiful woman.

God, what a fool he'd been.

How could he have let her play him so well?

Once he'd retired from the Air Force, she'd had a more difficult time playing around, and eventually he could no longer ignore the rumors and the discrepancies in her stories.

Eric had often wondered why she'd done it. Had he been neglectful? Had it been his long absences? Or perhaps she couldn't handle the stress of not knowing where he was and whether he would return in one piece? But those excuses had become invalid once he retired, and yet she hadn't stopped.

Maybe it had become a habit, or maybe she had gotten addicted to sex.

Sometimes he wondered whether it was the age difference.

He'd been thirty when he'd met Emma, and she'd been only twenty, but he'd always taken good care of himself and was in excellent shape.

Maybe Gilbert believed that was the reason their marriage had fallen apart, and that was why he was so opposed to Kaia's engagement to William.

Eric was so embarrassed about being played that he'd never told his brother about Emma's infidelity. He'd blamed it on his ex's insane tantrums and her combative personality, which had been true, but those hadn't been the deal-breakers. They'd always made up after her explosions, and the sex had been phenomenal.

Perhaps that was why he'd ignored what had been right in front of his eyes.

DARLENE

*D*arlene stifled a nervous giggle as she slunk around the lodge with a laundry bag slung over her shoulder. She wasn't doing anything wrong, and everything in that bag was hers, but she still felt like a thief with a load of stolen loot.

It was kind of exciting, especially given what it was for.

The Guardians in the control room might have seen her leaving her bungalow with her laundry bag, but hopefully no one had guessed what she had in it, and what she was planning to do with the stuff.

If anyone asked, she could say that the washing machine in her bungalow had malfunctioned, and she needed to do her laundry in the lodge.

The trickier part was to sneak into the parking lot behind the resort with no one seeing her.

It was late Saturday afternoon, so there was no way she could avoid bumping into guests roaming around or heading down to the beach, but they didn't know her, and they couldn't possibly guess what she was carrying or why.

Most of what she'd collected had come from her bed, so she

would need to launder everything later, but making a comfortable nest for her and Eric was worth the effort.

Her plan was to arrange everything first and then come back for him, but when she finally made it to the parking lot, her heart sank. The damn bus wasn't there.

"What now?" She looked around, searching for an alternative, but the only vehicle there was the resort's delivery van, and when she tried the handle, it was locked.

Maybe the bus was parked in the underground garage?

She'd never been there, but she'd heard that there was a small one that was connected to Emmett's underground cottage. Could the bus even fit in there?

Pulling out her phone, she texted William. *Do you know if the bus is parked in the garage? And if it is, how do I get in there?*

Hopefully, there was another way to get in because she couldn't go through the cottage. Kian and Syssi were staying there, including Kian's guards and their mates. Sneaking through unnoticed would be impossible.

William answered a moment later. *Did you lose something on the way back from the restaurant last night?*

Taking a deep breath, she decided to fess up. It was easier than coming up with an excuse on the spot and inviting even more questions. Eric was waiting for her at the lodge, and he might think she was standing him up.

Well, she intended to, but in a good way.

I didn't lose anything yet, but I plan to lose my inhibitions if you get my drift. I can't entertain anyone in my bungalow and the lodge is too busy, so I thought of the bus.

His return text had a smiley face and a thumbs up. *The bus is parked in the garage next to Kian's rented van. You need to go out of the lodge and turn right. When you get to the hedge, look at it closely, and you'll find the door. I know that it's unlocked, but I don't know about the bus. Text me if you can't get in, and I'll get you the keys.*

She typed back. *You are the best. Thanks.*

Another text came in before she had a chance to return the phone to her purse. *I don't know if anyone notified you about the dinner at the bunker with Syssi and Kian. If not, it's at eight. Tell Eric.*

Darlene glanced at the time on her phone. It was seventeen minutes after five o'clock. That should be enough time for a nice romp in the bus.

Chuckling to herself, she typed a message back. *We will try to be there. If we are not, tell them that we have eloped.*

A message with a laughing face came in a second later.

Her amusement didn't last long, though. When she got to the hedge, the door to the garage was so well hidden that it took her several frustrating moments of looking through the thick greenery and sweeping aside branches before she found it. Thankfully, it was unlocked just as William had promised.

It was cool and dark inside the garage, which suited her plans much better than if the bus was parked outside, and most importantly, it was more private. The chances of anyone walking in on them were tiny, but it was enough to add spice to the adventure.

When she found the bus door open, Darlene let out a relieved breath and climbed inside.

It took her several minutes to set everything up the way she wanted in the back of the bus, and when she was done, she took a step back and regarded her nest. Two blankets covered the floor, several pillows were casually tossed on top for added cushioning, and she'd also brought a thin blanket for covering up. Originally, it had been meant as a means to provide her with a small measure of modesty, but with how cool it was in the underground parking, it would also serve to keep the chill away.

Darlene had also brought a bottle of wine, two glasses, a box of tissues, and a pack of wipes. The only thing she didn't have was a condom, but hopefully, Eric had thought ahead and brought a bunch with him.

One would certainly not do it.

Pregnancy wasn't an issue, but he led an active sex life, and she didn't want to catch anything from him.

The setup was far from ideal, but it was naughty and fun, and it was highly unlikely that Eric had tried anything like this before. She might not have robust sexual experience to wow him with, but she could delight him with a novel environment.

WILLIAM

*a*fter Emmett and Eleanor's arrival, the conversation turned to paranormal recruitment and the Echelon system, and William started to relax.

This was familiar. This was where he was comfortable. He was with people who knew him, respected him, and knew what to expect from him.

Being with Kaia was exhilarating, but it was also exhausting.

William wasn't an old immortal, but he was old enough to be set in his ways, and change made him anxious. He might have thrived on new technologies and scientific discoveries, but the upheaval Kaia's arrival had brought to his personal life was draining.

He was sweaty even though it wasn't hot, and he felt lethargic although he hadn't done anything physically demanding.

"Is Echelon spitting out any relevant information?" Kian asked.

"I sifted through the lists our contact at Echelon provided me, and I have several prospects." Eleanor put her teacup on the table. "The problem is that I will need to recruit them like I did while working for the government." She looked at Kian. "First of all, I will need to travel to meet them, and I need your authorization for that, and I will probably also need to use compulsion to lure them here. How much of it am I allowed to use?"

The boss grimaced. "I don't like the idea of compelling people. Can't we lure them the old-fashioned way? A good salary should do it."

Eleanor gave Kian a one-shouldered shrug. "I can start by offering them a free spot in the paranormal retreat, but they will wonder how I found them. The headhunter cover worked very well for me before." She smiled. "No one ever asked me how I found out about them. They assumed I had access to their school and college records."

"You were a government agent," Syssi said. "It was natural for them to assume that. You can use that cover now as well. We can make you all the fake documents you need."

"What about my reason for contacting them? I need to come up with something that would sound reasonable. No one gives free retreats to random people without expecting something in return."

If Kian forbade Eleanor from using compulsion, he would be tying her hands and limiting her options. As a newly transitioned immortal, she couldn't thrall, so an ironclad contract was the only way she could ensure that the prospects didn't tell anyone about the lady recruiting paranormal talents for a secret project.

"Who are the potential prospects?" Syssi asked. "And what flagged them?"

"The best one has an interesting story." Eleanor lifted her teacup from the coffee table, took a sip, and put it down. "He was caught cheating on the roulette tables in Vegas, but they couldn't prove anything. He was just cleaning out the house with perfect hunches. They forbade him from ever gambling at any of the casinos there. His picture with the explanation of his uncanny lucky streak was sent to all the security offices of the large hotels, and that brief was what Echelon had flagged. He will be easy to deal with because he's either a master of deception or has a real precognition talent. After the fiasco in the casino, he won't be surprised when he's approached by people interested in his talent."

Syssi's eyes shone with excitement. "Does he live in Vegas?"

"No, he's actually a mathematics student at Caltech. Easy." Eleanor looked at Kian. "If you prefer to send one of the Guardians to get him, that's fine with me."

Leon got to his feet and walked over to the bar. "I wonder if he gambles in the small tribal casinos in the Los Angeles area. Did you check?"

Eleanor shook her head. "It's of no interest to me what he does with his talent. I only want to find out whether it's real. A Guardian could pose as one of Amanda's students and casually mention her lab to the guy. He might be able to lure him in for testing without even having to thrall him."

"Send me the information," Kian said. "I like your idea of getting him into Amanda's lab. Precognition is an easy talent to test."

"Who else?" Syssi asked.

"A woman in Nashville who claims to have precognition. I don't have anything official to support it, but Echelon flagged dozens of phone conversations with people who called her, asking for her help. What lends credibility to her claim is that she doesn't take money for foretelling the future, and she's not famous. People come to her by word of mouth. The others are weaker cases, but I don't mind traveling to see them if my expenses are covered."

Reading Kian's expression, William knew that the boss

worried more about Eleanor leaving Safe Haven than covering her expenses.

"Emmett will need to stay here," Kian said.

Eleanor cast her mate a sidelong glance. "That's okay. I will go and come back the same day. I don't plan to make a national tour out of that the way I used to."

"What if you need to bring a prospect in?" Anastasia asked. "They won't be ready to go right away."

"After I ascertain they are worth investigating further, Kian can send someone else to finalize the deal." She smiled at the boss. "It will complicate things, but since you don't want Emmett to join me on my travels, that's the best I can do."

ERIC

*a*s Eric saw Darlene walking toward him, he let out a relieved breath and pushed to his feet. "I thought you weren't coming back."

Her eyes darted around the lodge's common room. "Let's go. We don't have much time." She took his hand and led him toward one of the side doors.

"Why the rush?"

"Syssi and Kian are hosting your family for dinner at eight. Our presence is requested."

"Who told you that?"

She smiled sheepishly. "William. I couldn't find the bus, so I texted him."

He lifted a brow. "So, we are not going to the bus after all?"

"Yes, we are." She walked up to the hedge, reached behind a branch, and pushed open a hidden door. "It's parked in the garage."

It was cool and dark inside, which was perfect for their plans. "Is the bus open?"

"It is." She led him to the door and then up the steps. "And I've already prepared our nest."

When Eric saw the blankets and pillows on the floor, a grin stretched over his face. "Let's close the door."

It took him a couple of seconds to find the lever, and as he pushed on it, the door closed with a hiss.

"I hope it opens just as easily." The tremor in Darlene's voice had nothing to do with fear of being stuck on the bus.

It was all about the anticipation of what was coming next, and Eric vowed to make it so good for her that it would erase any other sexual experience she'd ever had, whether good or bad.

"It does." Turning around, he put his hands on her waist and smashed her soft body against his. When their mouths met, she melted into the kiss, and as he pushed his tongue past her lips, a throaty moan escaped her throat.

The need he heard in that moan made Eric wish that he could tear Darlene's clothes off, throw her down on the nest she'd made, and take her in every conceivable way, but it had been a while for her, and he was her first lover since she'd left her husband.

Darlene needed a slow and tender seduction, and he would give it to her. There would be many more times for them, and he would get his fill of her when she was ready.

Holding her tightly against him, he moved his hands up her back, pushed his fingers into her hair, and kissed her slowly. When they had to let go of each other's mouths to come up for air, he leaned away to study her face.

Her lips were swollen from their kiss, and her eyes were glazed with desire, and at that moment, she was the most beautiful woman he'd ever been with.

Dipping his head, he captured her lips again, and this time his kiss wasn't soft. It was hard and demanding, and as Darlene sagged in his arms, he gripped her waist and walked her backward toward the nest.

Gently lowering her to the pile of pillows, he kneeled beside her and slid his hands under her loose blouse. "May I?"

When she nodded, he dragged it up and off of her and then tossed it behind him.

The bra covering her ample breasts was lacy, soft, and almost sheer, and through the pink lace, he could see her slightly darker pink nipples puckered and awaiting his mouth.

"Darlene," he murmured as he sat back and pulled the bra cups down and under her breasts.

"Yes." Her chest heaving, she arched her back and offered him her bounty.

It was all the encouragement he needed, and as he descended on one of those plump berries and closed his lips around it, another needy moan left Darlene's throat.

"Eric." Her fingers threaded through his hair as she held him to her.

He feasted on her breasts for a long moment before hooking his fingers in the elastic of her pants and tugging them down her hips. He'd left them pulled around her knees and pushed his hands under her panties, cupping her generous ass.

When she trembled in his hold, he didn't know whether it was in anticipation of what he was about to do next or if she was cold. Trailing his fingers down the crack of her ass, he reached her moist petals from behind and got his answer.

"You are so ready for me," he murmured against her nipple.

"I am, and you have too many clothes on."

A dark laugh left his lips as he let go of her nipple and ripped his T-shirt over his head.

"Better?"

Her eyes ate the sight of his bare chest. "Much, but I want to see more." She leaned forward and grasped his belt.

"May I?" she asked mockingly, parroting what he'd asked her before baring her.

"Please." He puffed out his chest, making his pectorals bulge for her to ogle.

Her smile was wicked as she slipped the length of the belt from the buckle and unbuttoned his fly.

DARLENE

*A*s Darlene pushed Eric's jeans down to his knees, she paused before reaching for his boxers. Did she have the nerve to pull them down as well?

Instead, she looked into his eyes and put a hand on his chest. He must have spent many hours at the gym to be so chiseled, and seeing how toned and perfect his body was, she had the urge to cover her less than perky breasts and rounded belly.

Not that Eric seemed to notice any of it. As she ran her hands up his defined pecs, his eyes roamed over her body hungrily.

He let her explore for a few moments before folding his arms around her and drawing her to him, and when he kissed her, the passion in his kiss melted away her insecurities. He claimed her with such wild ferocity that she was left breathless and mindless, so much so that at some point, she found herself on her back with him pulling her pants and panties off her.

Evidently, Eric didn't need an immortal's ability to thrall his partners into oblivion. His expert kissing was just as effective.

His eyes never left her as he kicked off his own jeans the rest of the way. When he hooked his thumbs in the elastic band of his boxers, Darlene held her breath in anticipation of the reveal, but he pulled them down so fast that she only got a brief glimpse of his proud mast, and then he was on top of her, that hard length pressing against her center.

Was the guy an immortal pretending to be human? Who else could move with such speed? Or was it just an illusion that her mind had created?

Gripping the back of his neck, she arched into him, making him understand what she wanted him to do. Perhaps another time they could spend long moments on foreplay, but today, her patience had run out, and she was desperate for him to get inside of her.

"Eric," she moaned as he ground his shaft against that most sensitive spot, ratcheting her need to the stratosphere. "Don't tease me. I need you inside of me." She hooked her legs around his waist to get more of that delicious friction.

Cupping her cheek with one hand, he gripped himself with the other, but he didn't push inside her as she'd hoped.

Instead, he paused at her entrance. "I'm clean. I haven't been with anyone for over a month, and I got checked a week ago."

For some reason, knowing that he hadn't had sex since meeting her eased a knot of anxiety inside of her that she hadn't been aware of, and a relieved chuckle left her mouth. "I haven't been with anyone for months. I'm safe too."

A predatory gleam turning his brown eyes amber, he found her entrance a split second later, and as he slid his length inside of her, she gasped.

He stilled for a moment, his ragged breaths misting the air between them, but as she smiled up at him and arched up, he pushed all the way in, filling her so deliciously that a tear slid down the corner of her eye.

He kissed the tear away, and for a long moment, he just stared at her as if he wanted to tell her that he loved her, but that was a silly wish that had no hold in their reality.

They had this weekend, maybe one or two more, but love had no place in their summer fling.

And then Eric began to move, burning off her sad musings with the hard thrusts of his hips that demanded all of her attention.

With him claiming her core and her mouth, it didn't take more than a couple of minutes for her to climb beyond the point of no return, and as the climax exploded out of her, his thrusts became savage in their intensity.

As he swelled inside of her and shot his essence into her, Darlene climaxed again, shouting his name.

When he finally stilled, he let out a groan and shifted onto his side, taking her with him, so she was half sprawled over him. Her head resting on his chest, Darlene listened to the wild beat of Eric's heart until it slowed down and evened out.

Had she ever felt so satisfied after sex?

Not that she could remember. She came twice, only minutes apart. That had never happened before, and given that there had been barely any foreplay and the whole thing couldn't have lasted more than ten minutes, it was astounding.

Either Eric had some sex superpowers, or she'd been deprived for so long that she'd accumulated enough explosives to detonate from any spark.

"I'm sorry," he murmured, his hand caressing her back. "I really wanted it to last longer than that."

She lifted her head and smiled at him. "I don't think I could handle more. Already it was the best sex I ever had and the only time I climaxed twice in a row."

ERIC

*a*s Eric caressed Darlene's back after making good on his promise, he was satisfied that he'd adequately compensated for his embarrassing first performance.

He wasn't a young buck, but it had been surprisingly easy to get hard again for Darlene. She was soft and feminine, sexy and responsive, and being with her was as easy as water.

"Do you think I can find something to do around here?"

Her hand, which had been lovingly caressing his chest, stilled. "What do you mean? Do you want to participate in one of the retreats?"

He laughed. "That New Age stuff is not for me. Do you think your boss needs a pilot? That's pretty much all I know how to do."

She lifted her eyes to him. "I can ask. We are pretty isolated out here, and the nearest airport is the one you landed at. But I don't know if they can build a landing strip here. The area is rocky and hilly."

"Maybe I can do something else." He kept running his hand over the lush curve of her ass. "Do they need help in the kitchen?"

She narrowed her eyes at him. "Can you even cook?"

"Of course, I can cook. I know how to make scrambled eggs and defrost pre-made dinners. I'm also handy. I worked for my brother's construction firm for a while. But Gilbert and I can get along only when we don't spend too much time together. We are both too headstrong to cooperate."

Darlene let out a breath and put her head on his chest. "I don't think they are going to build anything more on this property. This project is done."

"That's a shame." He threaded his fingers through her hair and tugged her head back to nuzzle her neck. "Do they need a hairdresser?"

She chuckled. "Now I know that you're not serious."

"I'm serious. I want to find a way to be near you."

She lifted her head again. "I'm not going to stay here forever. This is a temporary assignment just until William's project is done."

"I didn't know that." His hand stilled on her back. "Do you know what they are working on?"

"No clue. It's top secret, and I'm just the administrative assistant."

He had a feeling that Darlene knew more than she was letting on, but she probably couldn't talk about it, and it was easier to pretend that she didn't know.

He knew all about keeping secrets. Most of his missions had been classified, and he couldn't tell anyone about the many times he almost hadn't made it but somehow had survived despite all odds.

"What does your boss do?"

"William? He runs the lab here and the one back home."

"I meant the big boss. Kian."

Darlene was in Safe Haven just for the project, and once it was done, she would go back home to Los Angeles. If he wanted long-term with her, he should look for work over there. He could always move his jet operations to one of the many private airports in her area, but he was curious to see whether she was interested in him following her.

The sex had been incredibly good, but for Eric, it was more than that. Just holding Darlene in his arms and talking with her was more pleasant than any interaction he'd had with a woman in ages. The question was whether she felt it too.

"Kian does many things. I know that he develops office buildings and hotels. Why?"

Eric shrugged. "Maybe I'll move to Los Angeles and get a job at his company."

As he felt Darlene tense in his arms, he got his answer. She wasn't interested in him following her to Los Angeles.

"As I said, I'm here for a few months, so if you want to see more of me, you can join a retreat. Not all of them are about New Age stuff. Safe Haven also runs retreats for people with paranormal talents. Do you have any extrasensory perception? Telepathy? Precognition? Remote viewing?"

He chuckled. "I have one paranormal talent, and that's staying alive. The guys in my unit called me the lucky charm. I somehow got out alive from situations that should have killed me, and so did everyone who flew with me. If it had happened once or twice, it could have been just dumb luck, but it happened so many times that it became spooky. After the last time it happened, I decided not to renew my contract for another term. I didn't want to push my luck."

She shivered. "I'm glad. Being a fighter pilot is dangerous."

"Not really. It's less dangerous than almost any other combat position. But I guess I was both lucky and unlucky. I was unlucky to get into more trouble than I should have, but I was lucky to walk away alive."

DARLENE

*W*as it too much to hope for that Eric was a Dormant?

Probably.

He made her feel alive, and being with him was surprisingly easy. Darlene had expected it to be awkward, and she hadn't even had much hope that the sex would be great, but he'd surpassed her expectations on every front.

Maybe that's how all players were, though.

Was that the secret of their success?

They made women feel so good about themselves that they became a coveted prize even when none of the beneficiaries of their attentions expected them to stay?

When Eric's phone rang, he reached for his discarded pants and pulled it out. "It's Gilbert."

"He's probably calling to tell you about the dinner at Syssi and Kian's."

Eric smiled at her before accepting the call. "Are you calling me to apologize?"

The phone was so close to her ear that she could hear Gilbert breathing on the other side.

"I didn't mean it the way it came out. Where are you?"

Eric trailed his hand down to her ass. "Darlene is showing me the sights."

She stifled a giggle by burying her face in his chest.

"Right. Anyway, I'm calling to tell you that we are all invited to dinner at Kian and Syssi's, and they are staying at what they call the bunker. Darlene probably knows where it is."

"I know about the dinner. William told Darlene about it. I guess that if you're going, you've gotten over your anger tantrum and reconciled yourself to accepting Kaia's choice."

"Not even close, but I have orders from Karen to behave. Kaia is in love with the guy, and Karen told me to back off and let it play out. If it's not meant to be, it will fizzle out on its own."

"Darlene says that William is a sweetheart, and that Kaia is lucky to snag him."

Darlene nodded her agreement and whispered. "The best guy I know."

When Eric squeezed her butt, she patted his chest. "After you, of course."

"That's better." He smiled.

"What's better?" Gilbert asked.

"Your attitude. I'm glad that Karen talked some sense into your stubborn head."

"Yeah, yeah. All is hunky dory now when William is thirty-two and looks younger than that. But in twenty years, he's going to be over fifty while Kaia will be only thirty-nine. That's a big difference. At that age, people's health starts to decline along with their looks. She's too young to see it now, and maybe he is too, but it's going to be a problem."

Eric winked at Darlene. "You're only as old as you feel. Besides, they are in love. What are you going to do? If you fight it, you're going to alienate her and make your entire family miserable."

Gilbert let out a long-suffering sigh. "Don't you think I know that? I need to apply pressure to force Kaia to re-evaluate her feelings and make sure that she really wants him. She had known the guy for seven days, and she accepted his marriage proposal. That's crazy, and it's very much unlike Kaia. He might have some unhealthy influence on her, and if she's unsure how to end it, she can use me as an excuse to get out of the relationship without souring things between her and her boss. That way, they can at least finish the damn project."

Darlene was impressed. Gilbert had pretended an anger tantrum not to stand in Kaia's way to love and happiness but to give her a way out if she needed it. The guy was either an excellent actor, or he was putting a spin on it because he felt embarrassed about the way he'd acted.

"Maybe they are really in love," Eric said. "Sometimes the simplest explanation is the correct one, and there is no need to search for hidden motives and undue influence."

"Maybe," Gilbert said. "That's what I want to find out."

Eric chuckled. "So, your posturing was all for show?"

"Not all of it, but some. I don't think that William is right for Kaia, mainly because of the age difference, but I won't stand in the way of her happiness if that's what she really wants."

Eric sighed. "Don't assume that all marriages where there is a big age difference between the partners end badly just because mine did. Emma was a psycho, and I was too blind to see that."

"You also dated her for only two months before proposing to her."

Eric closed his eyes. "We thought that she was pregnant."

"She tricked you," Gilbert said. "The woman was a master manipulator even though she was still a kid."

That explained so much. Eric had married a woman who had been much younger than him, and he'd done it after knowing her for a very short time. No wonder Gilbert was freaking out over Kaia doing the same. Well, the situation was reversed in that in his mind William was the cradle-robber, but it was similar enough.

"Yeah, she probably did, but at the time, I was in love and naive enough to believe her."

When Eric ended the call, Darlene lifted her head and braced it on her forearm. "How old were you when you got married?"

"I was thirty, and I don't want to talk about it." He pulled her on top of him. "So far, this has been one of the best days of my life, and I don't want to spoil it by talking about her."

56

WILLIAM

*a*fter leaving Kian and Syssi to prepare for dinner, William stopped by his bungalow to shower and change.

When he was done combing his hair, he removed his glasses, cleaned them with a wipe, and put them back on. But as he stood in front of the vanity mirror, he took them off again and put them on the counter.

He wasn't going to sit in front of a computer screen, and the sun wasn't glaring on the Oregon coast even at midday, let alone at seven-thirty in the evening. He had no valid excuse to hide behind the frames.

Not that he owed an explanation to anyone, but he felt that it was time to stop using the glasses as a crutch.

Given that he expected the battle with Kaia's stepfather to continue, it wasn't the best time to give up his imaginary shield, but since he was already facing so many changes, one more shouldn't make a difference.

Taking a calming breath, he glanced one last time at the folded glasses and then turned on his heel and headed out.

The lodge was less than ten minutes of an easy stroll away,

but William strode with purpose in his steps and made it in half the time. Walking down the corridor to the rooms the family occupied, he didn't know which of the three doors to knock on. The larger room housed the parents with the two boys, but the other two were the same size.

Which one was Kaia in?

Pulling out his phone, he started to text her, but as he heard a chorus of female laughter, he knocked on the door it was coming from.

Kaia opened up with a big smile and pulled him into a hug. "I missed you." She kissed his cheek.

Inside, Cheryl and Karen were seated on one bed while Idina was bouncing on the other with a doll clutched in each hand.

"William!" She jumped off the bed and lifted her arms to him. "I want to ride on your shoulders."

"We were just talking about you," Karen said.

"I hope only good things." He bent down and put his hands on the little girl's tiny waist.

As he picked Idina up, Cheryl gave him a discreet thumbs up from behind her mother's back.

Did she mean that what they'd talked about had been all good?

"Gilbert should be ready in a few minutes," Karen said without acknowledging his comment.

She'd changed into a pretty navy-colored dress, and with her dark hair curled and cascading down her shoulders, she looked effortlessly beautiful, but he didn't know whether it was okay for him to compliment Kaia's mother.

Cheryl had also changed into a new outfit, pairing black jeans with a short-sleeved white shirt. The fabric had tiny holes in it that were embroidered, but it wasn't lace. It had some other name that eluded him at the moment. Was it eyelet?

Kaia was still in the same outfit she'd worn that morning,

probably because she hadn't wanted to miss a moment with her family to get changed.

As the five of them stepped out into the corridor, the next door over opened, and Gilbert walked out, pushing the double stroller with one hand and holding a portable crib in the other.

"Let me help you." William reached for the crib.

"That's okay." Gilbert moved it out of William's reach. "Cheryl or Kaia can push the stroller, and I can carry the crib." He added a tight smile. "You are already carrying precious cargo. Make sure she doesn't fall."

The way Idina was gripping his head, there was no way she would fall, but little kids were impulsive, especially the hellion he was carrying on his shoulders.

"Hold on tight," he told her as he gently gripped her tiny ankles.

Idina's big personality was housed in a small, fragile body, and holding her, William wondered how parents dealt with the anxiety of knowing how vulnerable their children were. The girls in his clan transitioned early, and by Idina's age, they were already immortal, but boys remained vulnerable until puberty, and he wished there was a way to induce their transition earlier.

Maybe Okidu's journals held the answer to that, and perhaps they also had instructions for transforming the children born to immortal males with human partners.

The Fates had been kind to his clan lately, and many Dormants had been found, but there were still so many males without a mate and without immortal offspring.

"What are you thinking about?" Kaia fell in step with him.

"I was thinking about children and how vulnerable they are. Until they reach adulthood, their parents must live with constant anxiety."

"That never changes," Karen said. "You don't stop worrying about your child just because she's all grown up." She smiled at

Kaia. "On the contrary. The worst feeling for a parent is help-lessness. When our children are small, most of the time, it's easy to fix whatever is troubling them. The older they get, the harder it is to do, and at some point, they no longer listen to you, and you are forced to watch them making mistakes that they are going to regret later. As the saying goes, small kids, small troubles, big kids, big troubles."

Had she been referring to him? Did they still think that he was Kaia's mistake?

"Kaia says that you are sweet." Idina patted his head and then leaned down and kissed his forehead. "I like you."

Surprised, William lifted his eyes and looked into her smiling face. It was framed in soft curls that were now cascading down and blocking his view. "Thank you. I like you too."

Gilbert snorted. "It seems like you've won over all the ladies in my family." He looked up at Idina. "This one doesn't offer her affection easily. I wonder what magic you wield over the fairer sex."

William shrugged. "You should trust their female intuition. I'm a nice guy."

57

KAIA

"*I*s this where your boss is staying?" Gilbert looked with dismay at the small, one-room cottage.

Kaia had heard about the underground, but she'd never been there. Supposedly, Emmett had orgies down there before he met Eleanor and fell in love with her. William had said that there was more to the story and promised to tell her about it, but they'd been busy with other stuff, and they'd forgotten about it.

They were both guilty of getting completely immersed in whatever they were doing, whether it was work or sex, and they both tended to let other things fall by the wayside. They needed an Odu of their own to remind them of all the things they were forgetting.

"This is just for show." William opened the door and ducked low so Idina's head cleared the header. "There is a sizable bunker built under it, and the entrance is through the cottage."

Gilbert handed the travel crib to Kaia and took the stroller from Cheryl. "I thought that this was a free love commune, not a survivalist camp. What do they need a bunker for, and why is your boss staying underground when he could stay at the lodge?"

William glanced at Cheryl and then cast Gilbert an apologetic smile. "The bunker's history is a long story and not meant for young ears. And the reason my boss is staying there is that it's much more luxurious than the lodge and can house his entire entourage."

Cheryl snorted. "If you were referring to my ears as young, you are mistaken. I've heard and seen much more than you can ever imagine."

As Cheryl and Gilbert started arguing about what kind of content she was exposing herself to, and Karen got busy taking the twins out of the stroller, Kaia sidled up to William.

"Is Kian's butler here?" she asked quietly.

Nodding, William punched in the code to open the door.

"Yay." Kaia clapped her hands. "I'm so excited to meet him."

Cheryl walked over with Ryan in her arms. "Why are you so excited about meeting the butler?"

Thinking fast, Kaia said the first thing that popped into her head. "I've never met a proper British butler."

William had told her about the British television series and the characters that Okidu imitated, specifically the snooty butler. Hopefully, he was doing a good job of it and didn't look too robotic. Her sister was a smart girl, and she would notice if something was off.

As her family made its way down the narrow stairs carrying the twins, the folded stroller, the travel crib, and the big baby bag, Kaia hoped there was room enough down there for all of that.

When William opened the door at the bottom of the stairs, she had just a brief moment to look around as the greetings commenced.

"Good evening!" Syssi welcomed them with a big smile on her face.

The living room was sizable, but most of it was taken up by a long dining table. The couches and armchairs had been pushed against the walls, probably by the super-strong butler.

Where was he?

Kaia waited patiently for all the hellos to be over before turning to Syssi and whispering in her ear. "Where is the butler I've heard so much about?"

"Okidu is getting ready to serve dinner." Syssi threaded her arm through Kaia's. "Come. I'll introduce you." She led her through a swinging door into the kitchen.

The butler was dressed in a charcoal-colored suit, a white dress shirt, and a tie, with a white apron over his outfit.

"This is Kaia," Syssi said. "She wants to say hello."

He smiled broadly. "Hello, Mistress Kaia. How are you this lovely evening?"

He looked and sounded so human that she would have never guessed he was a cyborg.

"I'm great. What about you?"

"I am very well, thank you for asking. How is the work on my journals progressing?"

"We are making slow progress." She looked into his eyes, expecting to see camera apparatus behind the irises, but they looked perfectly organic. "Perhaps you can help us understand what you have written?"

He shook his head. "I just wrote down information that was stored in my memory banks. I know that they are instructions on how to build more of me, but I do not understand any of them." He smiled a little too broadly, and it looked fake but still human. "I am like a printer. The printer does not know what it prints. It just does its job."

She smiled. "I understand. Thank you for explaining."

He bowed. "I am always happy to help in any way I can."

Kaia turned to Syssi. "Is the printer analogy something Okidu was told?"

"I don't think so. Why?"

"Humor is a sign of intelligence."

"I agree." Syssi put her hand on Okidu's shoulder. "Please remember not to say anything like that near the others. They don't know about you."

He dipped his head. "Of course, mistress."

SYSSI

"Shall I start serving dinner, mistress?" Okidu asked.

Before answering, Syssi listened to the voices coming from the living room, but it didn't seem as if Eric and Darlene had arrived yet. "You can take out the soft drinks and the wine, but wait until the last two guests arrive to serve the food."

"Yes, mistress." He dipped his head and walked out of the kitchen with a tray of wine glasses.

When she made to follow, Kaia put a hand on her arm. "May I ask you something?"

"Go ahead."

Kaia struggled with what she wanted to say, opening and closing her mouth a few times. "How long have you and Kian been together?"

"About four and a half years. Why?"

"You have a daughter. I was told that's unusual."

Understanding dawning, Syssi nodded. "I wanted a child very much, and I didn't want to wait centuries to have one. Kian and I drank fertility potions that one of the clan's doctors had prepared for us, and we got pregnant within months." She smiled. "Kian thinks that it was a coincidence and that the potions were nothing more than snake oil, but I believe that they helped."

Kaia let out a breath. "I always dreamt of having a large family. Four kids was the minimum I considered, and I entertained the thought of having six. When I learned that it might not be possible after you know what, I started thinking of getting pregnant before doing the thing. But since my mother needs to do the same thing and her clock is ticking, I can't take the time to have a couple of kids before doing it. It's a relief that there is a treatment that might help me conceive sooner rather than later."

Syssi frowned. "Are you under compulsion not to talk about any of it?"

Kaia nodded. "The way it was worded, I can only talk about it with William. He tried to circumvent it so I could at least talk to Darlene, but it didn't work."

"Of course not. You need Eleanor and Emmett to remove the compulsion and reword it, so you can talk freely with those in the know."

"Yeah. I'll ask William to arrange that as soon as possible." She laughed. "I'm usually a direct person, and talking in circles is not my style."

"You're doing very well, given the limitations. It only illustrates how limited compulsion can be at enforcing the keeping of secrets. An intelligent person can find ways around it."

Kaia shifted from foot to foot. "Is the other method available to members of your family better?"

"I think so, but William is adamant about not thralling you. I think he's being overly cautious, but he keeps referring to your brain as a fine-tuned machine that shouldn't be messed with."

"I know." Kaia rolled her eyes. "I sometimes wonder if he's in love with me or my brain."

"Is there a difference between the two?" Syssi asked.

"Yeah, there is. I have a soul." Kaia put her hand over her heart. "And its feelings are no less influential on my character than my logical mind." She smiled. "Don't mind me. I know William loves everything about me. It just annoys me that he talks about my brain so much. I'm not as smart as everyone thinks."

Kaia's modesty was sweet, but it was unfounded. "I beg to differ. William is the smartest person I know, and he needs your help to decipher Okidu's journals. That means that you are at least as smart as he is, if not more."

The girl shrugged. "I'm a bioinformatician, and he's a computer engineer. There are things I know that he doesn't and vice versa. That's why we need to collaborate to find out what's in those journals." She frowned. "William is afraid that the knowledge gained from them might be dangerous, and I agree. I don't know what we should do if that's the case. The knowledge is valuable regardless of what it is used for."

"Precisely." Syssi threaded her arm through Kaia's. "Nearly every new invention or discovery has the potential to be either beneficial or harmful depending on the intent of those who use it." She led Kaia out of the kitchen. "And what's worse, it's impossible to bury it for long. Eventually, the technology or the idea always resurfaces, even if it's on a planet millions of light years away." She winked.

KIAN

"Where can I set up the crib?" Karen asked as soon as Syssi and Kaia had gone into the kitchen.

"I'll show you." Wonder rose to her feet with one of the twins in her arms. "Follow me."

"I'll come too." Callie cuddled the other baby boy to her chest.

With all the babies surrounding them, the ladies had their motherly hormones in overdrive, and Kian wouldn't be surprised if the two couples paid Merlin a visit upon their return to the village.

"Do you want to come?" Karen asked Kaia's baby sister.

Sitting in William's lap, she shook her head adamantly, her curly hair bouncing around her small face.

Idina was a fierce one, and Kian had taken a liking to her immediately. He liked feisty girls, and yet his perfect truelove mate was a gentle soul who never raised her voice or made any demands.

But then, that was Syssi's power. She only had to mention something in passing, and he jumped to fulfill her wishes.

Allegra was more like him than her mother, though. She

was demanding and uncompromising, but at least she knew how to get it all with a charming smile. He had no doubt that she had inherited that skill from her mother.

When he kissed the top of his daughter's head, she turned to look up at him. "Dada."

"Yes, sweetie. I'm your daddy."

"How old is your daughter?" Gilbert asked.

"She's six months old."

The guy pursed his lips. "She's talking early. My Idina was the same." He smiled at his little girl. "Right, baby?"

"I'm smart." She swung her leg up and down, missing William's shin by a hair. "Like Mommy."

He chuckled. "I get no respect. What about me? Are you smart like Daddy?"

She smiled, but her expression was a little evil. "I'm strong like Daddy." She lifted her arm and fisted her hands. "I'll build houses when I'm big. Like Daddy."

Kian's interest got piqued. "You're a builder?"

Gilbert's lips lifted on one side with a mocking smile. "I'm sure you know everything there is to know about me. The brief your people prepared on my family was quite extensive."

"That might be so, but I didn't read it. William is the one who heads the tech department, and I trust him implicitly. The only thing he needs to run by me is the budget, and I usually approve it without looking at it, either. His contribution to our organization is so massive that he can ask for the moon, and I'll tell my people to get it for him."

It was a shame that Syssi wasn't there to hear his speech. He'd followed her instructions to the letter, and Gilbert seemed duly impressed.

Looking at William, he gave him a once-over as if he was seeing him for the first time. "So, you're a big shot in the organization, are you?"

William gave him a shy smile. "I'm the authority on everything that has to do with technology."

"Nice. You're so unassuming that I would have never suspected that you were such an asset to your boss."

"I'm not really his boss," Kian said. "I answer to the board of directors, and William has one of the seven seats. Since I have to run every major decision through the board, it's more like they are my bosses than I'm theirs."

William was regarding him with a puzzled expression, probably confused by the bullshit he was spewing, and the moment Gilbert looked away, Kian winked and gave William the thumbs up.

"Our William is a genius," Anandur said. "He designed our entire defense system, and he's responsible for most of the patents we hold."

As Kian glared at Anandur for saying too much, William's cheeks got red, and he bounced Gilbert's little girl on his knees to hide his embarrassment.

"Kaia is a genius too," Gilbert said proudly. "I can't take credit for her smarts, but I'm proud to be her stepfather."

Evidently, he'd been too focused on the compliments to notice Anandur's slip up about the defense systems and therefore hadn't asked what they were defending themselves from and why.

Cheryl cleared her throat. "You and Mom are not married, so you are Kaia's and my honorary stepfather."

Pinning her with a hard stare, Gilbert put his hand over his heart. "It's what's in here that matters, not what's on a piece of paper."

"Amen to that." Anandur rose to his feet and walked over to the bar. "A shot of whiskey, anyone?"

"Don't mind if I do." Gilbert followed him up. "What do you have?"

As the two discussed the various whiskey brands on hand,

William closed his eyes briefly and let out a breath. "I should give Darlene a call. Maybe she can't find the place. They should've gotten here already."

"I'm on it." Brundar pulled out his phone.

"Who are you going to call?" William sounded anxious.

"The security office. They can find her and bring her and Gilbert's brother here."

William's expression turned panicked. "Don't send anyone looking for them. They'll get here when they get here."

The Guardian lifted one blond brow and kept typing a message on his phone.

A moment later, the device buzzed with an incoming message. "They are on their way. Max found them outside the lodge, and he's escorting them to the cottage."

"Thank the merciful Fates," William murmured under his breath.

Kian regarded him with amusement. "Is there something that you would like to share with us about Darlene and Eric?"

William shook his head. "I have absolutely nothing to share."

SYSSI

*T*hankfully, Allegra had fallen asleep in Kian's arms before dinner had started, and the twin boys had been sleeping peacefully in the spare bedroom.

Syssi had gone to check on them together with Karen, and they both had melted seeing the boys holding hands in the crib they shared.

Idina, on the other hand, didn't seem to be getting tired at all and continued listening intently to the conversations going on around the table and offering her opinion whenever she had one, whether it was on politics or economics, or the current bear market.

The adults had done their best to stifle their amused smiles at her astute observations, the best being about the bears and how they shouldn't be allowed in the market because they would just eat everything and scare the customers away.

When dinner was done, and Okidu had served hot beverages and dessert, Gilbert leaned back in his chair and patted his stomach. "Thank you for a lovely meal and the even lovelier company. I don't remember the last time I enjoyed an evening with friends so much."

"Thank you." Syssi smiled at him. "The feeling is mutual."

She wondered whether he had many friends, and for some reason she had a feeling that he did not, which reminded her of his comment about having a very small family and researching his ancestry to find more relatives.

She put her coffee cup down and turned to him. "You promised to tell me about your ancestry research and what you've found."

"Yes, I did." Gilbert put his hands on the table. "I was able to find out who my great-grandparents were, but that was as far as I got. I couldn't find anything about their parents."

She nodded. "You were fortunate to find even that. About three years ago, I tried to find out more about my ancestry, but I couldn't find anyone that predated my grandparents. They were no longer alive at the time, so there was no one to ask, and my parents didn't know much either. All I know is that my maternal great-grandparents came from Poland, and my paternal great-grandparents came from Ukraine, although back then, Ukraine was part of Russia."

Gilbert tapped his hands on the table with glee. "What a coincidence. You and I have common roots. No wonder I like you so much."

When Kian released a growl, Gilbert lifted his hands in the peace sign. "As a friend. I have eyes for only one woman." He draped his arm over Karen's back. "From the moment I first laid eyes on her, I never even thought of another." He leaned over and kissed her temple. "I found the love of my life, and she came with two wonderful girls." He looked lovingly at Cheryl and Kaia. "I got two amazing daughters in the bargain."

Looking placated, Kian gave him a tight smile. "Which one of your ancestors was Syssi's great-grandparents' countryman?"

"My maternal great-grandmother. My paternal grandfather was of British descent, and my paternal grandmother was Portuguese. On my mother's side, my grandfather was of

Austrian descent, and my grandmother was the daughter of Polish emigrants. They came to the United States shortly after World War I ended."

"Do you know where in Poland they were from?" Syssi asked.

He nodded. "They were from a small town named Gdynia. Today, it's a mid-sized seaport city, but back then, it was just a small tourist town that was part of the German Empire and was called Gdingen. After World War I, Gdynia was reintegrated within the Polish state."

"Interesting." Syssi took a cookie from the communal plate. "Your great-grandparents must have spoken fluent German."

"I assume that they did."

Syssi rubbed a hand over her chin. "I don't know which part of Poland my great-grandparents were from, but I remember my grandmother telling me that her mother could speak five languages, with German being one of them."

"She must have come from a wealthy family," Karen said. "Only the nobility could afford tutors for their children, and it was a status symbol to teach the kids several foreign languages. I bet she also knew French, English, and Russian. In addition to German, those were the main languages of the time."

"They still are," Eric said. "French is the language of love, English is the language of industry and commerce, German is the language of military precision, and Russian is the language of literature."

"Says who?" Kaia snorted. "I only know of French as being the language of love. I've never heard the other ones being described that way."

Eric shrugged. "That's how I think of them. I don't know whether I heard it somewhere or made it up."

Syssi thought of Sumerian and wondered whether it could be called the language of origins. Maybe it was the language that had launched the first human civilization, but it wasn't the original language from which all others had sprung.

That honor belonged to the gods' language. But then, even theirs might not be the original. Another advanced civilization could have started the gods' and another one before that started that one and so on.

It was probably a never-ending cycle, and the original fountainhead most likely no longer existed.

WILLIAM

*W*illiam was fascinated by Gilbert's showmanship. The guy enjoyed being the center of attention, drinking it in as if it was his favorite drug. He should have chosen a career in entertainment or in politics. But then, he probably owed his success to his people skills and to his politicking.

Getting permits to build in desirable locations required a lot of both.

"My great-grandmother's family owned a windmill near Gdynia," Gilbert said. "They might have been a little wealthier than their neighbors, but they weren't nobility, and they weren't rich. My great-grandmother's name was Perl or Perla, and she had a sister, Rosa. Perla married a man called Yanek Dorjinsky, and Rosa married his cousin Boris with the same last name. Both couples emigrated to the United States in 1923."

Syssi gasped. "My great-grandmother's name was Rosa, and she also came to the United States at about the same time."

Kian waved a dismissive hand. "Rosa was a popular name back then. It doesn't prove that you are related."

Ignoring her husband's dismissal, Syssi asked, "Do you know what happened to Rosa?"

Gilbert took a sip of coffee, put the cup down, and continued. "Boris died shortly after he and Rosa came to America, and Rosa remarried, but I lost track of her after that."

"What was the name of her second husband?" Anandur asked.

Gilbert lifted his hands in the air. "If I knew that, I could have found her, but my mother didn't remember what her mother had told her about her aunt, and my grandmother was no longer with us when I did my research. I even hired a private detective to try and find Rosa's descendants, provided that there were any, but since he couldn't locate her marriage certificate, he had nothing to go by. The town hall where she'd used to live with Boris burned down in 1927, and that was where the certificate had probably been kept."

"What happened to Perla after she came to the United States?" Wonder asked.

"She and my great-grandfather had only one daughter, my grandmother Sheila, who married an Austrian immigrant named Franz Wagner. They had a son who died as a baby and a daughter, my mother, Stephanie. She married Darren Emerson and had three kids. My brother Eric, my sister Gabi, and me. We don't have any family on our mother's side, and we have only two cousins on my father's side."

"That's why I want to have at least four kids," Kaia said. "I want to have a big family."

When William clasped her hand under the table, she gave him an encouraging squeeze.

"What about you, William?" Gilbert turned to him. "You want to marry my stepdaughter, and you haven't told us anything about your family."

Kaia pretended to frown. "You were raised by wolves, right?"

"I wasn't. My mother had me on her own, so I don't know anything about my father's side. But my mother has a big family with many cousins." He smiled at Gilbert. "Everyone here who is not part of your family is part of mine. Kian, Anandur, and Brundar are my second cousins, and Syssi, Wonder, and Callie are their mates."

"Mates?" Karen asked. "Is that a Scottish term for a significant other?"

"It's a family thing," Syssi said. "They have a tradition of calling their partners mates, and once you're exposed to it, you realize how much easier it is to use a gender and level of commitment neutral term. You can use it for a wife or a fiancée, you can use it for male or female, and you don't need to worry about offending anyone by using the wrong term."

"Pfft." Gilbert waved a hand. "People get offended too easily these days. Instead of worrying about serious things, they focus on minutiae."

"It's not minutiae to them," Cheryl grumbled under her breath. "But I'm all for simplifying things. I'm going to make an InstaTock post about using the term mate for every form of amorous partnership. I bet it will go viral."

"What's an InstaTock?" Kian asked.

She gaped at him as if he didn't know what a cell phone was. "Do you know what YouTube is?"

"Of course."

"And you know what a blog is, right?"

"Naturally."

"Instaock is a short video that is like an opinion blog. You record yourself either making a statement or commenting on someone else's, and then you add filters and background music to dramatize it, so it looks like a movie clip."

"That's an interesting concept," Kian said. "Maybe later you can show me an example."

"No problem. I have my own channel, and you are all

welcome to subscribe. The more subscribers I get, the more popular my channel will be. Instatock's algorithm will show my Instatocks to more people."

KAIA

*K*aia had seen several of Cheryl's vlogs and had done her sisterly duty of liking and sharing, but she wasn't a fan of social media in general and Instatock in particular. It was even more addictive than the others, and older teens Cheryl's age were obsessed with it.

Her mother leaned over Gilbert and picked his phone off the table. "Is the app you used to construct your family tree available on mobile?"

"It sure is." Gilbert took the phone from her. "I stored everything in the application, and I have some pictures I can show you. I went to Poland to try to claim the windmill for our family." He scrolled on his phone. "I didn't have proof enough to get ownership of it, but I took pictures." He passed the phone to Syssi.

She smiled. "It looks nice." She handed him the phone back. "They must preserve it as a historical monument, surely. It's not operational, right?"

Gilbert puffed out his chest. "I paid for the restoration in exchange for having a plaque with my great-grandmother's maiden name on it. I thought it would help my case in the future."

Kaia rolled her eyes. "That's so like you. You don't miss any opportunity to put your hands on real estate."

"That's what I do for a living, and I do it very well." He kept scrolling. "I also scanned old family photographs into the family tree application. This is my grandmother Sheila as a little girl with her mother, Perla." He passed the phone to Syssi again.

Her eyes widened. "Oh, my God. She looks exactly like my grandmother."

"Who?" Kaia leaned to get a look. "Perla or Sheila?"

"Perla." Syssi pushed to her feet. "I need to get my phone. I will be right back." She rushed down the hallway and returned a moment later. "I need to find her picture." She sat back down and kept scrolling until she found what she'd been looking for. "That's my grandmother as a young woman with my mother as a little girl." She passed the phone to Kaia.

"Syssi's grandmother looks a lot like your great-grandmother, Gilbert." Kaia enlarged the picture with her fingers.

Could Gilbert and Syssi be related?

It would be wonderful if they were.

If their great-grandmothers were sisters, then Gilbert, Eric, and Gabi were Dormants.

Hope surging in her heart, she passed Syssi's phone to Eric, who shook his head in disbelief. "That's one hell of a coincidence." He passed the phone to his brother.

Gilbert took one look at the screen, grinned like he'd just won the lottery, and passed the phone to Karen. "It seems that my ancestry research wasn't futile after all. I've found a relative, and she comes with a big, beautiful family." He offered Syssi his hand. "Hello, cousin."

Shaking it, she turned to Kian. "You know what that means, right?"

"I haven't seen the evidence yet." He waited until his wife's phone was passed over to him and turned to Gilbert. "Let me see the picture of your great-grandmother again."

"Here you go." Gilbert handed him his phone.

Kian put both on the table side by side and examined the old pictures for a long moment.

"It's not conclusive. They both have Slavic features, but these old photos are grainy and yellow. Besides, a physical resemblance is not enough to go by." Kian returned the phones to Syssi and Gilbert.

"The evidence might not be conclusive," Syssi said. "But if you take into account the other factors, the case in favor of this assumption is strong."

"What factors? Kaia is not a blood relative of his, and even if she was, her case is not conclusive either."

Gilbert regarded the two with a frown. "What are you talking about? I thought that William was Kian's cousin, not Syssi's. Or did you marry your second cousin, and you are both related to William?"

Gilbert's conclusion was logical given what he knew, but the suggestion was funny, and Kaia stifled a chuckle.

Syssi lifted her hand. "Give us one more moment, Gilbert." She turned to her husband. "I'm talking about the affinity. Gilbert and Karen fell for each other right away." She glanced at Darlene, who looked as stunned as Kaia felt. "I know that none of this is conclusive, and we need Bridget to run blood tests to confirm that I'm related to Gilbert and Eric, but given my strong urge to come here this weekend, I think that all the signs are pointing in that direction."

A blood test couldn't do that. They needed a mtDNA genetic test to confirm that Gilbert, Eric, and Syssi were third cousins, but given the tension in the room, Kaia felt that it wasn't the right time to mention it.

Kian nodded. "Let's get Emmett and Eleanor in here and

share what we know with our guests." He waved at Anandur, instructing him to do that. "Kaia's family will need time to process what they learn, so my regular mode of operation in instances like that is not an option."

"What the hell are you people talking about?" Eric asked.

Kian smiled at him. "Everything will become clear in a few moments." He turned to Gilbert. "While we wait for Eleanor and her mate, you can tell us about your father's side of the family."

Kaia could barely contain the tears of relief gathering at the corners of her eyes.

If Gilbert was a Dormant, her mother wouldn't need to leave him or have sex with someone else to transition. He could transition first and then induce her.

The whole family would become immortal.

But what if she wasn't a Dormant after all?

It would be just damn cruel if, at the end of the day, Gilbert, Eric, and their sister Gabi turned immortal while Kaia, her mother, and her siblings didn't.

63

WILLIAM

"*H*old on," Eric said. "Before my brother gets into our family's history, I want to know what Emmett Haderech and his girlfriend have to do with Syssi being our distant relative and why do we have to wait for them before you can talk to us? Do we have to sign some confidentiality agreement or something?"

"Or something." Kian chuckled. "It's crucial to our safety that what we are about to tell you remains a secret. It's a matter of life and death for us. Emmett and Eleanor are powerful hypnotists, and they can ensure that you don't breathe a word of what you hear to anyone outside your immediate family and us. You can't even tell your sister until she goes through the same process."

"It's not a big deal," Kaia said. "They did it to me, and I could barely feel it." She chuckled. "I thought that it was nonsense until I tried to say something that I wasn't supposed to, and the words wouldn't leave my mouth."

Eric leveled his dark brown eyes on her. "So, you know what this is all about?"

She nodded. "But I can't talk about it because of the

hypnotic coercion. It is not airtight, and I found a way to use different words and kind of talk around it, but I can only give hints, and without reference, you might have a hard time following." She glanced at William. "Do I have permission to tell them what I can?"

"Permission?" Gilbert spat. "You're asking his permission to speak? I knew that there was something shady under that innocent good-guy façade." He glared at William. "What kind of power do you hold over our Kaia that she needs to ask your permission to speak?"

Syssi put a hand on his arm. "Relax, Gilbert. It's about secrets that are connected to the research, and William is Kaia's boss. You shouldn't be surprised that she can't reveal anything about her work without his permission."

Gilbert didn't look appeased. "Why are you answering for him? Doesn't he have a mouth?"

William had had enough.

He wanted to build a good relationship with Kaia's family, but Gilbert was the type of guy that would just keep on pushing and attacking until he got pushback.

"I have a mouth," William said. "I prefer not to engage in futile arguments, and I don't want to do anything to upset Kaia, but I can't keep quiet when you keep attacking me. Kian has already told you that the information I shared with her is a matter of life and death for us, and I told her about it only after Emmett and Eleanor used hypnosis to ensure her silence. Furthermore, I'm not a hypnotist, so I can't grant her permission to talk around their hypnotic coercion or deny it. They are the only ones who can."

Surprising the heck out of him, Gilbert laughed. "I was wondering whether you had a backbone. I don't want my Kaia to marry a spineless guy who can't stand up to her or anyone else."

Asshole.

Perhaps he should have just thralled the guy. It would have saved him and Kaia a lot of aggravation.

Though if Gilbert turned out to be a Dormant and transitioned, William wouldn't be able to keep thralling him, and once the guy moved into the village, he would become a constant thorn in William's side. If Gilbert kept acting like an asshole, he would have to put him in his place the conventional way, but he had to do that without ruining their future relationship.

Easier said than done.

Kaia groaned. "You're so bad, Gilbert. You made us both miserable just to see how far you could push William?"

The smile slid off Gilbert's face. "I kept pushing to see how hard the two of you were willing to fight for your relationship, and I'm not done pushing yet. I'm still not happy about you deciding to marry your first boyfriend."

Kaia folded her arms over her chest. "William is not my first boyfriend, and you know it."

"*Pfft*. The fling you had at seventeen doesn't count. You weren't in love, and you didn't even claim to be. And if you bring up Anthony, your mother assured me that he was just a friend."

"He was." Kaia let out a breath. "Still is, I hope." She glanced at William. "I know that he's not dead. But I don't know whether I'll ever see him again."

64

KIAN

*T*he pain in Kaia's voice touched Kian. He wished he could help get her friend off the island, but he wasn't willing to risk Guardians' lives to free a human. In fact, he wouldn't have authorized a rescue even if Kaia's friend was a confirmed Dormant.

"There is always hope," William said quietly.

Idina had fallen asleep in his lap, and he looked as if he was afraid to move a muscle and wake her up.

"I'll take her." Karen rose to her feet. "Can I put her to sleep on the bed next to the boys' crib?"

"Of course." Syssi followed her up. "I'll turn down the blanket for you."

"Thanks." Karen took her daughter from William's arms and carried her to the bedroom.

When they returned, Eleanor walked in with Emmett, who was in his full prophet regalia.

"Hi." She glanced around the living room. "You had a party, and we were not invited?"

"Who's that?" Gilbert stared at Emmett.

"I'm Emmett Haderech, the spiritual leader of this community. And who are you?"

He knew perfectly well who Gilbert was, but Emmett enjoyed playing the part.

"I'm Kaia's stepfather." He turned to Kian. "That's your hypnotist? I wouldn't trust him to hypnotize a chicken."

Kian stifled a chuckle.

The comment was rude, but he understood Gilbert's reaction. He would have thought the same thing if he's seen Emmett in his white robe and long beard.

"Get up, Gilbert," Emmett commanded.

Gilbert shot to his feet.

"Sit down, Gilbert."

He dropped like a rock back on his chair.

Emmett smiled evilly. "Do you still think I can't hypnotize a chicken?"

"What the hell? How did you do that?" Gilbert looked at Karen. "He didn't even dangle a watch in front of my face or snap his fingers."

"He doesn't need to do any of that." Kaia walked over to Gilbert, stood behind his chair, and put one hand on his shoulder and the other on her mother's. "You all need to suspend disbelief for the rest of this evening."

Gilbert looked up at her. "Did you?"

"I did." She moved to stand between his chair and her mother's. "But you know me. I'm the girl who believes that aliens have been visiting Earth since time immemorial and that they have secret bases in the deepest regions of our oceans and on the dark side of the moon."

His eyes widened. "Is that what it's about? They are aliens?"

"Patience, Gilbert." She patted his shoulder. "Let Emmett and Eleanor do their thing first, and then you'll find out what this is all about."

Emmett pulled out a chair and sat down facing Gilbert. "So, who do I need to compel to keep their mouths shut?"

Kaia rose to her feet. "Let me introduce you to my family. This is Karen, my mother, and the guy you just compelled is my stepfather, Gilbert. On the other side of the table is my uncle, Eric, and that's my sister, Cheryl." She looked at Kian. "I can't tell him anything more unless I'm released from my compulsion."

"We will do that later." Kian motioned for Eric to move closer to his brother and for Cheryl to move closer to her mother. "All of Kaia's family members are potential Dormants. We need to tell them what their options are, and then they will need to go home and think things through. Your job is to make it so they can't tell anyone about it but can still discuss it among themselves. After you are done with them, you will have to change Kaia's compulsion so she can talk with her family and with everyone who knows about it already."

Emmett nodded. "Understood."

Eleanor sat down on the other side of the table next to Syssi. "Do you need me to reinforce Emmett's compulsion?"

Kian nodded. "I don't like sending them home with knowledge of us, but it's a complicated situation, and I can't expect the entire family to leave their lives behind, come to the village, and go for it. So, a double compulsion will allow me to sleep a little better at night."

"Got it." Eleanor nodded at her mate. "Do your thing."

"I need Eric and Cheryl to sit next to Gilbert and Karen."

When they did what he'd asked, Emmett lifted his arms, the wide sleeves of his white gown blocking the family from Kian's view. "Gilbert, Karen, Eric, and Cheryl, look into my eyes and listen to my voice."

65

DARLENE

*D*arlene's heart was pounding against her rib cage. It was really happening. Eric was a Dormant, and he was Syssi's distant relative.

They had a future together.

Provided that he wanted it.

Provided that he was a confirmed Dormant.

Provided that he transitioned successfully.

Darlene was terrified for him. Eric was younger than her, but he wasn't the grandson of a god, and transitioning would be risky for him.

Once Emmett and Eleanor were done compelling Kaia's family into keeping what they were about to learn a secret and changing Kaia's compulsion so she could talk with them about it, they left together with the Guardians and their mates to give the family privacy. Anandur and Brundar had probably stayed up in the cottage or right outside its door to guard Kian, but their mates had most likely retired for the night, and so had Eleanor and Emmett.

"I think drinks are in order." Kian rose to his feet and walked over to the bar. "Whiskey, anyone?"

As expected, all the men lifted their hands but none of the women.

"I'll get wine for the ladies." Syssi joined him at the bar and opened a new bottle of wine. "Can I give some to Kaia and Cheryl?" she asked Karen.

"Kaia can have as much as she wants, but Cheryl can have only a tiny bit."

"I don't like wine," Cheryl said. "And before you ask, I don't like whiskey either."

Syssi laughed. "I wasn't going to offer that. Do you prefer a soft drink?"

"Yes, please."

Once everyone had a glass in hand, and they'd all gotten comfortable on the couches and armchairs, Kaia lifted her hand. "Can I be the one who tells my family? I don't know everything yet, but now that I can finally talk about it, I can share with them what I know."

Kian waved a hand. "Go ahead."

Kaia leaned against the table and crossed her arms over her chest. "So here is the scoop. The gods from mythology were not invented by people. They were aliens." She glanced at Kian. "Am I right?"

"It depends on how you define aliens. The gods might have been the first intelligent creatures on Earth, and they created humanity by combining their genetic material with that of an earthly creature, so technically they weren't any more alien than humans, but we know that they came from somewhere else in the universe."

"Good enough." Kaia unfolded her arms and gripped the table. "The gods took human lovers and produced offspring who were immortal but not as powerful as the gods. However, when those immortals took human lovers, the children born to them were human, but the children of the immortal females carried the godly genes in a dormant state and could be turned immortal through a special activation process that I will explain later. But whether a dormant female was activated and turned immortal or not, her children carried the immortal gene, and her daughters passed it on through the maternal line down the generations. What it means is that there could be many humans who carry the immortal gene, and in our specific case, we all do. Bottom line, we can all turn immortal, but the process is not without risk, and it gets riskier the older the Dormant." She turned to Kian. "How did I do so far?"

"Excellent. From now on, it's your job to tell prospective Dormants about our history."

Karen shook her head. "It all sounds fantastical, but you asked us to suspend our disbelief, and I'm trying very hard to do that. I assume that Kian and Syssi and everyone else here that is not part of our family is immortal, correct?"

Kaia nodded.

Darlene wanted to raise her hand and remind him that she was still human, but it wasn't important at the moment, and it would only confuse things.

"Then my question is, how did they find us?"

"Dumb luck." Kaia smiled at William. "Or Fate, as William and his people believe."

"I can take it from here," Syssi said. "Immortals and Dormants feel a special affinity toward each other. So, when William and Kaia fell in love within days, William suspected that Kaia might be a Dormant, and he asked Kian's permission to share his suspicions with her." She smiled at Karen. "Your whirlwind romance with Gilbert is a good example of that. You said that he wasn't your type and that you couldn't understand why you were so drawn to each other, but now you have an explanation. Since you are both Dormants, you felt that special affinity."

Darlene glanced at Eric, and as she caught him looking at her, a silent communication passed between them. Was that special affinity responsible for how strongly they were drawn to each other?

Gilbert shook his head. "Forgive me for bursting the crazy bubble, but it all sounds like a script for a weird science fiction movie, and the affinity explanation sounds like total bullshit. What proof can you show me that you are really immortal?"

"I can take care of that." Kian leaned forward. "I'm glad that the little ones are asleep, or this would have scared them." He shifted his eyes to Cheryl. "I'm going to demonstrate the power immortals have over human minds by creating an illusion. What you are about to see is not real, but it will appear very real to you. I'm not going to tell you ahead of time what kind of illusion it will be so your stepdad won't say that I hypnotized you all and planted the suggestion in your minds."

"Okay." Cheryl eyed him with skepticism painted over her face. "But if we are all going to see it, why are you telling me about it?"

"I just don't want you to get scared."

She snorted. "I'm not a child." She cast a sidelong glance at Gilbert. "If anyone is going to scream like a little girl, it's this big guy."

He pouted. "I did that to amuse you. The remake of *It* was funnier than it was scary."

"Right." She rolled her eyes before turning to Kian. "Anyway, don't choose Pennywise the clown as your illusion."

"Noted."

66

KAIA

*E*xcitement thrummed in Kaia's chest as she waited for Kian to do his illusion.

William hadn't shown her any immortal tricks other than his elongating fangs, which in her opinion were a much better proof than an illusion, but perhaps not as entertaining.

The air shimmered, and a moment later, a blue, ten-foot-tall, half-naked Na'vi male appeared in Kian's chair, sitting in the same pose Kian had assumed, with one leg folded over the other and his chin resting on his fist.

Cheryl laughed. "That's what you call scary?"

"I decided to go for something less terrifying," the Na'vi said in Kian's voice.

Karen gaped. "Are you one of those natives from *Avatar?*"

"You see that too?" Eric asked.

She nodded and turned to Gilbert. "Just to make sure that we see the same thing. What is he wearing?"

"A damn loincloth."

"Yup. That's what I see as well."

Kian dropped the illusion. "Do you need more proof that I'm not human?"

"Do you bleed?" Eric asked.

"We do," Kian said. "And to answer your next question, we can be killed. Our bodies are very good at repairing themselves, but no one can regrow a heart or a head."

"What about limbs?" Eric asked.

"We can regrow missing limbs. We have a newly transitioned immortal in our village who had both legs amputated four years ago, and she is regrowing them. But it's a long and difficult process."

"That's amazing," Karen said. "I wish it was possible for humans."

"It might be," Kaia started, but as William shook his head, she remembered that their research was a secret even from most of his clan members.

Leaning back in his chair, Gilbert crossed his arms over his chest and grinned at her mother. "I kept telling you that I'm a god. You shouldn't have laughed at me."

Her mother chuckled. "You're not a god. You might be a descendant of aliens, but it's not a sure thing." She looked at Syssi. "Is there a conclusive test for that?"

"Normally, there isn't, but if our doctor can determine that Gilbert and Eric are my relatives, then they are Dormants for sure. For you, though, the only test is attempting transition and hoping it will happen."

Kaia was about to mention the need for a genetic test, but then Gilbert asked, "What's involved in attempting transition?"

Syssi glanced at Cheryl, sighed, and shifted her eyes back to Gilbert. "It's done differently for males than for females, but I need to explain a little more about immortals' physiology. The male immortals have fangs and venom. Their venom glands produce different compositions of venom depending on the trigger. If the trigger is aggression, the venom produced is more potent and can be used to incapacitate an opponent. If the trigger is sexual arousal, the venom produced is less potent, and it is used to provide intense pleasure to their partners. The venom is the catalyst for transition in both male and female Dormants, but since the one triggered by arousal is not as potent as the one triggered by aggression, female Dormants need more than just the venom to induce their transition. They also need to have unprotected sex with an immortal male so his seed is absorbed into their bodies along with the venom from his bite."

"Kinky." Cheryl lifted a brow at Kaia. "Did William induce you already?"

"There is no rush." Kaia wanted to strangle her sister for asking her that in front of everyone. "I'm young and healthy, so I can take my time deciding when and if I want to do it."

"So age is a factor?" her mother asked.

"It is." Syssi took the half-empty wine bottle, got up, and refilled Karen's glass. "The older the Dormant, the more dangerous the transition gets. Kaia has nothing to worry about, and Cheryl has plenty of time until it will become relevant for her, but the three of you don't have that luxury." She sat back down. "I was twenty-five when I went through my transition, and I almost didn't make it. My brother was forty, and he had a difficult transition as well."

"We haven't lost a Dormant yet," Kian said. "So, you shouldn't worry too much about that."

"How old was the oldest Dormant to transition?" Eric asked.

"I think Ronja was fifty-seven." Kian looked at Syssi. "Am I right?"

"I think so."

"Then we should be fine," Gilbert said. "I'm the oldest here, and I'm only forty-eight."

Kaia found it odd that Kian seemed much less concerned with the risks than Syssi. Maybe the reason was that he wasn't as caring as his wife, and he thought nothing of one of them dying.

Or he might know something that Syssi didn't.

"So let me get it straight," Eric said. "To transition, a male Dormant has to be bitten by an immortal male?"

Kian nodded. "Correct. A male Dormant needs to challenge an immortal male to a fight and spur his aggression."

"Does it matter if he wins the fight or not?" Eric asked.

Kian unfolded his arms and leaned forward. "It doesn't, but he needs to offer enough of a challenge to spur the immortal's aggression. If the Dormant is weak or scared, that might be a problem."

Gilbert puffed out his chest. "That won't be a problem for my brother and me."

Eric cast him a smile before returning his gaze to Syssi. "A female Dormant just needs to seduce an immortal male and not use birth control, right?"

"She can be on the pill, but no physical barriers." Syssi pushed a strand of hair behind her ear. "It also helps if a bond forms between her and the male, but it wasn't necessary for some of the female Dormants who were closer to the source than me, meaning that there were fewer degrees of separation between them and their godly ancestor."

WILLIAM

$\mathcal{K}$aren looked at Kaia. "What's stopping you from attempting it?"

William's jaw dropped. Was Karen encouraging her daughter to go for the transition?

He hadn't expected that.

Kaia laughed. "A few hours ago, you both wanted to take me back home because you thought I was crazy for getting engaged to William after knowing him for such a short time, and now you are asking why I haven't let him induce me yet?"

"We now know much more than we knew a few hours ago." Karen reached for Gilbert's hand. "We could be with each other forever."

He shook his head. "Didn't you listen to Syssi's warnings? Risky means that we might not make it through. We have three little kids. We can't take risks with our lives."

The excited gleam in Karen's eyes dimmed. "You are right." She turned to Syssi. "Since I'd rather not have sex with a stranger, Gilbert will have to transition first, correct?"

Syssi nodded. "The thing is that it will take about six months for him to grow fangs and functional venom glands, and that will mean you will be six months older by then. The sooner you do it, the better, but unless you two have an open relationship, that's the only way it can work for you."

"We do not have an open relationship." Gilbert pulled Karen's hand into his lap. "And I want to go first. If anything happens to me, our children would at least have their mother."

"Don't talk like that." Tears formed in Karen's eyes. "I can't bear the thought of losing you. If I could, I would go first."

"And leave me alone? No way."

"It can still happen even if you go first. I might die when I attempt it six months later."

Kaia lifted her hands. "Both of you stop. We all might not be Dormants at all. I will go first, and if I don't transition then you don't need to attempt it at all. But Gilbert and Eric can go for it regardless of whether I transition or not."

"I'll do it," Eric said. "I'm the only one here with nothing to lose."

"What about me?" Cheryl asked.

"You can't do it." Kaia gave her sister an amused look. "You need to wait until you're eighteen."

"No, I don't. I can have sex now if I want to. I'm the youngest, so it's the safest for me to transition."

Gilbert groaned. "Do you want to kill me before I get the chance to become immortal? You are not having sex until you're twenty-one."

"Right." Cheryl rolled her eyes. "Are there any cute boys my age in your clan?"

Syssi smiled at her. "We have one boy who is a little younger than you, but he's taken."

"Oh, well." Cheryl shrugged. "Then I guess I'm not transitioning anytime soon."

"By the way," Karen turned to William. "How old are you? I assume that you are not thirty-two."

He swallowed. "I'm much older than that."

For now, Gilbert and Karen were still stunned by all that they'd been told, so the number might not evoke an immediate shock, but once they'd processed everything, they would restart their campaign against his and Kaia's relationship. Perhaps he should start with a preamble? Like the age difference between Syssi and Kian?

"By how much?" Gilbert asked.

"Three centuries. But you need to understand that age is meaningless to immortals. Kian is two thousand years old, and Syssi is only twenty-nine, and they are truelove mates."

Eric whistled, and Karen gaped at Kian. "That's incredible. You've seen and experienced so much. What could you possibly have in common with such a young woman?"

"Love," Kian said simply. "I'd never experienced bonding my soul to another. Syssi is what was missing from a very long life that was all about duty to my clan. I'd never been truly happy until she came into my life, and then Allegra was born and made us both even happier."

Karen shifted her gaze to Syssi. "What about you? Did it bother you that your husband was ancient?"

Grinning, Syssi waved a hand at Kian. "Just look at him. I'm married to a demigod who worships me as if I were a goddess."

Kian confirmed with a nod. "And who enjoys every moment of his worshipful devotion."

Karen didn't look convinced, and apparently she'd thought that Syssi had called Kian a demigod because of his looks and not because he was the son of a goddess. If she'd made the connection, William was sure her response wouldn't have been a frown.

"What about chauvinistic attitudes?" Karen asked Syssi without even looking at Kian. "He's lived most of his life in times when women were devalued and oppressed."

A soft growl left Kian's throat. "Not in our clan. My mother is the head of our people, and the females of our clan have always been held in the highest regard. In fact, we value females more than we value males because they are the key to the clan's continuation."

"It's true," Syssi confirmed. "But that also translates into overprotectiveness, which could be perceived as discrimination. There is only one female Guardian, and Kian doesn't allow her to go on missions he deems too dangerous for her."

He crossed his arms over his chest. "I won't let Kri fall into the hands of Doomers, and if that makes me a chauvinist, I can live with it."

"Who or what are Doomers?" Gilbert asked.

"That's a story for another time," Kian said. "We need to focus on the topics at hand, which are your family's potential transition into immortality and William's relationship with Kaia. You need to stop making an issue out of the age difference between them. If you think about it for a moment, you will realize that on the inside, you are the same as you were at twenty. If you still looked twenty, you would feel that age as well."

"I have more life experience now than I had at twenty," Gilbert said. "And I see the world through the prism of my experiences. I can only imagine what that prism would look like in three hundred years, but I'm convinced that it would be very different from the prism of someone born into that future."

William shook his head. "I'm the same now as I was at twenty-five. Since we can't form long-lasting relationships with humans, and Dormants are rare, I've spent all of my adulthood alone and unchanging. Having Kaia in my life has opened a new chapter for me, and being in a loving relationship is as new for me as it is for her. In some ways, Kaia is more mature than I am because she has witnessed your loving relationship. I grew up without a father figure in my life, and I didn't have the privilege of watching my mother interact with a loving partner either."

"I love you," Kaia whispered. "Now and forever more."

"I love you too. Forever and beyond."

Karen sighed. "That's sweet, but I can't wrap my head around you being over three centuries old." She pushed to her feet and pulled Gilbert up. "I'm tired and overwhelmed, and I need to go to sleep. Maybe things will become clearer by morning."

"You shouldn't take too long deciding." Kian got up and offered Karen his hand. "The clock is ticking."

"I know." Kaia's mother shook his offered hand. "Is there a specific deadline by which we need to decide?"

"No, but the longer you wait, the riskier transitioning will be for you."

KAIA

$\mathcal{K}$aia got to her feet and wrapped her arm around her mother's shoulders. "We will discuss it tomorrow." She smiled at Kian. "We are still human, and unlike you, we need our eight hours of sleep to think clearly."

Needing less sleep was one of the things Kaia was looking forward to. So much more could be achieved with only four-hour nights.

"Words of wisdom." Her mother kissed her cheek.

"Do you need my help to get the boys back to the lodge?"

"Just help us get up the stairs, and we will be fine from there. Once we are outside the cottage, I'll put them in the stroller."

"We can help you." Eric got to his feet and walked over to them. "I'll carry Idina."

"I have a question." Darlene looked at Kian. "Can Eric sleep in my bungalow tonight? We need to talk things through as well."

"I don't see why not. I'll call the security office and ask them to make a key for him. You can pick it up on the way."

"Thank you."

"Thank you for everything," Eric said. "Even if we turn out not to be Dormants, it will be fun to entertain the idea of living forever, at least for a little while."

Kian grimaced. "Don't thank me yet. If you are not Dormants, we will have to erase from your memories everything you've learned about us and gods and immortals."

Eric shrugged. "Well, it's up to fate, right?"

"Absolutely." Syssi threaded her arm through Kian's. "The Fates wouldn't have orchestrated this encounter for nothing. I'm positive that you are all Dormants, and you will come to live with us in our village."

"Which is not on Mount Olympus," Kaia added.

"That's also something to talk about tomorrow." Eric offered Kian his hand. "I need to help Karen and Gilbert with the kids."

When her family and Darlene had said their goodbyes and walked out the door, Kaia returned to thank Syssi and Kian once again.

"I truly appreciate the warm welcome you have given my family." She offered Syssi her hand and got pulled into her arms.

"We are always happy to discover new Dormants who can join our clan, but in this case, I'm overjoyed to have found more relatives. Maybe having you in the village will convince my parents to finally retire and come live with us as well."

"Where are they now?" Kaia asked.

"In Africa. My mother is a pediatrician, and she volunteers in a clinic, while my father enjoys his hobby of photography in his retirement."

"Are they immortal?"

Syssi shook her head. "Regrettably, it was too late for my mother to transition, and my father is not a Dormant."

"How do you know? We would have never known about Gilbert and Eric if not for the story about your great-grandmothers. If Dormants feel a special affinity for each other, then your father might be a Dormant as well."

A pained look crossed Syssi's eyes. "It's irrelevant. He's too old to transition anyway."

She looked so sad that Kaia's heart ached for her. "Perhaps William and I will find the secret to immortality in Okidu's journals. William believes that the gods used genetic engineering to prevent their bodies from aging, and since the biological parts of the Odus' bodies can do the same, it makes sense that the journals contain that information."

The smile returned to Syssi's pretty face. "That would be wonderful." She sighed. "I hope. I wish we knew more about the world of the gods. We could learn from them how to manage a planet of immortals and avoid the pitfalls that a transformation like that will no doubt create." She chuckled. "I'm a seer, and I can't foresee a future like that."

"William told me that most of your visions are about catastrophes, so I'm glad that you can't see a future in which all of humanity is immortal. It means that it's a good possible future."

Syssi cast William a mock glare. "My visions are not all about catastrophic events. I also helped find a couple who were stranded in the desert."

Kian wrapped a protective arm around Syssi's waist. "We don't need to solve the puzzle of an immortal society to take care of your parents. If we find the secret to immortality, your parents will be the first we will offer it to, and knowing your mother, she will not shy away from being the first volunteer."

Syssi winced. "I don't know how it would help her. She already has the immortal genes. The problem is that her body is too old to survive the transition."

"Then I hope the journals contain a solution for that as well." He kissed the top of Syssi's head.

Once again, Kaia noticed that Kian looked less concerned about the safety of transitioning Dormants than his wife.

She was convinced that he knew something Syssi didn't.

If he were emotionally numb or uncaring, he wouldn't be as loving toward Syssi and Allegra.

Then again, he'd said that before meeting his wife, his life had been all about duty, so he might care only about her and his daughter.

Still, Kaia was willing to bet that Kian had information he wasn't sharing, but the question was why? According to what William had told her about him, the guy wasn't selfish, and he'd always placed the good of his clan ahead of his own. Therefore, if he was hiding something, even from his wife, it was to protect something or someone.

69

ERIC

*E*ric followed Darlene to the security office without paying much attention to where they were going and then stood outside while she got the key for him.

His head was spinning with all he'd learned earlier and all the questions he still needed to be answered. Other than not aging or getting sick, casting illusions, and manipulating minds, what else was different about immortals?

He'd spent many hours with Darlene, had sex with her, and she'd felt completely human to him. She also didn't look as young as the others. Even the two-thousand-year-old leader looked to be in his mid-thirties at most.

The only one who looked older was the butler.

Was there an underclass of immortals who aged faster than the others, like in the vampire stories?

Was Darlene one of them?

The butler had acted very subserviently, constantly bowing and calling everyone master and mistress, but Darlene hadn't. Maybe as a female, she enjoyed a higher status?

Kian had said that they valued females more than males, so

maybe it was true for the underclass of immortals as well. The males were servants, and the females were treated as equals.

"Are you okay?" Darlene asked. "You were fine back at the bunker, but now you seem to be walking in a daze. What's up?"

"What kind of an immortal are you?"

"I'm not an immortal yet. I'm a Dormant like you."

He let out a relieved breath but then wondered why she hadn't transitioned yet, and the possible answers his imagination supplied were all bad. "What's keeping you from doing it? Are you afraid to attempt it because of your age?"

She shook her head. "I'm quite new to all of this as well, and I decided to take my time. I wanted to finalize my divorce before hooking up with an immortal, and after that, I couldn't find anyone I really wanted to be with." She averted her gaze. "I wasn't willing to compromise or be someone else's compromise either. Never again."

He put his arm around her shoulders and drew her to him. "You are a prize, not a compromise. And that's not empty flattery. I'm drawn to you more than I've ever been drawn to anyone, and that includes my ex, who I thought was the love of my life when I married her."

"Thank you." She smiled up at him. "When you showed up with Karen and Gilbert, so full of charm and confidence, I wanted you like I've never wanted a man before. Now I know that it wasn't just your easygoing flirting and boyish charms. It was the affinity between Dormants."

"It's more than that."

"Yeah." She leaned her head on his arm. "It is."

They were walking at a snail's pace, but Eric wasn't in a rush to get to Darlene's bungalow. "I know that you are only thirty-five, but didn't Kian give you his speech about the ticking clock?"

She laughed. "I'm forty-nine, but my case is different."

So, his suspicions had been right, and there were different kinds of immortals.

"In what way?"

"I'm very close to the source, which means that my transition will probably be pretty effortless despite my age." She cast him an amused glance. "The force is strong with me."

If he wasn't still reeling from all he'd learned, Eric would have found another Star Wars quote to answer with, but his mind was still spinning too fast for him to respond to the reference. "What do you mean by closer to the source? Are the gods from mythology still living among us, and are you a recent descendant of one of them?"

Darlene smiled. "Most of the gods are gone, but you are right about me being a recent descendant of theirs. My grandfather is a god."

Eric stopped walking and turned to her. "For real? My girlfriend is a demigoddess?"

He'd thought she belonged to an underclass of immortals when the opposite was true.

He got himself a royal princess.

Or was it a divine princess?

Darlene didn't laugh. "Am I your girlfriend, Eric?"

"Of course." Stifling a chuckle, he took her hand and put it over his chest. "I didn't ask you officially, but I thought that we were going steady."

A smile bloomed on her face. "We are." She lifted on her toes and kissed his lips, but when he wanted to deepen the kiss, she pushed on his chest. "I want to make one thing clear, though. I'm not a demigoddess. That title belongs to my mother."

"There should be a special title for a granddaughter too—a demi-demigoddess, and I want to be known as a demi-demigoddess's boyfriend. It makes me feel important."

That finally got a laugh out of her.

"Fine. I'll petition the board of titles to add a demi-demigod."

He bowed his head. "Thank you. This oversight needs to be addressed."

"Seriously, though." Her smile turned into a frown. "Since I'm the granddaughter of a god, I'm less fearful about my transition, and I have the luxury of taking my time to some extent. You are younger than me by a good number of years, but given that you are Syssi's relative and her transition was difficult at twenty-five, you should do it as soon as possible. It's not a big deal for males. There is an initiation ceremony. You get into a wrestling ring with an immortal and try to offer him a challenge for a minute or two. Once he gets aggressive enough for his fangs to elongate and his venom glands to fill up, he will take you down and bite you."

Did she think so little of him?

He might not be a professional wrestler, but he could hold his own in the ring.

"Unless the immortal gets into my head and overpowers me that way, it will take him much longer to subdue me. If the fight is fair, I might be the one who will overpower him." Still holding on to Darlene's hand, Eric resumed walking.

70

DARLENE

arlene loved how cocky Eric was, but she knew he was wrong. "Immortal males are much stronger than humans. Even William could overpower you with ease, and the guy is the typical computer nerd who hates exercising."

Eric's expression turned worried. "Could he hurt Kaia? If he's so strong, he might do so without meaning to."

"I don't think that's a problem. These immortal males have been hooking up with human females for centuries. They know that they need to be careful."

"How would you know? You said that you've never been with one."

"I haven't, but my half-sister was still human when she fell in love with an immortal, and she said that he was the best lover she'd ever had, and she's had quite a few."

"Oh, yeah?" He lifted a brow. "Your sister was a player?"

"Define player." Darlene pressed her keycard to the lock on the gate and waved at the camera.

"Someone who never stays long with one partner and is always chasing the next one."

The gate opened without Eric needing to press his card to the reader as well.

She smirked. "Like you?"

"Yeah. Like me," he admitted. "But those days are behind me."

"Because of me?"

He nodded.

Darlene's heart did a happy flip, but she reminded herself that Eric was still stunned by all he'd learned and that it was much too early for him to make promises he might later regret. The truth was that she was excited about a possible future with him, but she'd been hurt before and needed to proceed with caution.

"Cassandra is not a player," she said. "And she never was. She works too hard to have time to chase anyone, and she's so beautiful that I doubt she ever had to lift a finger to attract a guy."

"What does she do?"

"She's the creative director of Fifty Shades of Beauty. It's a cosmetics company that caters to a wide range of skin tones." Darlene opened the door to her bungalow.

Eric grinned. "I know who your sister is. I've seen her picture in one of the gossip magazines, and she is one hell of a looker." He followed her inside. "She looks a little bitchy, though." He waved a hand over his face. "She has resting bitch face."

Darlene laughed. "Cassandra has a temper, and she's assertive, but she's a good person. When a woman looks like that, she needs to fend off a lot of unwanted attention, and the resting bitch face comes with the territory."

"You are a beautiful woman as well, but you are not haughty, and you don't look down your nose at people. You have a kind expression with a little flirtatiousness mixed in." He cupped her cheek. "You have smiling eyes."

Darlene swallowed. Eric had sex on his mind, and she did too, but they needed to talk. She hadn't allowed herself to fall for him before, but now that her armor had been penetrated by the sword of hope, the flood of emotions pouring in and out was overwhelming, and she saw a future with Eric that she hadn't before.

Would he still talk about long-term when she did so as well? Or would he back away and laugh off his previous declarations of intent?

She pushed on his chest. "Do you want coffee?"

"You know what I want."

She rolled her eyes. "We need to talk. We can do that over wine or coffee. Those are your options."

He shook his head in mock dismay. "You are a tough negotiator. I'll take coffee, black." He smiled. "Because manly men don't put sugar or cream in their coffee."

She chuckled. "You are manly enough for me regardless of your choice of beverage. Do you want sugar and cream or not?"

"Yes, please." He sat on her couch, picked up one of her fashion magazines, and then put it down.

"I don't think you should wait any longer to transition, even if you are the granddaughter of a god. The longer you wait, the riskier it will get regardless of how close you are to the source."

Was that his way of backing out? The classic I'm-not-good-for-you excuse?

Darlene put the pod into the coffeemaker and pressed the button. "You should go first, and when your fangs and venom glands are functional, you can induce my transition."

"That will take too long." He sighed. "I don't think Karen should wait for Gilbert to transition either, but there is no way either of them would even consider her having sex with another male, even if it's for health reasons."

Darlene put the mugs on a tray, added the creamer and a container of sugar, and brought it to the table.

"Would you consider that for me?" she asked.

"I wouldn't be happy about it, but I wouldn't stand in your way or give you grief about it. I don't want to be responsible for holding you back, especially since it could make the difference between surviving it or not."

Darlene's heart sank.

His answer sounded so reasonable, but this was not how a Dormant or an immortal male would have reacted. They were extremely possessive, and they couldn't fathom their mate being with anyone else even if her life depended on it, which meant that Eric wasn't her truelove mate, and she wasn't his.

But perhaps she was wrong?

What would Kian have done if he were in Eric's shoes?

Would he have gambled with Syssi's life and had her wait for him to transition first?

Darlene didn't think so.

Kian adored Syssi, and if sex with another male had been the only thing that could save her life, he wouldn't have stopped her from doing it. He might have asked one of his friends to put him in stasis so he wouldn't be awake for it, but he would never have done anything to risk her life.

Sitting down on the couch next to Eric, Darlene fixed her coffee the way she liked it. "So, are you going to do it?" She lifted the mug to her lips and took a sip.

He nodded. "I have to. I'm the younger, single brother, and I'm expendable. Gilbert has a family."

"Don't talk like that. You are precious to me and to your brother and his children. They need you."

"What about you? Do you need me?"

"I just said that you are precious to me."

"It's not the same as needing me."

"I need you." She closed her eyes briefly and then leveled them at his. "I want to be honest with you. Before I knew you might be a Dormant, I planned on having a short fling with you and using you as a stepping stone in my journey of sexual experimentation." She smiled. "The immortal men everyone kept introducing me to were all too handsome and looked too young. I couldn't see myself getting naked with men who looked my son's age and were perfectly put together."

He frowned. "So, I was the imperfect specimen that was less intimidating?"

"Yes," she admitted. "But it was much more than that. I was immediately drawn to you. Heck, I haven't flirted with anyone with such enthusiasm since I was a college girl. I kept thinking that it was a shame that you were not an immortal, but then I told myself that you were a player and that you were not long-term material anyway."

Eric reached for her hand. "I hope I made you realize how beautiful and desirable you are."

"You did, and I want to see where this thing between us goes. I don't want to take some random immortal into my bed. I prefer you."

A mischievous smirk lifting one corner of his mouth, he leaned toward her. "What if I'm in bed with you and the immortal?"

As the image he painted with his words appeared in her mind, Darlene's cheeks caught fire. "You can't be serious. Are you suggesting a threesome?"

"What if I am? Are you feeling adventurous, Darlene?"

KAIA

The decision to attempt transition as soon as possible solidified in Kaia's mind as she stood under the hot spray in the shower.

She needed to get induced first, and she needed to do it fast. If she failed to transition, her mother wouldn't need to rush into anything, and Gilbert could take his time as well. And if she transitioned, her siblings would have someone to take care of them if the unthinkable happened and her mother or Gilbert didn't make it.

The stress of it was making her heart race and her hands shake as she lathered up the soap. She'd already lost one parent, and she wouldn't survive losing another.

Immortality would be a curse if she needed to live with the pain for eternity.

Would it have been better if William had never found her, and they'd all lived out their lives as humans?

It would surely have been less stressful. In a way, it was easier when no choice needed to be made. Perhaps she should talk it over with her family tomorrow and suggest that they all forget about it. William or some other immortal could thrall the memories away, and they could keep on living in blissful ignorance.

But that was a coward's way out, and as much as she feared for the lives of the people she loved, she couldn't ask them to choose a route she wouldn't choose for herself.

If she were twenty years older, would she have still decided to go through with it?

Probably.

What about thirty years older, when it became really dangerous like it was for Gilbert and her mother? Most likely, she would have decided to chance it then as well.

Kaia had much less trouble with risking her own life than watching the people she loved risk theirs.

Then again, she had proof that the soul continued on and that death wasn't the final step in the journey, so dying wasn't as terrifying to her. Most people didn't have the luxury of remembering their past lives, though, so even though their souls would live on, the person they were before would no longer exist, and that was scary.

Besides, what did it matter if the soul continued in a different body when all the people she loved would be lost to her anyway?

Bottom line, dying was frightening even for people like her who knew it wasn't the end.

Gah, her mind was running in circles.

She'd made her decision to go ahead and attempt transition, and she had to stick with it.

When she got out of the bathroom, William was waiting for her in bed with a fresh cup of tea and a worried expression on his face. "You were in there for nearly an hour. Are you okay?"

"Yeah, I am." She climbed into bed, picked up the cup, and took a long sip. "Thank you for the tea. It's perfect."

"It's lukewarm by now."

"That's precisely how I like it." She leaned against the stack of pillows William had arranged for her. "I made up my mind. I'm going for the transition right away. We can start working on it tonight."

William's eyes widened. "We can't."

"Why not?"

"We need to finish the research first."

"Why? You said that it'll be easy for me. I'll take a break for a few days and then go back to work as an immortal."

"It's not that simple." He put his teacup on the nightstand and turned to her. "You need to be under medical supervision when you transition, and we don't have the clinic set up here yet. If the equipment were here, I would ask one of our doctors to fly over, but without it, they wouldn't be able to do much for you."

"Why do I need medical supervision? You said that it would be as easy as having a cold or flu."

"It will most likely be like that, but on the remote chance that it isn't, and things go south, I want you to have the best medical help possible, and that's Doctor Bridget back in the village. I suggest that we finish the research first, then move into the village, and only then start your induction."

Kaia let out a long breath. "You are not thinking it all the way through, William. Even if the clock wasn't ticking for my mother and Gilbert, there is still the issue of my future after the research is done. If it turns out that I'm not a Dormant, and you erase my memories of you and everything I've learned about immortals, I can go back to my old life and take the job at Stanford, but if I wait too long, that job will be gone. I don't want to miss the deadline for that. Opportunities like that don't come often."

"You are right." He sighed. "It's just that I don't even consider it a possibility that you are not a Dormant."

As William wrapped his arm around her shoulders, Kaia put her head on his chest. "I know, but even though I love your optimism, I need to plan my moves while taking both options into consideration, and I need to find out as soon as possible whether my life is taking a serious detour or staying on course. I also need to know what is expected of me once I transition. What am I going to do? Can I still work in research? Do I have to move in with you into the village? What if I don't like it there?"

"Whoa." William chuckled. "One question at a time, please. I'm sure that you are going to love it in the village because everyone does. None of the transitioned Dormants have complained about living there. And as for what you are going to do, that's obvious. We will continue deciphering the rest of the journals, and then you and I will build an Odu prototype together."

WILLIAM

*G*iven how brightly Kaia smiled, that had been the right thing to say.

Kaia's eyes shone with excitement. "I would absolutely freaking love to build an Odu with you. Now I really want to transition."

William laughed. "Immortality is not exciting enough?"

"You know what I mean." She slapped his forearm playfully. "I want to be immortal, and I want us to be truelove mates forever, but I'm a little scared of transitioning, and I'm very scared of my mom or stepdad not making it through. Changing my career trajectory is not an easy pill to swallow either, and I need a spoonful of honey to make the medicine go down. The prospect of building an Odu with you after we decipher the blueprints is just that spoonful."

"I'm glad that I came up with that."

Kaia narrowed her eyes at him. "So, it was just something you said to make me feel excited about the future? You didn't plan on building an Odu before?"

"I did, and I hope we will not only decipher the instructions but also figure out how to avoid the pitfalls. We need the Odus to be intelligent enough to communicate and learn simple tasks, but we don't want them to be able to learn too fast or too much, or they will become dangerous. I also don't want to make them indestructible. I'm sure that their indestructibility played a big part in the banning of the technology to make them. You and I will have to think long and hard about all those issues and how to solve them."

"We should form a committee of experts. Do you have anyone on staff who is versed in ethics?"

"I don't, but you are right about us needing an ethicist on the team." He leaned over and kissed her temple. "To be frank, I don't think I would have had the guts to tackle such an undertaking without you. Having you working on it with me makes me feel more confident about achieving those objectives. You just came up with an idea to form a committee that wouldn't have occurred to me, and you will probably come up with more things that I failed to address. Combining our brain power and checking each other will be greatly beneficial to the future of this and other research."

Kaia let out a breath. "Your confidence in me is flattering, but I would have never dared to work on a monumental invention like that without you either. Any mistake we make could have dire consequences, which is why we need more capable people on our team who are from different disciplines." She pushed up on the pillows and tugged the blanket up to her chin. "I don't think that we should make the new Odus look as human as the old ones. In fact, we can't. We don't have the ability to make organs and skin yet. Besides, the more robotic they look, the less intimidating they will seem."

"So no sexy mannequins?"

She eyed him from under lowered lashes. "Male or female?"

William worked hard to stifle a smile. "Both. We could make a sexy French maid female model and a hunky Australian male. We will make a fortune."

"Why Australian?"

He shrugged. "I overheard Darlene talk with some of the other clan ladies about hunky Australian actors. I thought it was a thing."

"Thunder from Down Under," Kaia said. "It's a male stripper show in Vegas, and the guys are supposedly from Australia. I thought that you got the idea from there."

Imagining Kaia drooling over some half-naked muscular guys, William felt a wave of jealousy rise up in his chest.

"I haven't been to Vegas in decades, and I've never heard of a male stripper show. Have you seen it?"

"I've seen ads for it," Kaia said. "But I wouldn't go to a show like that even if I could."

"Why not?"

Smiling, she snaked a hand under his T-shirt and caressed his chest. "Watching can be fun, but I prefer touching."

William lifted a finger. "Hold that thought." He picked up his phone from the nightstand. "I need to text Kian and let him know that you want to transition as soon as possible."

Kaia groaned. "Now? He's probably asleep already."

"He's not. It's not even midnight yet."

"Still, can't it wait for tomorrow?" She circled her finger around his nipple, eliciting a pained groan from his throat.

He wanted nothing more than to let Kaia keep playing, but this couldn't wait.

"Your family is leaving in the afternoon, and so is Kian." He pulled her hand from under his shirt and kissed her knuckles. "If you want to transition right away, I need to stop the project, send the rest of the team on vacation, and take you to the village. Your family needs to know where you're going and why, and Kian needs to approve it."

"Gah." She flopped onto her back. "Why does everything have to be so complicated?"

He chuckled. "You and I are the definition of complicated, but that's what makes us special."

"True." She waved a hand. "Call your boss."

"I'll text him and ask him to call me back. I don't want to wake Allegra up or interrupt Kian and Syssi's fun time." William typed while he talked. "We need him to approve your plan, and aggravating him right before asking him to do it wouldn't be wise. The guy is grumpy on a good day."

73

KAIA

*W*illiam's phone rang a moment after he'd sent the text.

"What's the emergency?" Kian barked into the phone.

Kaia doubted that he'd even read the text. There hadn't been enough time.

"Everything is okay. Kaia is here with me, and I'm activating the speaker so she can hear you."

"Hello, Kaia. How are you doing?"

"I'm great. I want to transition as soon as possible."

"I'm glad. Why the urgent message to call you back, though?"

Kian didn't think it was a problem, so why did William?

William shook his head. "It's not that simple. The clinic is not ready, and I don't want Kaia to start transitioning without medical supervision. I would have to stop the project and take her to the village, and I need your approval to do that."

"That's indeed a problem," Kian said. "What's the rush? Why can't you wait until the project is done?"

"I can't," Kaia said. "My mother will want to wait for Gilbert to transition first and induce her when his fangs and venom glands are operational. But if she's not a Dormant and can't turn immortal, he might not want to risk transitioning at his age. But if I transition, he might hurry up, or maybe they would consider using the services of an immortal male. I don't think they would, but they might. My sisters and brothers pose another issue. If my mother and Gilbert know that I will be there for my siblings in case they don't make it, it will make their decision to try it easier."

"I see." Kian sighed. "What are you going to do about the other team members? You can't leave them to work alone."

"I will have to send them on vacation," William said. "Kaia is so young that she probably won't need more than a week or two to recuperate from the transition."

"It can also take up to two weeks for the transition to start," Kian said. "So, the break could stretch into a month, and I don't like that."

William looked at Kaia. "Can we finish it on our own? Or do you need them?"

"We can do it by ourselves, but it will take a little longer, though not by much. Their help is marginal."

"You heard the lady," William said. "I can dismiss the team, and we can continue working on the project in the village."

Kian groaned. "That was one hell of an expensive setup for one week's worth of work."

"I know." William didn't look apologetic at all. "But the setup is not just for this one project. You wanted a scaled-down duplicate of the lab in the village, so we will have an emergency location in case the village is compromised. I would have never invested so much effort and resources into building it for one project that I knew wouldn't take more than a few months. Besides, we didn't know how good Kaia really was. I expected her to be the shining star of the team, but she exceeded all of my expectations."

Kian chuckled. "In more ways than one. Syssi says that we

should all meet tomorrow morning and decide on a course of action together with Kaia's family."

"That's a very good idea," William said. "When and where?"

"Here, at ten in the morning. Syssi will arrange for brunch to be delivered."

"I'll let my mother know." Kaia looked at her watch. "I'll text her."

"Goodnight," Kian said. "Don't start anything yet."

William's cheeks reddened. "We won't."

When Kian ended the call, Kaia smirked. "Are you sure about that? We can throw away the condoms and have fun tonight."

"Not yet." He put his phone down on the nightstand. "I'd rather play it safe. We'll wait until we are in the village."

He was such a nerd, but he was her nerd, and she loved him just the way he was.

"Fine. Have it your way." She threw the blanket off and got out of bed.

"Where are you going?"

"I left the purse with my phone in the living room. It's probably dead because I forgot to hook it up to the charger."

"I'll get you a clan phone when we get to the village. They keep a charge twice as long."

"Oh, yeah? How did you manage that?"

He smirked. "I can tell you after you text your mother, but I'd rather do other things."

She lifted a finger. "Hold that thought. I'll be right back."

74

WILLIAM

"Wish me luck." Kaia stopped in front of the lodge. William squeezed her hand in encouragement. "Good luck. Just remember to speak quietly and remind your family to do the same. The lodge is filling up with guests for the next retreat, and someone might overhear you."

"I'm going to talk to them in my mother and Gilbert's room. It's sandwiched between my sisters' and Eric's room, so there will be no ears on the walls."

"Good, but people passing through the corridor could hear you through the door if you don't keep your voices down, and that's especially true for Gilbert."

She smiled. "Yeah. He likes to dominate the conversation, but I'll remind him to keep it down."

He leaned and kissed her cheek. "I'll see you at the bunker in half an hour."

She gave him a smile. "I love you."

"I love you too." He stole a quick kiss before opening the door for her.

When he got to the cottage, he found Anandur sitting outside on a bench that hadn't been there the day before.

"Good morning." He offered the Guardian his hand. "Is this your new post?"

"I'm waiting for Wonder to get ready. We are going to have breakfast at the lodge and then go for a walk on the beach." He stretched his long legs in front of him and patted the bench. "How do you like my new addition?"

"It's a great idea. It gets stuffy down there."

"I know, right? The air-conditioned air is drying out my skin. I need fresh air and some sun on my face."

William could never tell when Anandur was joking and when he was serious, so he chose to smile noncommittally. "Is Brundar staying to guard Kian?"

"He and Callie are coming with us. Your buddy Max is sending two guys to replace us."

Poor Max. William had encouraged him to pursue Darlene, and the guy had done so with notable enthusiasm, but now that Eric had the potential of turning immortal, Darlene was probably going to stay with him.

"Enjoy your day." William opened the door and walked inside.

When he pressed the intercom button, the door opened right away, and he took the stairs down to the bunker.

"Good morning, boss." Darlene rose to her feet, walked over to him, and gave him a hug.

She was the only one in the living room, so the others must be still getting ready.

"You look happy." He leaned to hug her back.

"I am happy. Eric decided to go for the transition as soon as possible, and Kian told me that Kaia decided to do the same."

"She did. I guess Eric's reasoning is the same as Kaia's. They are both doing it for Karen and Gilbert."

"Good morning, William." Syssi walked into the room with Allegra in her arms. "Kian is on the phone with Shai. He will be here in a moment."

William hoped so. They didn't have much time before Kaia arrived, and he needed to run by Kian the plan he'd come up with during the night.

As Syssi put Allegra on a baby mat on the floor, the girl smiled at the toys hanging from the baby gym and started babbling at them.

"Would you like some coffee while we wait?" Syssi asked.

"Thank you. I would love some."

"Did you hear that, Okidu?" she asked before sitting down on the couch next to Darlene.

"I did, mistress," Okidu answered from the kitchen. "I shall serve freshly brewed coffee momentarily."

"Thank you," Syssi called back.

Darlene sighed. "I wish I had an Odu. Heck, I wish every household in the village had one."

"Your wish might come true one day," William said. "With the speed science is progressing, today's science fiction may very well be tomorrow's reality."

She grinned. "If everything goes well and I transition, I will still be around when that happens."

He couldn't tell her that it might happen much sooner than that.

Darlene had a general idea of what they were working on, but she didn't know it was connected to the Odus. All he'd told her and the others at the lab was that he needed to decipher some of the gods' writings that had genetic components to them he didn't understand. They assumed that it was information contained in Ekin's tablet, which was the source of all their advanced knowledge.

The truth was that there were still sections of the information contained on the tablet that he hadn't decoded, but he understood enough of it to know that they had to do with alien technology and not biology.

Some of the difficulty was the language barrier, and some of it was Ekin's style of writing things down in a code that had been known only to him. William suspected that he hadn't done it to obscure his writings but as a form of shorthand.

He'd been working on that tablet for many decades, and he hadn't decoded even half of it. If he could dedicate all of his time to the tablet, he would probably progress at a much faster pace. But the reality was that he barely had time to keep up with the demands placed on him at the lab, let alone dedicate hours to decoding the rest of the information contained on that ancient device.

Perhaps once they were done with Okidu's journals, Kaia could help him with that as well. It wasn't her exact field of expertise, but as a bioinformatician she was trained in managing data, developing algorithms, and classifying components of biological systems, like DNA sequences and documenting protein expression. She was well-versed in programming statistical models and interpreting data sets, which made her even more qualified for the job than he was.

KIAN

*T*he smell of freshly brewed coffee lured Kian out of the bedroom he used as his temporary office.

"Do you need me for anything else?" he asked his assistant as he walked toward the living room with the phone pressed to his ear.

"No, that's it."

"Thanks for coming in on a Sunday, Shai. I appreciate your dedication."

"No problem, boss. I'm glad I checked your emails. Otherwise, we wouldn't have found out about it until Monday, and a whole day of production would have been lost."

"Well done. Have a great rest of your weekend." Kian ended the call.

"Good morning," William said. "Trouble?"

"Nothing serious." Kian pulled out a chair next to Syssi. "Supply chain issues."

William nodded. "It's affecting every sector."

"Indeed." Kian accepted a mug full of coffee from Okidu. "Thank you." He took a grateful sip. "So, what did you want to talk to me about before Kaia's family gets here?"

"I need your input on what to do with the other bioinformaticians. Kaia says she and I can finish the project on our own. She expects that it will take a little longer, but not by much. I would rather send them on vacation and get them back to work once she's done with her transition."

"Can't you give them something else to do?" Darlene asked. "If you send them on vacation, you will need to erase their memories of what they've worked on so far, and when they return, they will have to start from scratch and wonder what happened to their memories. It would be a mess."

Kian couldn't agree more. "She has a point."

After the enormous investment in building the lab and the smaller investment of hiring the bioinformaticians, it would be incredibly wasteful to close up shop after one week.

"What can I get them to work on?" William asked. "I don't want them to continue the current project without Kaia and me being there to supervise them."

"You could send Marcel to take over," Kian said. "He knows what we are doing here, and you can supervise his work remotely from the village."

As William rubbed his jaw, Kian noticed that he didn't have his glasses on. Had he forgotten to put them on this morning?

Come to think of it, he hadn't seen him wearing them last night either.

Good for him. The guy was starting to care about his appearance. His hair was cut in a fashionable new style, and his new clothes fit him well instead of being a couple of sizes too large.

"I'm not a hundred percent comfortable with that," William said. "But I guess it could work as a temporary solution. Even if they don't make progress in our absence, they will still be here and working."

"Then it's settled." Kian took another sip of his coffee. "The damn supply chain issues are also to blame for the clinic not being ready. We have a paranormal retreat starting in three weeks, and if we are lucky enough to find a Dormant among the participants and we don't have a functioning clinic, we will have to bring them to the village, which defies the whole purpose of doing it here."

The medical equipment needed was pretty standard, and it had been ordered over two months ago. Normally, he would have expected delivery in a couple of weeks, not months, but things were crazy all over the globe, and the shortages were difficult to explain.

"Don't you have a clinic in your old location?" Darlene asked.

"We do, but we don't want to bring Dormants there. It's located in the keep's underground, and they would have to be locked down there for the duration of the trial to see whether they could be induced or not. We've done that before, but that was when the entire Guardian force was living in the keep and manning the security office."

"That's not what I had in mind." Darlene put her cup down. "My idea was to transport the equipment from that clinic to this one, and once what was ordered arrived, to put the new stuff in the old clinic."

"That's a great idea," Syssi said. "It's an immediate solution."

Kian grimaced. "I don't like putting old equipment in a new clinic. I'll have Shai check with the supplier again tomorrow, and if it's not going to get here in time for the retreat, I'll do as Darlene suggests and transfer the equipment from the keep."

"Which one of our doctors will be working here?" Darlene asked.

"Julian and Bridget will be on call and get here as soon as we have a transitioning Dormant," William said. "Gertrude agreed to move out here and run the clinic. She's an excellent nurse who has a lot of experience with Dormants. She should be fine for a few hours until we get one of the doctors here."

KAIA

*K*aia had expected her mother and Gilbert to argue against her decision, to tell her that she needed to wait to make sure, but she should have known better. When push came to shove, her family united to provide support for its members.

"We are coming with you," Gilbert said in a tone that brooked no argument. "Your mother and Cheryl can call in sick, and we will stay with you until you transition safely. Did you really think we could go back home when we knew that you were doing something so dangerous?"

"It's not dangerous for me. I'm nineteen."

"I would like to meet the rest of William's family," her mother said. "And I want to be there for you, but I can't take a month-long vacation."

Cheryl smirked as she turned to their mother. "It's not a vacation when you are sick. Tell them that I got the chicken pox, and you caught it from me and that you are highly contagious."

Their mother shook her head. "We are both vaccinated, and

even if we get sick, chicken pox only lasts a few days, not a month."

Cheryl didn't back off. "Fifteen to twenty percent of people who got the Varicella vaccine still get it, but in a milder form, and some get complications like pneumonia, that last a long time."

Karen narrowed her eyes at Cheryl. "It seems that you've researched the topic. Were you planning on using chicken pox as an excuse to ditch school?"

Cheryl lifted her hands. "Not for me. It was for Claudia, and her parents approved. Do you remember when she went on a month-long trip to Japan with her family last November?"

"Yeah, I asked you how she could miss so much school, and you said that you would take notes for her."

Cheryl smiled sheepishly. "I answered the question you asked. You didn't ask me what she told the school."

Grinning, Gilbert clapped her back. "That's my smart girl."

"Don't encourage her." Their mother wagged her finger at him. "She's too sneaky for her own good."

Idina, who'd been ignoring the entire conversation so far, lifted her head and gave Gilbert a sweet smile. "Am I your smart girl, Daddy?"

"Of course, you are." He lifted her off the bed and threw her in the air.

Idina squealed happily while their mother glared at Gilbert. "I hate it when you do that."

"People." Kaia lifted her hand. "We need to go. We have ten minutes to get to the cottage, and we still need to put the twins in the stroller. We can keep talking on the way."

"We will just carry them," Karen said. "We will leave the stroller here."

Gilbert planted Idina on his shoulders. "We are ready." He opened the door. "Duck!" They both did to clear the doorway.

"I'll take Evan." Cheryl took him out of his playpen.

"And I'll get Ryan." Kaia lifted their brother and hugged him to her. "I'm so glad that you are all coming with me. I don't have to say goodbye." She kissed his soft cheek.

Her mother slung the strap of her enormous baby bag across her body and followed them out. "I don't know if that's actually going to happen. What if Kian doesn't allow us to come unless we all want to attempt the thing right away?"

"I don't think he would do that," Kaia smirked. "I'm too valuable to his clan for him to do anything to alienate me, and I will make it very clear that I want you all with me."

"What if there is no room for us all?" Cheryl asked.

"That could be a problem," Kaia admitted. "We can all stay at William's place, but I don't know how large it is and how many beds he has."

"We will ask all those questions when we get there," Gilbert said. "Maybe some of William's relatives can take us in."

"Where is Eric?" Cheryl asked. "He said that he was going to get something from his room and never came back."

Kaia stopped. "I forgot about him. Should I go back and get him?"

"I'll call him," their mother said.

Eric had been a little strange this morning. He'd spent the night at Darlene's, so he should have been in a great mood, but he seemed subdued, contemplative, with none of his usual banter.

Maybe he was scared of the transition?

"Where are you?" her mother asked.

"You could've told us that you were leaving," she said into the phone. "We thought that you ran away." There was a pause, and then her mother said, "We will be there in a few minutes." She ended the call. "He's already there."

"He's acting strange," Kaia said. "Did he say anything about being scared of transitioning?"

"Not to me," Gilbert said. "He seemed eager to go first."

Eric was doing it for the same reason Kaia was, but unlike her, his transition wouldn't be without risk, and she was worried for him.

77

ERIC

hen Eric arrived at the cottage, he found a new guard sitting on a bench that hadn't been there before.

"Good morning." The guy gave him a once-over as if he was checking him out.

"Good morning. Did the rest of my family get here already?"

"Not yet, but you can go ahead, Eric. Darlene and William are there."

"I'm at a disadvantage." He offered the guy his hand. "You know my name, but I don't know yours."

"Max." The guard shook his hand firmly. "So, you are a Dormant, eh?"

That answered the question of whether the guy was one of the immortals or just a human security guard.

Perhaps he could answer some of the questions Eric had, which he wasn't sure Kian or William would answer honestly.

"Can I join you? I'd rather wait for my family out here, so we can all go in together."

"Be my guest." The guy scooted to make room for him.

"Why aren't you with them? I was told that you were having a family meeting about who attempts transition first."

"We did, but we were all crammed into one small room, and I needed air. I went for a walk and lost track of time. When I realized what time it was, I came straight here." He frowned. "Who told you about us? We just found out last night that Gilbert and I might be related to—damn, I can't say her name."

Max grinned. "I know who you mean. And as for how I found out, you will soon discover that the clan is like a hive, and rumors spread faster than wildfire. When you live as long as we do, juicy gossip that breaks up the routine is eagerly shared."

"How old are you, if I may ask?"

Max chuckled. "You didn't take me out, you didn't buy me dinner, and you want to know how old I am? How rude of you!"

Eric didn't know whether the guy was joking or coming on to him.

"My apologies. I'm new to all this. Is it rude to ask someone like you how old they are?"

Kaia was right. It was possible to talk around the compulsion, but it was a drag.

"It's not rude," Max said. "But it's not something we do. We don't celebrate birthdays either. Perhaps it's because the passage of time is not as meaningful to us as it is to humans." The guard crossed his arms over his chest. "Patience is one of the first things you will learn as an immortal. There is very little reason to rush."

Eric had a hundred more questions he could ask the guy, but his phone rang.

He pulled it out and accepted the call from Karen.

"Where are you?" She sounded irritated, and rightly so.

He'd told them that he needed to get something from his room, which was code for him needing to use the bathroom, but when he was done, he should have gone back and told them that he couldn't stand how stuffy the room was with all of them crammed in together.

"I went on a walk and lost track of time, so I came straight to the cottage. I'm sitting outside on a bench and having a great conversation with a guard named Max."

"You could've told us that you were leaving. We thought that you ran away."

"I would never leave you stranded. Are you on your way?"

"We will be there in a few minutes." She ended the call.

Eric put the phone away.

"The correct term is Guardian," Max said. "We are much more than guards."

Eric tilted his head. "What do you do aside from guarding the research facility and Kian?"

"Many things." Max gave him an assessing look. "You were a pilot in the Air Force, right?"

"Did you read our family dossier?"

"I was just told the highlights. The clan could use another experienced fighter jet pilot. We only have one with military experience, but the last time he flew a fighter plane was over eighty years ago."

Eric's hackles rose. "What do you need fighter jet pilots for?"

Max shrugged. "A contingency in case of an attack from above."

"Who do you expect to attack you?"

Max snorted. "Everyone. If humans found out about us, they would hunt us down to find out the secret to immortality. And if our enemies found us, they would just annihilate us. That's why it is so important to guard the secret of our existence and our location."

Eric put his hand over his heart. "I can't tell anyone even if I wanted to. I'm under a strong compulsion to keep my mouth shut. But I wouldn't reveal your secret even if I could, and even if my family wasn't about to join your ranks. I will never endanger your people."

"Good to know." The guy clapped him on the back. "I wish you and your family the best of luck."

78

KIAN

*K*ian nearly spat out the sip of coffee he'd just drunk. "You all want to join Kaia in the village?"

"Of course." Karen wrung her hands. "If my baby is going through a difficult ordeal, I want to be there for her and hold her hand. I know that she has William, and maybe she doesn't need me, but I need to be there for her." She turned to Syssi. "You can understand, right?"

"I do." Syssi turned a pair of pleading eyes at Kian. "They are all potential Dormants. They will arrive at the village sooner or later, so why not sooner?"

"Because they are not all getting induced at the same time."

"I also want to transition as soon as possible," Eric said. "I'm the younger brother, and I'm a bachelor." He looked at Darlene. "For now." He winked at her.

"What about the test your doctor can perform?" Gilbert asked. "If we can verify that Eric and I are Syssi's relatives, then I'm going for the transition as well. I won't even wait for Eric to do it first." He smiled at his brother. "We can do it together." He shifted his gaze to Kian. "Once that's done, Eric can induce Darlene, and I can induce Karen."

Kaia cleared her throat. "Can your doctor perform a genetic test? Because that's the only way to confirm that Gilbert, Eric, and Syssi are related. A blood test is not enough."

"On a limited scale," Kian said. "We talked about getting some new equipment for her, but I don't know if she ordered it. I can give her a call." He crossed his arms over his chest. "But that's not the important issue here." He turned to Gilbert. "Even if you and Eric are confirmed Dormants because of your relationship to Syssi, it's not as simple as you think. Darlene is also a confirmed Dormant because her mother is immortal, but Karen is not." He wanted to add that they were both not so young and shouldn't wait, but he didn't want to state the obvious and offend them.

"Do you have a better plan?" Gilbert asked.

"Kaia needs to transition first. If she does, then Karen is a confirmed Dormant, and you will need to consider letting someone else induce her. The six months she will have to wait for your fangs to become functional might be the difference between her making it or not, and the same goes for Darlene."

Karen sighed. "I'm glad that Cheryl took the boys and Idina to watch a show in the bedroom. It would have been very awkward to talk about having sex with a stranger in front of her." She looked at Kaia. "It's still awkward with you here, but at least you are an adult." She glanced at her mate. "I don't think I can do that. Even if Gilbert is okay with that, I'm not."

Gilbert's lips were pressed together in a tight line, but he didn't say a word.

Kian could understand how the guy felt. If he were in his shoes, what would he have done?

The answer was simple. He wouldn't have risked Syssi's life because of jealousy.

He would have asked Bridget to knock him out while someone else induced Syssi, and then he would have tried not to dwell on it when he woke up. Syssi's life was more important than any other consideration.

Darlene was less of a problem because her grandfather would obviously help her with donations of his blood. But his and Annani's help would also be needed with the older members of Kaia's family transitions.

Toven might also be willing to help Eric because it seemed that Darlene had chosen him as her mate, and Annani might be inclined to help Gilbert because he was Syssi's relative and Karen because she was his mate.

But even with the gods' assistance, Karen shouldn't wait another six months to go for it.

"You don't have to decide anything right now." Syssi reached for Karen's hand. "A week or two won't make a difference, and in that time, you should consider your options. I know it's a difficult option to consider, but given that your life is on the line, I think it's a small price to pay."

"Would you have done that?" Karen asked. "If you were married to Kian, and that was the dilemma you were facing, would you have waited for him to transition first and assume a higher risk for your own transition, or would you have agreed to be serviced by another male?"

"I would have waited." Syssi smiled at Kian. "I would have trusted the Fates to see me through."

WILLIAM

*F*or a long moment, no one said a thing, and William suspected that everyone was thinking about what they would do in a similar situation.

He glanced at Kaia, but she was so young and full of vitality that it was difficult to imagine her in her mother's situation.

But what if she contracted some exotic disease, and the only cure was having sex with another man? What if only the Kra-ell had the antigens for it, and the only way for her to get it was to have sex with one of them?

He would encourage her to do it, but then he would cut out his own heart and give it to her if that was what she needed to survive.

"I wouldn't have let you wait," Kian growled. "I would have done everything to keep you alive."

"I know," Syssi said softly. "I'm glad that we didn't have to do that."

"It's settled then." Kian clapped his hands on his thighs. "We are all leaving today and going straight to the village. Kaia and William will start working on Kaia's transition. Gilbert, Eric, and Syssi will give Bridget samples of their blood, and if they are related, I will choose initiators for them, and we will have a double induction ceremony. Darlene and Karen will have to decide whether they want to wait for their mates to have active fangs and venom or use a surrogate, but they can take a few days to think it through."

"How are we going to get there?" Karen asked. "Can Eric fly us to Los Angeles, and someone will pick us up from the airport?"

"That's one possibility," Kian said. "The other option is for your plane to stay where it is, and you will all fly with us on our private jet."

"We don't have enough room," Syssi said.

"We are not going to use the same jet." Kian rose to his feet and walked over to the bar. "I'll ask Morris to pick us up with the large jet." He poured himself a drink. "Does anyone else want one?"

"It's too early for alcohol." Karen gave Gilbert a warning look. "You are not immortal yet."

He lifted his hands. "I wasn't going to ask."

"I can't just leave my plane at the airport," Eric said. "I rented the space for the weekend, and I need to vacate it this evening. I also have a client who needs it this Tuesday."

Kian nodded. "You have to understand that if you transition, your old life will end. You will have to move into the village and find a new occupation, preferably the kind you can do online. Your appearance will change dramatically, and only so much can be explained away by plastic surgery."

"I don't want to move," Cheryl said from the other room. "I have great friends that I'm going to miss."

Groaning, Karen closed her eyes. "I should have known that she was listening. It was too quiet in there."

"Don't you want to be immortal?" Kaia asked. "Are your friends worth giving up eternal life?"

Cheryl stood at the mouth of the hallway leading to the

bedrooms. "I guess not. Can I still keep in touch with them on Instatock?"

"You mentioned that social media platform before," Kian said. "When we get to the village, I want you to show me your channel."

Cheryl grinned. "Gladly." She turned around and went back into the bedroom where her siblings were watching some noisy kids' show.

Kian turned to William. "Have you heard of it before?"

He shook his head. "I don't pay attention to all those social media channels that keep popping out. It's all about nonsense like dance challenges and making silly faces. It's not for adults."

"Speaking of the village," Karen said. "Where exactly are we going to stay? Do you have accommodations for guests?"

"We have plenty of fully furnished vacant houses." Syssi pulled out her phone. "I'll text the person in charge of housing to have two prepared for you."

"I still didn't get an answer about my plane," Eric said.

"I'll fly back home with you," Darlene offered. "We can book a commercial flight to Los Angeles, and someone will pick us up from the airport."

William looked at Kian. "Is that acceptable to you?"

"It has to be. I'll take Kaia's family with me today, and I'll send the jet back with Marcel tomorrow. You and Kaia need to finalize things with the team, and you need to pass the baton to Marcel."

William looked at Kaia. "Are you okay with that?"

She nodded. "Kian's plan is solid." She turned to her mother. "Are you going to be okay in the village without me?"

"Of course, sweetie." Karen sighed. "I hope these homes come equipped with washers and dryers. I brought just enough clothes for three days."

"Don't worry." Syssi smiled. "You will lack for nothing. We shop online and get things delivered just like everyone else."

"Well, our deliveries go through one extra stop, but we still get them the same day."

"I'm excited." Karen looked at her mate. "Are you?"

He snorted. "I thought that having three little kids at our age was as adventurous as we would get, but I was wrong. We are about to embark on the most thrilling adventure yet."

KAIA

 $\mathcal{T}$ his time around, there were no tears when Kaia had parted with her family.

The big red-headed Guardian and his Amazonian beauty of a mate stayed behind to leave enough room in Kian's jet for all of her family members, and they would accompany William and her to the village tomorrow afternoon.

When the bus disappeared behind the curve, William wrapped his arm around her. "Are you okay?"

Smiling, Kaia leaned her head on his shoulder. "I'm going to see them tomorrow, and I have you by my side. It doesn't get any better than that."

He hooked a finger under her chin and turned her face up to steal a kiss. "I have every intention of making things even better."

The mischievous spark in his eyes gave her a good clue as to what those intentions were.

Kaia yawned. "It's been a long day. I'm ready for bed."

He chuckled. "It's only seven in the evening."

"I didn't say that I wanted to go to sleep, only that I wanted to go to bed."

His grin widened. "Great minds think alike." He leaned closer and whispered in her ear. "Are you ready to throw away the rubbers?"

"Am I ever! But you said that you wanted to wait for us to get to the village."

He shrugged. "We are leaving for the village tomorrow, and transition doesn't start overnight. I'm willing to chance it if you are."

She wanted to say that yes, she was ready, but a sudden sense of foreboding changed her mind. "You know what? Let's play it safe. I have an idea that you're going to love, and that doesn't involve condoms." She stretched her neck and whispered it in his ear.

"Sweet, merciful Fates." William's eyes blazed with an inner light. "Would you be really mad if I swung you into my arms and ran back to our bungalow?"

"Mad? I'll be thrilled."

She didn't get to finish the sentence before William did exactly as he'd promised.

Winding her arms around his neck, she threw her head back and laughed, the sense of foreboding washed away by a wave of happiness.

Kaia had always known that her future was bright, but now it seemed brighter than ever.

She was looking forward to spending eternity with the man she loved, building Odus and countless other innovations, and somewhere along the way, perhaps with a little help from the clan's physician, children would come as well.

COMING UP NEXT
The Children of the Gods Book 64
Dark Whispers From Beyond

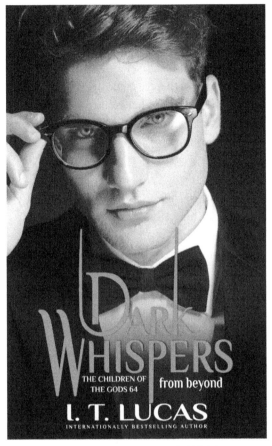

To read the first 3 chapters JOIN the VIP club at
***ITLUCAS.COM** —To find out what's included in your free*
membership, click HERE or flip to the last page.

Dear reader,

Thank you for reading the **Children of the Gods**.

As an independent author, I rely on your support to spread the word. So if you enjoyed the story, please share your experience with others, and if it isn't too much trouble, I would greatly appreciate a brief review on Amazon.

Love & happy reading,

Isabell

Also by I. T. Lucas

PERFECT MATCH

**TRY THE CHILDREN OF THE GODS SERIES ON
AUDIBLE**

2 FREE audiobooks with your new Audible subscription!

FOR EXCLUSIVE PEEKS AT UPCOMING RELEASES & A FREE COMPANION BOOK

Made in the USA
Coppell, TX
12 August 2022

81331246R00184